"How 'bout a little night of love, querida?"

"Beat it mister!" Her brown eyes flashed at him, and she looked away, muttering, "I'm waiting for someone."

"So?" He winked lecherously. "This carcass doesn't take long to pleasure, sweetheart. Five minutes in the back room oughta do it."

He could see he had rattled her, although she was striving to cover it. Her mouth curled contemptuously.

"I've bitten a few rotten coins, mister," she hissed, "and don't need to hook up with the likes of you."

So began the acquaintance of the indomitable Roxana Van Buren and the unconquerable Sam Brady.

D1466802

BLUE MOON

PARRIS AFTON BONDS

FAWCETT COLUMBINE • NEW YORK

For Your Encouragement,
Jean Mays, Toni Thomas, and Sylvia Walsh,
I thank you.

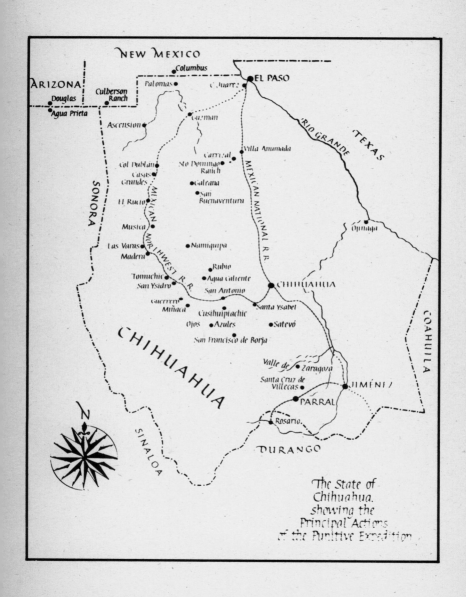

The State of Chihuahua showing the Principal Actions of the Punitive Expedition

BLUE
MOON

Once upon a time, or so begin the fairy tales, there was a bluestocking spinster and a gin-sodden cowpoke. Sourly, suspiciously, the two sat eyeing one another across a smoke-hazed, liquor-stinking barroom. Each pondered the mad quirk of foolishness that had brought them to that seedy cantina on Calle de Noche Triste in Juarez, Mexico. . . .

1

1916 . . . the age of the hobble skirt that shackled women below the knee . . . the peak of the militant Suffragette movement . . . the time of revolutions, the Sinn Fein in Ireland, the Bolsheviks in Russia, and the Villistas in Mexico.

Well-bred Roxana Van Buren of the aristocratic old Dutch family was busy staging her own revolution: at thirty, she was going to work—or rather she was attempting to, though it appeared her mother's body might block the doorway with a precipitous fainting spell, a ploy the woman had used frequently when dealing with her husband's tyrannical decisions. A ploy that seldom worked.

Augustus Van Buren's Solomon-like wisdom, his Old World polish and old money, the influence of his powerful political standing as a Supreme Court Justice, all made him well-nigh invincible. He was committed to his position in life, to his wife, and to their children.

Consequently, Roxana, Wally, and Rowena were raised in a most secure, albeit patriarchal family structure, which made it difficult to break away. Wally was following in his father's political footsteps, Rowena had married the young doctor of whom her father had so heartily approved, and Roxana . . . well, Roxana had remained within the bosom of the family all those years.

Poor Audrey Van Buren had come reluctantly to the conclusion that her oldest daughter was a spinster. Certainly, her mother had done her best by Roxana, affording her the finest education at Sacred Heart Convent in New York and completing her formal education at Liège, where her daughter had learned to speak passable French and had spent vacations from school visiting the cultural spots throughout Europe. And Roxana was attractive enough—unless one compared her to Rowena, beside whose golden beauty all females paled. It wasn't that Roxana had never had a suitor; in fact, several came to call after Rowena married. Roxana simply wasn't interested.

It was the education that had definitely affected Roxana's mind. Rowena was graduated from finishing school with a refined and knowledgeable interest in music and the arts. Not Roxana. The girl had been inordinately bookish. True, Audrey had been caught up in romantic novels as a young woman, even to the point of naming her daughters for Sir Walter Scott's heroine Rowena and Edmond Rostand's Roxana. Still, by the time she was a married woman of twenty-five with three children to her credit, she no longer was preoccupied with such foolish notions.

But Roxana was past thirty! And this . . . this latest tomfoolery of Roxana's . . .

Audrey had hoped Roxana would be satisfied with the little ragsheet in which she had become involved the last few years. Along with those awful Suffragettes, Roxana had cranked out flyers that dealt with all sorts of controversial subjects: the values of a vegetarian diet, politics, prison reform, free verse poetry, and—Lord, help her—birth control.

But now . . . Audrey covered her forehead with the back of one hand and fluttered the other, murmuring, "Please, my smelling salts, Roxana."

"Your smelling salts are useless, Mother."

"A small bit of sherry, then. Your father will never countenance this latest idea of yours. It's so—so vulgar, dear."

From beneath lowered lashes, Audrey watched Roxana cross to the side table's stock of expensive liquors. She despaired for her eldest child's future. Roxana was neither as diminutive as she herself or Rowena, nor did she possess their delicate beauty. Tall and big boned, she moved with an untutored grace. Her father's deep brown eyes, with their direct scrutiny, looked out of a face with prominent cheekbones and jawline. On her father, the features were distinguishing. On Roxana they seemed rather severe.

Not even the inheritance of Audrey's untamable curls softened Roxana's appearance. With a little sigh, Audrey thought that her daughter could at least have been blessed with the Reschler mouth, on which Charles Dana Gibson himself had complimented both Audrey and Rowena, telling them he would like to paint those bowlike lips as a trademark for his Gibson Girl look.

Roxana restored the sherry bottle to the sidetable's cabinet and handed her mother the crystal glass. "I would hardly term employment vulgar, Mother. Hundreds of thousands of women are in the labor force."

Audrey swallowed the soothing sherry before she tackled the sensitive subject. "Yes, dear. But in genteel professions. Teachers, governesses, seamstresses."

"And what of the women working in factories or sweatshops or as domestics?"

"Well, if the alternative is starvation, then, of course, I understand it. But any woman who isn't forced by economic circumstances to make her own living and insists on a career . . . And to want to enter a masculine-dominated field—it's not only unladylike at the very least, it's a disgrace to the family. A muckraker! Imagine! Why, Roxana, dear, you'll be regarded as some kind of freak."

"I suppose I am already, Mother."

.   .   .

Roxana couldn't help herself. As the eldest, she had received the brunt of her father's well-meaning but despotic discipline. Wally, as a son, was allowed to make his decisions as he grew older. Rowena, as she grew more beautiful, had no need to make decisions. Like their mother, what Rowena didn't achieve directly she was able to wheedle through various subterfuges.

For a while, during those miserable years of puberty, Roxana had meekly endured her life. Her body reflected her misery by refusing to shed its baby fat and even rebelliously putting on pounds. She thought whoever said that large frames carried extra poundage better than smaller ones had been wrong. At five feet nine inches she looked like a behemoth. She wallowed in both her unhappiness and the rich foods served up at her mother's famed dinner parties.

Roxana retreated more and more into the world of books. Her love of the printed word went beyond her mother's absorption with romances. She not only read everything she could get her hands on, she also wrote—poetry, short stories, and articles, which she hid from her family and never had the courage to submit. The iconoclastic spirit in her ached to reform the injustices of the world, and what better way to do it than with the power of the pen? It didn't matter if her writings never reached the influential eye of the public. At least she felt better for having taken her own private stand.

On one occasion her father discovered in a desk drawer an exposé article she had written entitled "Our Insane Treatment of the Insane." He had merely lifted that derisive brow and said in his dry, disparaging voice, "My dear, I would think a young lady could better employ her time in womanly pursuits and leave journalism to those who are qualified."

Inside she seethed with revolt and resentment against the godlike male. For almost thirty years she submitted quite naturally to the arbitrary decisions of the superior sex. She may have had a strong mind of her own, but her strict upbringing had suppressed it. How, when raised by the doctrine of the imperfection of woman as opposed to infallible man, could she suppose that there was an alternative to the woman's circumscribed life?

Then one day something very simply changed her. She happened to watch a parade of Suffragettes marching toward the White House. It was spring, and they all wore gloriously white dresses with yellow ribbons or yellow flowers, the color representative of their cause. Suddenly, it occurred to her: how could a woman be so lacking in self-esteem as to cede to a male the right to control her life?

After that, she began to make her own decisions. She came and went, and did as she pleased. Her activities expanded to include a whole new world of people, both male and female, who shared her wide interests. She was busy reading, writing, making speeches, attending public meetings normally forbidden to well-bred young ladies. The pounds melted off.

One day, glancing at the mirror before she hurried out, she saw a svelte figure. Her astonishment was followed by light laughter. "I knew you were inside that mastodon's body all the time," she told the reflection, "just waiting to get out." She continued on her way without another thought to her new appearance.

She came to value her new-found independence almost passionately. Her father made his disapproval of her activities obvious, but, surprisingly, he had not interfered.

Yet.

The newspaper field was considered particularly unsuitable for women. Like saloons, newsrooms were strictly masculine environments, where profanity was common. Roxana ignored the disgusted looks of the aproned pressmen and the newspapermen who worked in their shirt sleeves, hats perched on the back of their heads. Regally, she threaded her way across the newsroom cluttered as it was with paper, spittoons, and pencil shavings.

She was ushered into the office of the editor of *The Washington Post*. February's feeble yellow sunlight worked through the dusty office window panes, dappling the bald pate of old McClarney. He greeted her with wary courtesy and offered her a chair across from his desk. She seated herself with the majestic assurance of a queen mounting a throne, placed the tip of her umbrella on the floor between her high-buttoned kid boots, and leaned forward to fix him with a penetrating gaze.

He popped his suspenders irritably, and she knew she was facing old-time editorial prejudice. If a woman had to be hired, men demanded, why couldn't she write her articles at home? With her working among the men, they would have to doff their hats, wear coats, and watch their language.

From his side of the desk McClarney studied the Van Buren woman. What he saw was a woman with a steady expression and an air of determination about her. He was familiar with the little weekly paper she and her cohorts issued from one of those bohemian Georgetown apartments. He was also familiar with her background. Daughter of a powerful Supreme Court Justice and of a mother who was the capital's most influential socialite. He was treading on spring ice.

He cleared his throat. "I understand you want to write for the *Post*."

"Yes." She thrust some of her bylined stories in front of him. "As a journalist."

He scanned the clippings. "We, umm, have had several female free-lancers these past few years and would, of course, welcome your contributions. Perhaps to the society page. Meg Anderson does a splendid column but could use a stringer."

Roxana's long eyes narrowed. The term "stringer" was derived from the old method of payment for copy actually printed. The length of each item was measured by a string, and at the end of the month, correspondents were paid according to the total number of inches of string they sent in to the editor. While a woman could sell a considerable amount of material to papers on a piece basis, it was almost impossible to get a salaried job, and even then she was required to do her writing at home.

Roxana clamped her hands more firmly about the handle of her umbrella. "Your time is valuable, Mr. McClarney, so I will get right to the point. I want to be hired by you, to work alongside the other newsmen, to have my own desk. I want to be a front-page reporter. Women are quite as capable of gathering news as men, sir."

"Miss Van Buren, I appeal to your better judgment; to your gentility; to the desirability of the female sex remaining sheltered and protected from the sterner aspects of life; to—"

"Rubbish. Pure rubbish."

Blinking, he ceased his platitudes. "I'm afraid it's out of the question."

Her smile was tart. "Why?"

She was making him uneasy. "You can't go every place a man can go."

"Joseph Pultizer hired Nellie Bly to gather news for the *New York World*."

He ran a finger under his stock collar and said dryly, "I suppose you want to be a war correspondent and travel to Europe to cover the battles?"

She shrugged lightly. "Why not?"

"Because a woman can't dig a trench fast enough!" he snapped, losing all patience. He now had a glimmer of what people meant when they spoke of the Van Buren spinster's determination. But he hadn't gotten to be editor because he was a soft touch. He leaned forward. "I have a war correspondent posted in El Paso— you know where that is?"

"I'm fully familiar with the continental geography, sir. It's in western Texas on the Mexican border."

"Rooney is covering the revolutionary skirmishes in northern Mexico as our senior war correspondent. Do you know anything about Mexico's political potboiler?"

Although she read several papers a day—among them the *New York World* and the *Times*—she understood only a little better than most Americans the situation in Mexico and its turbulent history. She knew that Villa's Revolucionarios and the de facto Mexican president Carranza had battled each other across the northwestern states of Chihuahua and Sonora for some time now, even before the United States had finally recognized Carranza's right to the presidency. Every week or so American-owned property in Mexico was disposed of by Pancho Villa or some other Mexican guerrilla bands in a manner most distressful to President Wilson.

The Carranza forces were almost as bad. A Federal soldier had murdered an American and displayed the man's severed head on a pole for all to see. The wealthy William Randolph Hearst, owner of the *New York Journal*, possessed a medieval fief, cattle herds, and silver mines in northern Mexico and wanted the country pacified, by intervention if necessary.

A Villista escapade a couple of weeks earlier, dragging sixteen American mining engineers off a train in Chihuahua and mutilating and executing them, had enraged the American public and caused Congress to order 12,000 soldiers to El Paso's nearby Fort Bliss, to protect the border. Wilson might be keeping his pledge to keep the United States out of Europe's Great War, but American soldiers were looking at a possible war right on their own back porch.

"El Paso is overrun with those journalists not on the European front covering the war," McClarney rattled off, hoping to free himself from the woman's siege. "Journalists from all over the world are trying to get an exclusive interview with Villa. Get that interview for the *Post* and you've got yourself a job as a cub reporter."

Thrilled, Roxana rose to her feet. "I will get your interview, Mr. McClarney."

He played his ace in the hole, hoping it would be the discouraging factor. "Naturally, the *Post* will give you a fifty-dollar advance, but otherwise you'll be on your own until you prove yourself."

She looked down at the man, undaunted. "I'll find a way to finance myself, I assure you."

Augustus Van Buren slammed a blistering shot that whizzed by the Vice President and won the point for the justice. Roxana could hear the pounding of the ball against the gymnasium's walls on the story above her bedroom. Once the handball game was over, her father and Tom Marshall would have their usual cognac in the library before the Vice President departed.

Then she knew it would be only a matter of minutes before her father stormed back up the stairs to confront her. His eruption earlier that morning had been heard all over the second floor. "Roxana's going to do *what?*"

Apparently her mother had not introduced the subject of their daughter's job that smoothly. The Vice President's arrival for the weekly handball match had only momentarily postponed the confrontation between Roxana and her father.

"You're going to do what?" demanded her father from the doorway.

Roxana tossed the gaiters in the camelback trunk along with the balmoral skirt and the chemise and drawers and faced her father. Despite the dirt streak on one white canvas shoe, he still managed to have that immaculate, dapper appearance. A distinguished man whose mere lift of the brow could intimidate a lawyer before the bench. And now, after all those years, she alone among the females in the family was defying his authority.

Strangely enough, it pained her to do so. More than she had imagined. One didn't change habits overnight. But it was more than that. For all his dictatorial ways, she knew he loved her. And she loved him.

"I am going to El Paso, Father. To work as a reporter for the *Post.*"

"I've put up with quite a lot of your eccentricities, Roxana, but this is the ultimate. I forbid you to go."

"I'm past the age of forbidding."

He stood staring at her, this feminine replica of himself in appearance and, perhaps, in personality. He knew she was not one to indulge in whims. If she had been a man, she would have made a hell of a lawyer. Like himself, she possessed a mind that took abstract pleasure in the precise application of logic to patternless chaos. Why then couldn't she see that this idea of hers was manifestly chaotic?

He tried one more time, meaning every word he said, for he was just as firm of word and mind as his daughter. "If you go, Roxana, I'll not advance a penny toward your upkeep."

She picked up the white eyelet gloves on the bed and tucked them into a corner of the trunk. Her stomach was knotting and tears were welling just below her lids. "I wouldn't expect you to, Father."

"Have you thought of the damage you're doing to your reputation, to the family name?"

"I'm sure the name Van Buren will survive admirably despite your eldest daughter's peccadillos."

"Roxana . . ." He paused, hating to utter words of such finality. "If you go, all funds will be forever terminated, including inheritances."

She closed the trunk lid.

2

As the thousands of miles sped by the Pullman sleeper window, Roxana had reason to doubt her wisdom in leaving her family, friends, and, yes, even her source of all sustenance. The familiar—the majestic forests, the rolling hills, the pastoral countryside of white fences, red barns, and rich black earth—gave way to bleak prairie that stretched monotonously beyond the limit of vision. No landmarks existed by which to judge the train's progress. The days faded one into the other with only intermittent communities to indicate humanity's toehold west of the Mississippi.

She spent the time reading, researching all she could about the political factions warring in Mexico. John Reed, who, with Carl Sandburg, had briefly operated a socialist newspaper, had just returned from Mexico and written a book on its latest revolution before he left to cover the coming revolution in Russia. *Insurgent Mexico* explained much—but from a biased point of view. She decided she didn't understand the revolution any better than before.

The train at last entered Texas. Even halfway across, five hundred and eighty-five miles of empty plains and desert still separated El Paso from the captial in Austin. After the Southern Pacific crossed the Pecos High Bridge, the landscape altered drastically, and Roxana, her mouth open, felt it was grand and gorgeous, fit for the most eminent artist. The mauve Santa Rosa mountains were starkly visible in Mexico, their nearest peak fully one hundred miles away.

The train track continually wound upward, twisting through deep canyons with perpendicular walls, red rocky bluffs, and sugarloaf peaks. And rock, endless rock. Here and there a mass of dirty gray fluff that was a sheep searched for tufts of the short mesquite grass and sotol.

When yuccas and ocotillos dotted the moonscape, she knew she was nearing her journey's end, El Paso, a narrow garden of green along the Rio Grande River. The city of sixty-two thousand souls, saved or otherwise, wrapped around Mount Franklin, the ragged tail end of the Rocky Mountains, like a well-worn horseshoe.

With the other passengers, mostly men, Roxana left the train at Union Station. As she stood trying to take stock of her situation, the engine's steam hissed about her long skirts and people surged around her. Counting the *Post*'s fifty-dollar advance and spending money she had saved, she had only thirty-three dollars left after the train trip. She also had no job and no place to stay. She did have the name of Charley Rooney.

Outside the soot-stained depot an Arctic wind whipped down from the Rocky Mountain pass, blowing tumbleweed and newspapers through the streets. Sand slithered before the breeze along the potholed pavement. She hugged the black peau de soi coat more tightly about her. Hardly the tropical weather travel books portrayed of the Southwest.

A pigtailed Chinaman huddled in a hack, waiting for passengers. Though she was spending precious coins, she hailed him to take her to the Sheldon Hotel, where Rooney was headquartered. A cavalry sergeant on the train, returning to Fort Bliss after a leave of duty, had told her that the colorful Sheldon Hotel served as the base for the soldiers of fortune and adventurers like Tracy Richardson and Tom Mix, while they rounded up supplies for Villa. It was also the haunt for the hundreds of newspapermen from all the over the world who waited for Villa to once again attack El Paso's sister city of Juarez, Mexico.

Roxana meant to be one of those reporters gathered at the Sheldon.

It seemed the officious desk clerk would have it otherwise. "I'm sorry, madam, but we have no rooms available." He gestured toward the empty key racks. Above them a placard advertised BULLET-PROOF ROOMS.

"But—"

"None."

She drew herself up to her full height and glared at him through her toque's veil. "Then would you page Mr. Charles Rooney for me."

"You'll find him in our coffee shop."

The coffee shop was packed with men in bowlers and straw boaters. The cigars jammed in their mouths bobbed with their rapid-fire talk and belched smoke throughout the room. A white-aproned Mexican waiter led her through the maze of tables to one girded by half a dozen men, who all stood immediately when she paused before them.

"Mr. Rooney?" she asked, looking from one masculine face to another.

The man with a face like a cliff tipped his straw boater. "You got him, miss."

The gentlemen shuffled quickly to draw up another chair for her, and she primly took a seat. Silence hung over the table as she surveyed the men who watched her. "I was trying to get a room here," she began, "but was told there were none to be had."

"That's right, ma'am," the man on her left supplied. "What the reporters don't have, the refugees out of Mexico do—least ways, those who can afford the rooms."

A horse-faced man, who identified himself as with Pathé News, said, "It's this way. Between the Americans and the Mormons, the Chinese and Mexicans fleeing up out of Mexico, and the doughboys brought down to protect the border, there's not even a couch to be had. Pool rooms are renting billiard tables for beds—in shifts of eight hours."

A Reuters News Service reporter advised in a very proper English accent, "My dear woman, I'd go back wherever I came from."

She looked to Rooney again, who watched her with pale-lashed eyes. He wore a loud, plaid suit that sported a cheap watch fob at the waistcoat pocket. "Mr. Rooney, *The Washington Post* has employed me to help cover the civil war going on across the border, so I'm not going back until I get an interview with Pancho Villa."

The end of Rooney's stubby cigar dropped perilously close to his jutting chin.

"Well, I'll be damned," said a newspaperman wearing a International News Service badge.

"A woman reporter!" gaped a man with red garters holding up his long sleeves. "What'll those monkeys in the East come up with next?"

"And I was hoping, Mr. Rooney, that you could help me get established here," she continued.

"And I'm hoping William Randolph Hearst'll give me a million dollars," Rooney bit out. His cigar bobbled with each word, depositing ashes on the table. "Good luck, lady. News reporting is a very competitive business. No place for a woman."

She rose stiffly, gathering her gored alpaca traveling skirt. "I'll get the interview with Villa while the rest of you are still sitting here drinking coffee."

Rooney smiled grimly. "First you gotta find him, lady. And then you gotta beg him not to execute you, 'cause he 'specially hates American reporters."

She could still hear the raucous male guffaws as she sailed majestically out of the coffee shop.

· · ·

To her dismay, the reporters had been right. There were no FOR
RENT signs anywhere. Although El Paso's revenue was touted as
the five C's—climate, cotton, cattle, copper, and lastly con-
sumption—the numerous tuberculosis sanitoriums were filled
with roomers who were not all consumptive patients seeking the
pure air and sunshine of the West.

To the victims of the White Plague, El Paso may have been
famous as the Sun City, but to most it was infamous as Sin City.
Its peccadillos and gamy predilections far outshone anything Ab-
ilene, Kansas, or Tombstone, Arizona, had to offer. Yet there
were those who claimed that in the earlier days the prostitutes
were a civilizing influence on frontier El Paso. The madams'
names always appeared on the list of donors to charitable causes.
However, only a few of the prostitutes' patrons could appreciate
the quiet charm of good taste.

So it was there, in El Paso's Tenderloin District, that a few
rooms could be had. Some of the most famous madams of the
day had stately mansions in midtown along Utah and Ninth.
Brothels like Madame Palmer's Gentlemen's Club, the posh
Marlborough House, and the Manhattan Club were elegant places
where men went for the best steak, the finest wine; where the
doxies wore ballgowns and cattle deals were settled and real estate
sold. The men didn't have to go upstairs, although most probably
did.

Roxana decided she wasn't that desperate for lodging.

She looked once more at the folded *El Paso Herald* she held
in her hand and then looked up at the two-story red brick building
with the grilled balcony. It was the right address on Oregon Street,
according to the newspaper ad. The bottom floor was devoted to
the Elite Confectionery, an ice cream parlor, which, so said the
hack driver, Pancho Villa had occasionally patronized four years
earlier as a exile from his political opponent, Carranza. In fact,
one of Villa's wives, La Luz, and their children still lived on
Oregon Street.

It seemed only fitting then that this was where she might find both lodging and work, if she was lucky. She climbed the narrow staircase, careful to keep her suede gloves off the dusty railing. On the second floor she halted before the door marked 203. On its opaque glass paneling were stenciled the words ROCKY MOUNTAIN DETECTIVE AGENCY and below it the picture of an eye.

The Pinkerton Detective Agency had made that symbol, the private eye, famous: "The eye that never closes; it follows to the end of the earth to arrest, then spends every available dollar to put the offender behind bars."

A little man in a tweed suit greeted her knock. He sported a bristling mustache and his hair looked as if it were pasted down. Quickly he assessed her, without seeming to. A wife who wanted to put a tail on her wandering husband? "Do come in," he said with an old-fashioned dignity that put clients at ease.

Roxana took a seat in an overstuffed chair with worn arms. The office resembled the backstage of a theater but for the fruitwood desk that had seen better days. A variety of cloaks and hats hung from pegs. A dressing table's tarnished mirror reflected pots of rouge and cold cream and other makeup. Wigs capped the table's curlicue cornices along with a holstered pearl-handled derringer and a set of nickel-plated, blue steel handcuffs. The place appealed to her dramatic instincts.

"Mr. Bernard Rouche at your service, madam. Tell me, how can I help you?"

Everything depended on the little man on the other side of the desk. If he scoffed at the idea of a female detective, what then? Her funds were depleting rapidly. Even now her stomach was growling in a very unfeminine manner. Oh, for a rib-eye steak from the Willard! She clutched the delicate silver chains of her bag. "I would like to apply for the position of an—operative," she said, using the terminology printed in the ad.

His bird-bright eyes rounded, but he controlled his surprise. "Of course."

The Rocky Mountain Detective Agency was in need of someone to manage its El Paso office, and the Chicago headquarters had sent him out to run it until he could hire a qualified person. Someone knowledgeable in the art of shadowing, disguise, and playing a role. Someone with tenacity, ingenuity, and organizational ability. Someone who would keep his own counsel.

Mr. Rouche had not reached such a high position as a principal with the agency without being one of the best in criminology, espionage, and investigation. In addition, he was shrewd and a good judge of character.

He studied the young woman across from him. The features could be called handsome but were decidedly of an intellectual cast. Her body, though reposed, radiated a surplus of energy. Her face was honest, which would cause one in distress to select her instinctively as a confidante. Undoubtedly, she would be able to worm out secrets in many places where it was impossible for male operatives to gain access.

"How soon can you begin, madam?"

3

From the dust-filmed window of the Rocky Mountain Detective Agency Roxana could barely see tree-shaded San Jacinto Plaza, where live alligators were kept in the fountain. Down the street a boy in knickerbockers filled potholes with manure from the corrals behind the Grand Central Hotel. On the street's opposite side a *carbonero*, a coal merchant, led two burros, all but obscured by the two panniers of coal, to the public water trough.

Because of El Paso's isolation, change came slowly. In spite of the lingering wisps of frontier gunsmoke, the anachronistic town possessed a cosmopolitan flavor. It was the Chinese Mecca of the Southwest, and several blocks over in the Segundo Barrio was Chinatown, settled by coolies brought in to finish the railroad. Between Second Streeet and the Rio Grande was Little Chihuahua, crowded with all the refugees from the Villistas' wrath.

The town was also the mining center of the Southwest, and students from all over the world who were studying at the State

School of Mines and Metallurgy were seen everywhere, as were the soldiers in khakis from nearby Camp Cotton.

The Pass had always been a meeting place, a crossroads, where Indian, Spaniard, and Anglo met and mingled. Conquistadors and colonists, wild Indians and devoted friars, trappers and traders and Forty-niners played their parts in its history. Gunmen and gamblers, cavalrymen and fancy women still held the stage.

And now a female detective had insinuated herself in their midst.

In one week Rouche had taught her much about the modus operandi of a detective before he returned to Chicago. She learned from him about collecting the preliminary facts on a case, interviews and data from clients; about keeping basic records containing the clients' problems and requirements, together with the precise plan of operation for the fieldman. Too, she learned the little tricks of secreting information—rolling a message and hiding it in a plug of tobacco or in her tresses.

Like the Pinkerton Agency, Rocky Mountain had its Rogues Gallery—photos with detailed records and descriptions on the reverse side. The description system was a method invented by the Frenchman Bertillon, who had discovered there were twelve measurements on the human body that did not change in an adult. Roxana learned how to take these particular measurements as well as to perform the more mundane tasks of filling out vouchers and applying for drafts.

The benefits of working for the agency included free railroad passes through the American Express Company, which protected the railroads, and the use of the agency office as a "residence." A white iron bed now reposed behind a Chinese silk screen, and she had purchased a hot plate for heating soups and tea from the prestigious White House department store, where liveried doormen helped wealthy patrons in and out of both carriages and cars.

Now she had both lodging and a job that paid on a regular basis. Still, she had yet to render a service for the agency or to file a story about the Mexican revolutionaries. She had considered several angles—maybe interviewing one of the Mormon refugees of the 1910–11 exodus out of Mexico. The Mormons had settled several colonies in Mexico in the 1880s when the Arizona church members fled prosecution for polygamy.

Villa's wife Luz sold candy and soda pop on the streets to raise money for the Villista cause, but a story had already been done on her.

There was Hippolito, Villa's brother. When Villa last overran Juarez, he had given Juarez's bullring and gambling concession to Hippolito, as well as the tribute paid by the sporting-houses. But Hippolito appeared to be an absentee landlord.

Roxana pressed her forehead against the pane's cold glass and agonized over how she was going to outwit several hundred newspapermen all angling for the scoop of the year. She knew her story couldn't be ordinary. It had to be sensational. She was competing with superb journalists like Damon Runyon with International News Service, Floyd Gibbons of the *Chicago Tribune*, and Jack London with *Collier's Magazine*.

Immediately below her a cream-colored Reo automobile pulled against the curb, and the uniformed driver got out to open the rear door before the Elite Confectionery. A heavyset man in a silk-bound Homburg and black beaver Chesterfield coat emerged. His negligent gesture of acknowledgement to the driver and his stately carriage that did not really require the ivory walking stick suggested a man long accustomed to wealth.

Moments later the knock at the door drew her attention to the immediate problem of running the agency. She opened the door to find her first client—the man in the Homburg. He removed his hat to reveal silver gray hair that matched the thick brows and clipped mustache. "Miss—?"

"Van Buren. Please come in, sir."

He was heavily jowled, with brooding eyes that carefully inspected the bizarre office. "The manager of the agency? I wish to speak with him." His speech had a foreign inflection that started

Roxana guessing. Certainly not French. But definitely an aristocrat. The imperious nose, the high brow, and classical mouth.

Perhaps he was a Spanish grandee like Don Luis Terrazas. The former governor of the state of Chihuahua had fought victoriously against the French many years before, and Benito Juarez had rewarded him with a ranch empire. Chicago firms had ordered a million head of his cattle, and it was said that one could not cross Chihuahua without stepping on his property. But Villa's vendetta against Hispanics had forced Terrazas to flee Mexico. With his entourage of hundreds, Terrazas had fled to El Paso, where he and his family and servants had occupied a full three floors of the hotel Paso del Norte.

Roxana shut the door behind the gentleman and indicated the overstuffed chair. "I manage the office, sir. How can I help you?"

His gray brows beetled down over the shrewd eyes. "You are a detective? A woman detective?"

She nodded and seated herself in the swivel chair behind the desk. Expecting just such incredulity from clients, she reached for the package of cigarettes she had purchased and withdrew one. It had taken no little practice that past week to acquire the art of inhaling without choking. Disapproval lurked in the hidalgo's velvet brown eyes. "Women are quite capable of thin"— she cleared her throat in order to stifle a rising cough—"of performing many of the same tasks as men."

The man leaned forward, bracing his hands on the cane's gold knob. She could see he was mulling over his decision to use the agency's services. At last, sighing heavily, he spoke. "I am Don Arturo Asunsolo of Durango, Mexico. Or at least that was our home, until four years ago. Villa's raids forced us to abandon our hacienda. Until it is safe to return, we have taken a home up in Sunset Heights, while my youngest daughter finishes her education at St. Joseph of Loretto Academy."

A Spanish grandee. She had guessed accurately.

Suddenly, the grandee's shoulders slumped and he looked very old. "This is what has brought me here today. My daughter.

Angelina disappeared from the Academy two days ago. The El Paso police have filed a missing persons report but are doing nothing to find her." He shrugged his shoulders. "We are not Americans, they say. They say that dozens of people go missing every day in El Paso, more than they can hope to find."

He looked up and fixed Roxana with an old eagle's piercing gaze. "I want to find my daughter."

"The agency will do all it can, Don Asunsolo."

"I will pay a reward. A handsome reward of five thousand dollars if you find her—alive."

There was not much to go on. A snapshot taken the month before, when a nephew from Chihuahua came to visit. The good-looking young man was at the center of the photo, with his Asunsolo cousins gathered on either side before a table spread with tureens, platters, and salvers of food.

The six Asunsolo children were replicas of their father. Most in their twenties, they all bore that aristocratic countenance. Roxana studied the four sons and two daughters. Marta at thirty-one was the eldest. And Angelina at seventeen the youngest—and the most handsome of the children. No, beautiful. A delicate beauty of dark almond eyes that danced and lovely, childish lips that possessed that Mona Lisa curve of secret laughter.

"Angelina was the sweetest, most considerate of my children," her father said before he left, "and I cannot imagine anyone wanting to hurt her. I have to find her, or my heart will never know any peace."

Roxana had to admit to herself that she was as unsure as to where to begin the search as Don Arturo. She lay awake on the narrow bed that night asking herself questions and finding no satisfactory answers.

Abduction? But no ransom had been demanded.

Murder? Who would have wanted her murdered?

Or could Angelina Asunsolo have run away? Why?

The next morning Roxana studied the photo again and once

more glanced over the information she had gleaned from Don Arturo. The sheaf of foolscap was less than half filled with her precise copperplate handwriting.

No distinguishable markings. Black hair, brown eyes. Slight of figure. Last seen at Academy February 6th during matins. No clothing or personal articles missing. Was wearing school uniform of white middy blouse and navy blue skirt and deceased mother's black-pearled crucifix.

The four sons, Roxana had learned, all lived at home and held clerical positions at the American Smelting and Refining Company. Marta, the eldest daughter, lived in Juarez with her husband, a lawyer, Jesus Sanchez.

That gave Roxana three places to visit: A.S.&R. in Smeltertown, which was on El Paso's western perimeter; the Sanchezes across the border in Juarez; and the St. Joseph of Loretto Academy.

Smeltertown, built mostly on the cooled fiery red dump slag from the refinery, was composed of some of El Paso's most dilapidated shacks and a few nice houses; the shacks for the laborers of American Smelting and Refining, the well-constructed yellow buildings for a few of its management. The four Asunsolo brothers were part of that management, their positions obtained, Roxana suspected, through their father's prestige and authority.

A.S.&R. had subsidiaries in several northern Mexican cities, and A.S.&R.'s board of directors likely felt it only politic to appease an old man who still carried a great deal of influence with the Carranza government—though it was difficult to determine how long that government would control the capital of Mexico City, with Villa disrupting the peripheral population.

Smeltertown's smokestack was claimed to be the tallest in the country, and as Roxana descended the wooden stairs from A.S.&R.'s offices, the acrid smell of sulphur belching from the smokestack enveloped her. For some illogical reason, she was reminded of dried apricots.

But then, most of her reasoning seemed illogical. Why didn't Angelina have a young man in whom she was interested? The girl was old enough. And exquisitely beautiful.

Yet the four brothers, each of whom Roxana had interviewed separately in A.S.&R.'s conference room, had insisted that Angelina had refused the attentions of all the eligible suitors.

And the ineligible?

"Why, there were none!" Esteban, the oldest brother, had proclaimed indignantly. "My father would never have allowed it."

From Luis, Roxana elicited the information that a stable hand had once tried to kiss Angelina and was surprised by their father, who horsewhipped the man himself.

Perhaps an inheritance? Could one of the siblings have murdered the sister? Pascual stated that his three brothers and himself were the only beneficiaries of their father's will. Marta and Angelina had received their portion upon their mother's death from diphtheria more than two years before.

Renaldo, the youngest of the brothers, grudgingly opined that Angelina was not completely an angel. "She was the last of the children—the image of my mother. And my father, he has spoiled Angelina terribly. But who cannot help but give her what she wants?"

Roxana took the electric trolley across the International Bridge to Juarez. Its buildings and houses still bore fresh scars from machine-gun bullets and bursting shrapnel where twice Villa had taken the city, which reflected the extremes of poverty and wealth. Whoever controlled Juarez controlled northern Mexico, rich with mines and the gateway for military supplies imported from the United States.

The Sanchez home was only a couple of blocks away from the Cárcel Publica and Juzgado de Letras, where Licenciado Sanchez's law office was located. The front of the Sanchez home was unimposing, a flat adobe wall painted a garish green, which turned its back on the dirt street. But inside, the heavy ornate furniture, grilled ironwork, and mosaic tiled floors immersed Roxana in Old World charm.

She followed an Indian woman whose huarache sandals shuffled down a palm-planted corridor to the *sala*, where Marta Sanchez greeted her. Marta was a paler version of her younger sister. She possessed the same sculptured bone structure, but the eyes did not dance secretively, the mouth did not laugh at the world.

The woman could only reaffirm what her brothers had said. Angelina would not have run off, for there had been no reason. She was happy, had all she could want, and did not have a boyfriend.

"My sister found all the young men"—Marta searched for the word, her hands groping expressively—"silly. After Enrique—"

"Enrique?"

"There." Marta pointed to the snapshot Roxana held. "The young man in the center of us. Enrique Ronquillo. All these years Angelina has idolized him. But since he is our cousin, that is all there is. If she finds a man like Enrique, then she will marry."

If she was still alive, Roxana privately added.

The Mother Superior, her veined hands momentarily concealed by the drape of the white habit, shook her head sadly. "We are all mystified by Angelina's disappearance, Miss Van Buren. She was a perfect student. All A's. She had many friends here, and I can think of no one who would have wanted to harm her. A happy child, she was."

But she wasn't a child. She was seventeen, due to be graduated from the Academy that spring. Roxana asked to speak with the friend closest to Angelina.

Maria Josefa, a plump girl with pretty features, was from South America. She faced Roxana in the Academy's vestibule. The sunlight filtering through the stained glass in the fanned window above the doorway betrayed the girl's agitation: the eyes that looked everywhere but at Roxana, the teeth that gnawed nervously at the bottom lip, the dimpled hands that twisted about each other. "I told the police everything I knew, Señorita."

"I'm sorry," Roxana said gently, "but I haven't talked with the police." She gestured toward the hand-carved bench against one stucco wall, and Maria Josefa stiffly took a seat at the opposite end of the bench from her. "I'm a friend of the family, Maria Josefa, and they're very worried. Could you please tell me all you know, again?"

"*Pues,* like I said, it was just before matins, and Angelina said she had left her rosary beads in her room. She returned to her room but never did come back for matins." The girl shrugged. "That's all I know. *Verdad.*"

"Did Angelina have a boyfriend?"

"No. No one."

The girl was lying. It was obvious. Rouche's words came back to Roxana. *Listen carefully to lies. They are sometimes very revealing of the truth.*

Roxana didn't like what she was about to do. But her job was to find Angelina Asunsolo. She fished in the chatelaine bag attached by the silver chain to her belt and came up with the package of cigarettes. She extended the pack to Maria Josefa. "Do you smoke?"

Maria Josefa glanced down the hall toward the Mother Superior's office. "Never."

"Good." Roxana lit one. "Smoking's bad for the lungs."

"But sometimes it helps the nerves," Maria Josefa mumbled. "I'll take one."

Roxana passed her the cigarette. "Why are you nervous?"

The girl inhaled deeply, then exhaled in one long breath that was almost a sigh. "Oh, you know. I'm worried about what happened to Angelina. It could happen to anyone. To me, even. After all, I was her roommate."

"What did happen?"

Maria Josefa glanced sharply at Roxana. "Why, I told you, I don't know."

"But you were worried about something. What?"

"Oh, anything could have happened. The Chinaman that brings the laundry. He could have abducted her and carried her off to one of those opium dens in Chinatown." Maria Josefa rattled on between agitated puffs of the cigarette. "You know, those Chinamen have no women of their own. They left their women to come here and earn their fortunes. A veritable sex emporium, the Mother Superior says the opium dens are."

Roxana had two leads. Enrique was the prime lead. From Don Asunsolo, Roxana learned that Enrique's parents were in the import/export business in Chihuahua, and that Enrique traveled extensively over the southwestern United States for the family business.

"I cannot believe Enrique would encourage Angelina to such a sin as incest," Don Asunsolo declared, his gold-knobbed cane jabbing emphatically with each word. "Enrique is an honorable young man."

Honorable enough to let Don Asunsolo know that his daughter was with him?

Roxana wired Enrique's parents in Chihuahua. As often happened, the telegraph lines were down, cut by one of the guerrilla factions that warred back and forth across northern Mexico. While she waited for the Ronquillos' reply to her wire, she pursued her second lead.

A funeral was in process in Chinatown, where fewer than three hundred males and four or five females were crowded alongside the adobe and wooden shanties of the Mexican Americans.

Tunnels with two-foot-thick walls and ceilings formed honeycombed passages beneath El Paso's Chinatown. One tunnel was even said to run under the Rio Grande into the heart of Juarez's dens of inequity. Those tunnels served as underground railroads for the Mexican-Chinese smuggling trade. Through them Chinese were smuggled out of Mexico and on to New York, Chicago, or San Francisco.

The funeral's bright red snakes of firecrackers heralded writhing fifty-foot papier-mâché lions and dragons. The street was blocked, and Roxana had to wait while the infernal din first passed Tony Lama's Shoe & Boot Repair, then the Overland Street Laundry. It was at the Chinese hand-laundry that she had a flicker of hope in gaining further clues to Angelina Asunsolo.

A bright vermillion card with spidery black figures announced in two languages:

WASHED SHEETS—$1.00
LADIES STARCHED DRAWERS—50 CENTS

Inside, the shop smelled of steam and starch, with the faint odor of sandalwood incense. Incredulous, Roxana watched as a little man in flowing black robes and coarse black slippers sprinkled a pair of trousers by spewing water from his mouth.

Folding the sprinkled trousers, he asked politely, "Melican lady wants clothes washed?"

Was this the laundryman whom Maria Josefa believed could have abducted Angelina for the sinister purpose of white slavery? "Do you know Señorita Angelina Asunsolo?"

The Chinaman's parchment skin creased in puzzlement. "I check."

He opened a little black rice-paper book, and his finger ran down the oblique Chinese characters. They were placed both on the laundry and in the book, using personal description to identify his customers: Unhappy Lady Who Coughs, or Fat Man With Long Fingernails, or Stick Figure Man With Hair Lice.

The Chinaman shook his head. "No, missy. I do her lawnly?"

"Señorita Asunsolo is a student at the Loretto Academy. You do their laundry."

The slanted lids seemed to slide closed like a reptile's. "I not know Missy Asunsolo."

Roxana counted on a long shot. She pulled out of her bag the yellow copy of the telegram she had sent to Chihuahua. Winking conspiratorially, she said, "I have a letter she wants me to deliver to her friend."

"Ahh, so! To Gus."

His hand reached for the paper, but she slipped the telegram back into her bag, saying, "Yes, she asked me to deliver it personally to Gus at—at—" Roxana wrinkled her forehead. "Oh, my! Where did she tell me? I'm so forgetful!"

"The Caballo Blanco," the Chinaman volunteered in his desire to accommodate.

"That's it. Thank you so much."

It took Roxana a good half hour of questioning El Pasoans to find out that the Caballo Blanco was a cantina—the White Horse Saloon. And that it was located in the most dangerous part of Juarez.

4

The cowpuncher weaved his way out of the Caballo Blanco's latrine. The cantina's adobe walls reeked of urine where drunken patrons had missed their aim. Cantinas at that hour always smelled like a stinking morgue.

At the knife-notched bar a strolling musician in a sugarloaf sombrero and a food-stained white pajama shirt solicited donations for his songs. Tipping back his cornet, the musician launched into a brassy rendition of "Adelita," a song of the Mexican Revolution. The music deafened the sibilant drone of the rainfall outside.

The cowpoke's gaze deserted the musician to search the smoky cantina. It was Friday night and the place was choked to the craw with Mexicans. Here and there tottered an American soldier or a looped cowpoke. His casual scrutiny swept to the cantina's darkened corner. The prostitute was still there. An incredibly sleazy woman with an artificial rose tucked into the frowsy black curls and rouge layered on lips and cheeks, which were no doubt as cratered as Swiss cheese. The red satin gown with black fringe had seen better days, as no doubt had the *puta*.

In other days the cowpoke would have felt more compassion for the whore. After all, this woman had been someone's infant daughter. Who was he to question what life had made of the malleable infant?

From the viewpoint of his table, he studied her through the haze of her cigarette smoke and a couple of times caught her uncertain glance ricocheting off him. He knew that evening she had had several offers from inebriated customers and had refused them. Such a gesture normally would go unnoticed. But Mexican whores were usually sharper than street Arabs and didn't miss an opportunity, all of which pricked a nerve ending in the cow-puncher's extraordinary instincts.

He lurched through the crowd to the corner table. The chair tilted precariously as he sprawled in crumpled comfort across from the *puta*. Her heavily mascaraed eyes widened, then narrowed into slits. "Beat it, mister!" she hissed.

An American woman! Working this side of the border? He grinned drunkenly. "How 'bout a little night of love, *querida*?"

Her brown eyes flashed at him, and she looked away. She was younger than he had suspected. She rapidly exhaled the cigarette smoke and lapsed into a fit of coughing before she managed to choke out, "I'm waiting for someone."

"So?" He winked lecherously. "This carcass doesn't take long to pleasure, sweetheart. Five minutes in the back room oughtta do it."

The sharp intake of her breath drew his attention to the wares so nicely displayed above the black spangled neckline. The flesh was firm and smooth, as if in the first bloom of youth. Reluctantly his gaze deserted the delectable globes and swept back up to the face. He could see he had rattled her, although she was striving to cover it.

"He's paid me to wait," she muttered.

"Who?"

"Gus," she tossed out and then looked like she could have swallowed her tongue.

At once he was alert. He flipped a Mexican 'dobe on the table, saying, "I'll match whatever Gus is giving you, sweetheart."

The woman's wide mouth curled contemptuously. She picked up the silver piece. He noted that her hands were nicely shaped and the nails clean. "I've bitten a few rotten coins, mister," she cracked from the side of her mouth, "and don't need to hook up with the likes of you."

Well, refinement wasn't everything.

She tossed the silver piece back to him, and he caught it in midair. "I can take a hint, sweetheart." He shoved away from the table, nearly toppling the chair again, and staggered back to his own table to take up his watch. But Gus didn't come through the bat-wing doors the rest of that evening.

Unfortunately, Concha did.

If the six-foot *puta* weighed an ounce, she weighed two hundred pounds. Her ebony locks were as greasy as tallow. For the cantina's male patrons she had the proverbial heart of gold—and a knife for her competition. Sourly she eyed the woman who unwittingly had taken her table. From between her abundant and pendulous bosoms, Concha produced her stiletto-sharp conversation piece and advanced menacingly on the unsuspecting whore who occupied her table.

The bartender's white apron momentarily obscured the cowpoke's vision, then it flashed by to show the slow-motion play that was in progress: Concha hovering murderously over the *gringa puta* . . . the *gringa's* eyes unnaturally wide, her mouth parting in the beginning of a gurgled scream . . . the drunken men turning with excitement in their chairs to watch the coming brawl . . . a small scarlet pinprick at the *gringa's* throat.

After years that seemed but a blur of mescal haze, the cowpoke moved much quicker than he would have thought he could. In less than the breadth of a cough he had Concha's thick wrist clutched in his fingers. "She's mine for the night, Concha."

The surprise faded from the painted jowls, and Concha's fat-padded thumb and forefinger came up to pinch his jaw with several playful shakes. "So, you gonna play big stud tonight, eh?" She jerked her head toward the American woman, who sat with eyes glazed, watching the two. "A good lay, the *puta*, no?"

"Si, Concha." He grinned wickedly. "She's good in the bed—but doesn't know half the tricks you do."

He released Concha's wrist and reached for the bare arm of the American woman. "Get your shawl."

She tried to pull away, and he leaned down, his mouth next to her ear, his hand indecently cupping the side of her breast. Beneath his fingers he could feel her stiffen, but he continued to paw the cheap, gaudy satin over her breast in what was almost an obscene gesture. "These men already feel cheated of one fight, and I'm sure as hell not going to fight them for you. You coming with me?"

She nodded mutely. He pulled her to her feet, and her shapely hindquarters captured his eyes. When she tried to move away, his arm tightened about her waist. She was taller than he had expected but seemed slight, especially with Concha hulking along behind them.

"I go weeth you two and teach some tricks, eh?"

Hell! "Afterwards, Concha."

"You geet eet up twice for Concha, I think!" the gargantuan woman snorted and thumped his crotch with her thumb and forefinger.

She lumbered off, and he started down the dimly lit hall with the American woman in tow. The gas lamp's smoky yellow light lent a stricken, sickly look to her face. Beneath his fingertips he could feel her pulse throbbing erratically in her wrist. What was the connection between her and Gus? Was she a part of Felix Sommerfield's ring?

Then good ol' Gus Gruenwald had more than one espionage agent working El Paso. The Germans were willing to try every trick in the book to embroil the United States in a war with Mexico while they rolled over Europe—even to using prostitutes to pump information out of the American soldiers stationed at Bliss.

When a doughboy staggered out of the privy, he thrust the woman up against the wall, burying his face in the hollow of her shoulder and groping at her breast while the soldier stumbled on by. Against his temple her breath was hot and shallow and rapid. The hallway's odor of puke and urine could not entirely overpower the woman's faint scent of jasmine. Her pelvis fitted like a puzzle's piece against his own, and he didn't move immediately when the hallway was deserted once more.

Then he felt the short cylinder pressing against his ribs. The pistol's barrel jiggled slightly, and he knew she was trying to make up her mind.

"I've never been shot by a woman before."

It wasn't said flippantly, and it unnerved her just enough for his elbow to swing inward, knocking the pistol between their feet. At the same time his right hand fastened about her throat, the crux of his thumb and forefinger closing off her windpipe. "Don't scream, old girl, or we're both dead meat for the knife-happy Mexs out there."

He felt the taut muscles in her neck slacken. "Good," he murmured.

He relaxed his hold, though his hand still grasped her throat firmly but gently, like a hunting dog's teeth on a buckshot duck. Her flesh beneath his callused fingers was soft, smooth as Cathay silk. He eased forward, pressing her hips against the wall. He didn't especially want to kiss the bright red slash that was her mouth, but he liked and wanted the feel of feminine softness against him. . . .

He should have expected it from the whore. Her knee shot up hard and swift, smashing into its target with perfect aim. He doubled, jerking to his knees, the pain a rainbow of explosive lights, his groans an echo of her tapping red heels fading off down the hallway.

He staggered to his feet, grabbed up her pearl-handled derringer, and lurched toward the rear door. Calle de Noche Triste, Street of the Sad Night, was a dark ribbon of mud. Rain, which would have been snow had it been any colder, curtained the vision beyond twenty-five yards.

Something in him warned that it wasn't wise to stand silhouetted in the lighted doorway. And so he stood there a moment longer, his old anger defying—welcoming—whatever crouched in the night. *Bring it on.*

But there was only the muted raucousness of the cantina.

His three-inch rowel spurs jangled on the wooden stairs as he stepped into the rain-slick street. The rain pummeled his hat. He turned up his face to let the ice-cold water explode on his cheekbones and spatter into his slitted eyes. The drops dribbled down his neck and channeled under his skeepskin jacket. Its cleansing effect felt good and he laughed.

Sloshing down the street, his mind turned to the American woman. Inexplicably he thought of Rowena. An image of her sitting before the piano crept through the corridors of his brain, until Sam Brady slammed an iron door on it.

Wallace Van Buren's father was a Supreme Court Justice, the Honorable Augustus Van Buren. All sorts of important personages came and went to the imposing three-story Van Buren House in Washington, D.C., so the friend Wally brought home from West Point for the Thanksgiving holidays was just another face among the Congressmen, foreign ambassadors, and naval and military cadets.

Well, almost.

Rowena, Wally's younger sister, noticed Sam Brady at once. His clear blue eyes could bestow at times, when he was either angered or scouting out uncharted ground, a black look that made him formidable and, thus, even more handsome. In the aristocratic Van Buren home the young man raised on a modest Kansas ranch was definitely scouting out uncharted ground.

When his father died in the Spanish-American War, Sam at

fourteen had been given the responsibility of running the ranch. However, he was beckoned to the life of the military by his father's Medal of Honor, which he removed periodically with reverent, callused fingers from a cigar box of youthful treasures.

The day came that Sam handed his mother the article placed by the district's Congressman in the *Kansas Weekly Courier*. She knew then her only son was already caught up in that Dash and Daring that had claimed her husband but was for her nothing but organized violence.

On July 7th there will be a competitive examination for the appointment of a cadet at the United States Military Academy at West Point. All honest, strong, God-fearing boys of this district may take part.

Beginning then, Sam initiated a program of study after his day's chores were finished. Often his head hurt from so much studying. At nights, after putting away his textbooks, he worked his way through the legal commentaries of Kent and Blackstone, trying to absorb the basics of law.

He took the test at Topeka and his months of intensive studying stood him in good stead. During the oral portion his voice rang strong and true with no faltering. His sheer determination and confidence were an invading force of vitality that influenced the judges in his favor over two other applicants who had scored as well.

Sam's ambition was for more than just the first-rate education at the government's expense that the military academy would provide. For him there was the strange alchemy of West Point that beckoned him as a plebe that summer of 1903. Those four years of tradition bound by West Point's credo, "Duty, honor, country," made the measure of him. The work was constant; the studying a lingering, chronic plague. He did well on the rifle range and on military topography, but poorly at French, saddled by his Midwestern twang.

Despite or maybe because of his middle-class background, he was a challenge to the utterly beautiful young girl who was accustomed to having callers invade the Van Buren parlor merely to be allowed to sit mutely before her and her mother, cousin, older sister, or whatever duenna could be found at the moment. Rowena noted that the cadet with wildly curling caramel hair was lacking in social graces. That would be the first thing Mrs. Augustus Van Buren would point out if Rowena displayed even mild interest in the young cadet. Her father would merely raise that bushy arch of an eyebrow that made grown men squirm.

So that Thanksgiving eighteen-year-old Rowena played the piano more prettily, laughed more gaily, and was more full of high spirits than ever. But in no way did she commit herself even by a mere look that favored Sam Brady among any of the other young men who called. A lady never committed herself. Neither did she slight even the lowliest of her callers, for kindness was the essence of good breeding. Thus impartially did the well-bred young lady portion out her attention to each and every visitor.

For his part, Sam knew, with the same certainty he had known he was destined to be a soldier, that the beautiful golden-haired Rowena was the woman meant for him. He was a young man of immense patience, and he bided his time that Thanksgiving, then accepted Wally's next invitation to come down for the Christmas holidays.

Sam sat in the parlor and watched Rowena's wing-collared beaux warble carols around the piano, which was draped with Christmas garlands. The sound of her lovely voice made his breath catch oddly, and the gaslight playing over her bare, alabaster shoulders suffused his cheeks with hot color.

He was in love. At night, when he lay on the big tester bed in one of the guest bedrooms, his thoughts dwelled on the lovely Rowena. Quality, intelligence, grace, kindness. A soft, modulated voice that did strange things to his insides. A tender white neck that beckoned to be stroked. The golden ringlets that would surely curl about his fingers of their own accord. For him, there could be no other woman.

He was a direct young man and he knew the time was coming

to make his intentions known. Wally already knew. A morning or so later the stocky young man cornered Sam, who was shaving. "You got it in the worst way for Rowena, don't you, old man?"

Sam never took his eyes from his reflection. "I'm going to marry your younger sister, Wally."

Wally stared at Sam's reflection. "Well, bully!" he pronounced in his best Teddy Roosevelt voice. "Does Rowena know how you feel? Forget that question—my younger sister is very astute where men are concerned. I'm sure she is more than aware of your interest. She has probably done her damnedest to encourage it. It wouldn't surprise me if she isn't playing that dashed chap from the British Embassy—Hadley—off against you."

He paused, choosing his words with care, then said, "Nothing I'd like better than to see you marry Rowena. But you have the Honorable Justice to face. My father has plans for his daughters that don't include a mere soldier." Even for his own son, the Honorable Justice Van Buren had chosen West Point only for its academic training. After graduation, Wally would become a lawyer, then—who knew? Perhaps President, like a distant Van Buren had been a generation earlier.

Sam dipped the brush in his hsaving mug. "But I don't plan to be a mere soldier." One cheek muscle stretched the skin smooth before the path of his straight-edged razor. "I plan to be a general, Wally, and I want Rowena at my side."

"It's a damned good general you'll be, Sam."

Wally and his fellow cadets had found a striking martial quality in Sam. They had conferred on him the honor of class presidency, and the Academy officials had awarded him the highest cadet office available each year.

From the beginning Sam had quickly developed the right idea of command and authority, aided by his robust build and keen searching eyes with their intense gaze. His personal magnetism won him followers and admirers. His exercise of authority was of a peculiarly impersonal nature: dispassionate, hard, and firm. His manner, when most of his fellow cadets were a trifle shaky-voiced and shamefaced about snapping orders and were far from having acquired the "habit of command," indicated clearly that he believed he had an unquestionable right to obedience. But then, he was older.

That instinctive grasp of the "right to obedience" had led him steadily upward through the West Point ranks, until as a First Classman, he was appointed Captain of Cadets—surely one of those uniquely favored First Captains so often destined to make history.

With the girls who came up to West Point for the hops, Sam Brady was even more popular—and, if anything, even more stiff and formal, for Wally knew Sam had not allowed himself the time to enjoy the fairer sex. He was cautious and uneasy. For all their flirtatious motions, the young ladies were unable to defrost his icy command manner. Wally should have known his sister Rowena would succeed in defrosting his friend.

Sam waited until the last day of the holidays to make his intentions known to Rowena. Actually, by then she was quite peeved that he had evinced no obvious interest: no longing looks or flowery speeches. And she was downright incensed when Sam did speak his mind. Did he suppose he could conquer her without paying his respects, without calling on her and courting her?

She had repaired to the drawing room to play the piano, all the while hoping passionately that Sam would approach her before he and Wally had to leave for West Point. When he presented himself at the drawing room's French doors, he was terribly handsome in his full dress white uniform with his military hat tucked beneath his arm.

Her heart fluttered erratically. Putting a stilling hand to her throat, she said quite calmly, "Good evening, Captain Brady."

He made the cadet's formal bow, the old military one with one leg placed in front. "Good evening, Miss Van Buren. I'm leaving today and wanted a word with you before going."

"Leaving so soon? We do hope you've enjoyed yourself with us." She rose from the piano with a swish of her magenta taffeta skirts and crossed to the damask and rosewood sofa. "Here, let me pour you some tea. Do sit down. The Christmas holidays have always been special, what with so many friends dropping in to visit. Sugar? Cream? No, you don't take either, I remember now."

She was running on, but she couldn't seem to put a halt to her tongue. With those blue eyes regarding her so steadfastly, her veneer of sophistication was severely threatened. "There you are. Careful now, you wouldn't want to spot your lovely uniform."

Balancing the teacup's saucer on one knee, he spoke directly, for that was all that he knew how to do. "Miss Van Buren, within six months' time I'll graduate and be posted to some unknown destination. After that I most likely won't have the opportunity to call on you for some time. So I must tell you now that over the weeks I have spent here I have come to admire you greatly. You are everything that I would want in a wife. If you share any of the same feelings, I would like to call on you formally with the intention of asking your father for your hand in marriage upon my graduation this June."

Rowena sat stunned. Where were the yearning looks and the wistful sighs? The cadet had not even given her the opportunity to practice coquetry, to ply her feminine wiles. It was either yes or no. Not that her family would ever seriously consider permitting her to marry the young man who possessed no significant family background.

"I'm honored by your proposal, Captain Brady," she said at last, salvaging some of her feminine pride, "but we don't really know each other well enough for such a precipitous decision. Perhaps, after a while . . ." She let her words trail off, thereby lending encouragement, for she was more than attracted to Sam Brady.

He stood and sat the teacup on the drop-leaf table. With a stiff bow, he said, "I thank you then for your gracious hospitality, Miss Van Buren."

Pale pink flooded her cheeks as she rose easily to her feet. Her tulip-blue eyes mirrored her confusion. "Wait, I—I can give you no definite answer. That would be up to my father." She lowered her head shyly. She hated to lose this young man who possessed such an air of self-command, who was somehow different from all the posturing swains who had called on her. "But I would welcome your attentions."

Boldly, he took one of the soft, slender hands that gracefully clasped the other before her bosom and held the cool hand between his large ones. He was excited, more than his demeanor betrayed, and he felt like his hands were a pair of warm oysters. "Miss Van Buren . . . Rowena . . . you have done me great honor."

Rowena's lashes dropped. A sweet silence of expectation pervaded the drawing room. When Sam would have kissed her hand, the front door slammed open, and the older sister, Roxana, burst in. Without pausing, she pushed open the French doors. Sam groaned inside.

Roxana Van Buren rubbed him the wrong way. She was one of those females who knew nothing about gentleness or the other maidenly attributes that endeared a woman to a man. Cyrano's fair Roxana wasn't matched in beauty by this Roxana. At twenty, Roxana Van Buren was impossibly opinionated, with not a soft line to her. A big-boned young woman, even her speech came out as clipped and brisk as her name. Fortunately she was absent from the mansion more often than she was present.

Her face was unbecomingly flushed by the cold, and her nose was a bright, shiny red. Beneath the fur turban, her brown hair was frazzled by the blustery wind. She tossed the matching barrel fur muff on the sofa, saying, "Have you finished proposing, Captain Brady? Wally and I have a wager riding on the outcome."

"Roxana!" Rowena gasped. "Have you not the common decency to see—"

"I have common sense," Roxana said crisply, crossing to the silver tea service to pour herself a cup. She ignored Sam's black look and continued, "More sense than you or Captain Brady apparently have."

The romantic moment was spoiled, and Sam took his leave shortly thereafter. But at least he knew that the first step in his plan to marry Rowena was effected. That afternoon, her father received him formally in the library. Sam came right to the point, declaring his love for the youngest daughter as well as his wish to court her.

The Supreme Court Justice fixed Cadet Captain Brady with the eye that had reduced many a brilliant lawyer to stuttering uncertainty. But the young man faced him with determination—with that vast assurance that allowed Sam to believe in himself without thinking overwell of himself.

The shrewd patriarch, who was of old Dutch stock, listened to Sam's short declaration. When Sam was finished, Justice Van Buren sat silently, flexing the fingers of each hand as they met together to form a pyramid. At last, he spoke—as diplomatically as a politician, as tactically as any military man.

"Rowena would not survive happily on a frontier post, Mr. Brady. Her illusions of love would be shattered before they had a chance to gain substance. If you are so determined, I ask that you wait a year after your graduation. Then . . ." he waved a hand negligently, "then if you two are still of the same mind . . . why, yes, I will grant my permission for the engagement."

Sam recognized a powerful opponent in the father. He could have matched him argument for argument, quite ably. Yet, he knew he stood to win much more by waiting the year and letting Rowena come to him of her own free will than by a manipulative tug of war between him and Rowena's father.

That spring, graduation was celebrated with dinner at Delmonico's with Sam at the head of the table as Class President. He was commissioned a second lieutenant in the cavalry in the Regular Army, and found himself posted to Fort Fillmore in the New Mexico Territory.

When the rain drip-dropped through the one-room adobe

quarters, turning the walls to mud . . . when the sandstorms, despite battened windows and locked doors, settled their fine grit over the table's food . . . when a baby made that dreadful crouping noise and the nearest doctor was forty miles away at Fort Bliss, El Paso . . . Sam wondered if Augustus Van Buren wasn't right about Rowena's disposition on the territorial frontier.

Still, he had faith in Rowena's strength of character. She wasn't a Van Buren for nothing. Each month on the most important day on post—the arrival of the Express Mail, when the ranchers rode into the fort to collect their mail and the soldiers eagerly gathered for long-awaited letters—Sam always found one from Rowena. Her lighthearted letters promised nothing yet revealed much: her insight at her own foibles, her secret amusement at her parents' pretentiousness, and always those polite closings that betrayed her slight uneasiness in handling this self-assured Midwesterner.

The soldiers whiled away the isolation with poker. But Sam, bored by cards, read his way through the post library and devoted himself to learning the Indian languages from the Navajo and Mescalero Apache, and Spanish from the civilian scouts. He thought often of Rowena, trying to imagine her so very different life and the pressures that no doubt were being applied to her. He kept faith with himself and with her own strong sense of will.

At the end of the first year he applied for a six-weeks' leave and returned to Washington, D.C., where he took a room off Fourteenth and Constitution for the duration of his stay. Wally, who had been appointed to the bar, filled him in with gossip of old West Point friends, and Roxana, involved in another suffragist program, was friendly enough in her distracted manner. Justice and Mrs. Van Buren were polite when he called, and Rowena's eyes twinkled at this knight who was so determined to carry her off.

His steady pursuit won the day, and in a thrilling moment when his lips sought hers, she relented and became engaged to Sam Brady, with her parent's reluctant blessing. There was still that year of engagement before the wedding, and Justice Van Buren no doubt hoped that a change of heart might still be effected, especially since Sam was promptly posted to the Philippines. Eight years earlier the United States had acquired the islands as spoils from the Spanish-American War, the same war that had taken Sam's father.

Determined to acquire the polish he lacked, Sam booked passage at his own expense aboard a British steamship bound for Liverpool. He sailed in advance of the *Missouri*, which was going by way of the Suez Canal, so he could spend a few weeks sightseeing.

He explored London diligently, crowding his days and evenings there full: Westminster Abbey, the Bank of England, the palaces and museums, the London Tower. Paris came next: Notre Dame, the Madeleine, the Pantheon, Les Invalides, the Bois de Boulogne, the Opera. What interested him most, though, were the art galleries; he spent some time each day in the Louvre and the Luxembourg, fascinated by such a collection of the world's masterpieces.

At last, he sailed for Manila. Within a year Rowena would be joining him as his bride at his post in Zamboanga, and he could imagine no place more perfect for a honeymoon than that exotic and languorous port of the south seas with its coral shores. The officers lolled at their ease in cantonments by the Sulu Sea, chewing betel nut and accepting drinks from native servants bearing brass trays. Their days were wafted by cooling trade winds, and the smooth white sandy beaches were only twenty paces from the splended bamboo palisades that were the bachelor officers' quarters at Camp Vicars. The verandas in the BOQ were filled with palms and ferns and hung profusely with rare orchids.

From the canteens, pretty, dark-eyed native girls dispensed cigars and candy, among other favors. Many soldiers in the Philippines had native girls for mistresses. Having a mistress carried no stigma; marrying one did. Sam never took a mistress. For him there existed only the golden loveliness of Rowena.

Instead, he worked hard to acquire the Maranaw dialect and learned to use the wide, sharp bolo swords. Because of his unusual attitude, the military governor of the Moro province, Major General and Assistant Adjutant General John J. "Black Jack" Pershing—named for the black cavalry troop he had commanded—offered Sam an appointment as aide-de-camp on his personal staff.

What the brusque Pershing, who had little respect for posturing, thought of this zealous shavetail, he never said. But his reliance on Sam became more and more evident as the Fifth Troop took to the mountains and jungles to storm hostile Moro *cottas*, or forts. That year Sam rode the narrow jungle trails with Pershing, acquiring the habit of partaking of afternoon tea and learning when to show initiative and when to obey orders.

Like Pershing, Sam inspired confidence among his men. He still found his own inspiration in his father's Medal of Honor.

At times he was lonely, and Mrs. Pershing and the other officers' wives clucked over him, consoling him that it was only a matter of months before his intended arrived. Homemade pies found their way to his table, as well as hand-sewn curtains for his bare quarters, which sat on stilts.

If one officer's wife offered to console him a little more than the others, he honestly never noticed it—at least not at first.

After a while, though, Alice Waterman's attentions became obvious. She was a pretty little woman, strawberry blond, with fluttering hands. Pancake hats over her pompadour hairdo did little to protect her pale skin, which pinked easily in the tropical sun. She was ambitious for her husband's success in the military. Like Sam, her husband was a lieutenant, but he lacked that quiet capability that was Sam's. She saw promotions pass her husband by, and she despaired. And she envied. And she almost hated. And because she did, she went out of her way to make certain no one suspected her ill will for Sam, least of all him.

Yet those little kindnessess she showed him backlashed. Alice Waterman fell helplessly in love with Lieutenant Sam Brady. He was everything her husband wasn't. And it galled her that he could be so unaware of her as a desirable woman. She personally mended his dress whites when his orderly could just as easily have done it. She left little bouquets of exotic wild flowers on his table, and his careless thanks hurt. She had only to brush his hand covertly and all the emotional pain subsided. She felt that if she could ever bring Sam to her bed, he would understand her, see her for the good person she was, and love her in return.

Even Sam, at last, became aware of the intensity of passion Alice silently bore him. Tactfully, he put as much distance between them as possible. Even so, he was forbiddingly handsome when glaring steadily at her from beneath those winged brows that, with the eyelashes, were so much darker than his butter-yellow hair.

The night the typhoon struck, her husband was on maneuvers, and she went to Sam for help in battening down the storm shutters over windows that were mere sliding panels of translucent sea shells. The house was swaying on its stilts. Fighting the sea-wet wind, she and Sam were thrown together, her heavy white skirts whipping about his long legs. When he caught her, her whispered "Sam" was lost on the wind. But her lips clung to his, begging.

He tried to set her from him, but her arms were tenacious cables about his shoulders. The heat from her hungry mouth slowly infused Sam's repressed sexual drive. Too long without a source of expression, his desire leaped to the surface in a furious blaze. He forgot all that he stood to lose, everything that was dear to him, in the mindless frenzy to couple with the woman entwined about him. Their passion was consummated with the wind shrieking outside the fragile house.

Afterwards, even as the typhoon still raged, Sam abruptly left her to return to his own quarters. He felt as if he had hurt Rowena, though she could never possibly know about the incident. He debated and agonized over writing her. He wanted badly to get the incident off his conscience. Common sense told him that he might needlessly hurt her. He loved her, and the last thing he wanted was to hurt her.

Rowena did find out, because Alice, humiliated by Sam's

rejection, once she had let him take and use her, announced to her husband and ultimately to every major newspaper in the United States that Sam Brady had raped her.

Women's suffrage might be on the move and the anarchist Emma Goldman might be touring with her titillating lecture on free love, but virtually every American female followed the story of the court-martial. Some did solely because of its sensationalism; others simply because of the photograph of the handsome officer. Then, too, in that year of 1909, some had sweethearts or husbands posted in the Philippines.

"You have been charged with a heinous crime," the president of the military court said, looking grimly at the accused officer, then to the officer-lawyers who flanked him. "What have you to say in your defense?"

Staring straight ahead, Lieutenant Brady replied in a firm voice, "I ask the trial court to let my record speak for itself." He would not attempt to vindicate himself. It was not a passivity that held him silent but rather a profound belief in military justice, a certainty that he would be judged innocent.

During the court-martial, Sam Brady's defense was magnificent, proving Sam's sterling character with witness after witness. Not one Moro woman could be found to testify she had slept with the lieutenant, which was certainly not the case with most of the soldiers, married ones included. It was the fate of those married ones that prejudiced public opinion against Sam. Feminine readers "back home" were forced to speculate on what their own spouses and sweethearts were doing in their spare time.

Alice Waterman stuck to her story of rape.

At last the court-martial came to its close. The president read the verdict in a stentorian monotone. "The court finds you, Lieutenant Brady, not guilty of rape . . ." A long pause gave Sam false hope. ". . . but does find you guilty of indulging in conduct unbecoming to an officer and a gentleman."

The next day, under a white hot sky, Sam was drummed out of the service in an emotion-laden ceremony. In front of the division in formation, General Pershing sliced off Sam's brass buttons and epaulettes and broke Sam's sword over his knee. Then the division was commanded to about face, their backs to Sam. As the muffled drum rolled, he was escorted out the post gate by two officers. His belongings were flung out after him.

So did one of the finest soldiers of the era forfeit his military career, along with the aristocratic Rowena Van Buren.

There it was, too, that the white sands of the Sulu Sea slowly covered a Medal of Honor that had been hurled into the azure water from a bamboo balcony.

5

After the rain the early March weather was warm, so Roxana wore a broad flat straw hat, a shirtwaist blouse, and a gray flannel skirt with box pleats that showed her trim ankles. Of course, a lady was never caught out without her gloves and parasol. From a wide, silver-buckled belt hung a leather purse in which she carried cigarettes and matches. She never gave a second thought to the paradox of gloves and parasols and cigarettes and matches. She was a mass of contradictions; wasn't everyone? So, she had determined some years before that she would no longer wage a senseless, useless battle trying to gel herself into a single mold.

Into the purse she tucked the Southern Pacific's schedule and stepped out of the Union Station's shadows into the street. She knew now that the day Angelina disappeared there were three trains out, two running west and one east. The two westward bound trains passed through Tucson.

She still had not reached Enrique's parents, but if he traveled the American Southwest for the family's import/expert business . . .

Was Angelina with Enrique, and if so, where were they now? Or was she with this Gus Gruenwald?

What if she was dead? The odds were that a body would have turned up by now. Roxana shuddered, wondering if she would have the fortitude to go to the morgue to view a corpse.

Gus Gruenwald was her one and only lead. He had not shown up at the Caballo Blanco. No one there had known where to find him, but an American soldier had drunkenly mumbled something about Gus having some kind of contract with the Army.

The muscle ridges that flanked Roxana's spine from the small of her back to the base of her skull tightened into stiff columns. It could have been the unpleasant memory of the night before— of the swaggering Mexican guerrillas, most of whom had never seen Villa, or so they said; of the menacing, hefty whore and her switchblade; of the besotted, leering cowboy who had pawed her so disgustingly. She had been fortunate Rouche had taught her some of the simpler tricks of the trade, like aiming for a man's groin.

The uneasy feeling persisted, and instinctively she glanced around. Soldiers in steeple-crowned campaign hats, pigtailed Chinese, sombreroed Mexicans, carriages, a few automobiles, horses, the electric trolley—they all packed the street, making distinction impossible. Yet she had the impression of a cowboy's unshaven face and bleary eyes beneath a soldier-Stetson white hat.

For a moment her gloved hand ran along her throat, where his fingers had pressed. Beneath the shirtwaist's stiff collar was the knife's pinprick, already healing over. She shrugged away the eerie feeling and hurried to catch one of the streetcars that made five daily trips out to Lanoria Mesa, where, at the foot of the Franklin Mountains, sprawled Fort Bliss.

With its five thousand soldiers, the fort housed the largest body of troops in the nation. Heavy traffic had reduced the two roads from town to the army post into miserable thoroughfares. Mayor

Lea had convinced the county to pave them, and construction was underway, so that when Roxana swung off the open streetcar, white dust coated her clothing and skin.

At the adobe sentry station the guard, his khaki trousers tucked into canvas-gaitered boots, obstinately refused to let her enter the post grounds until she displayed her press credentials, reluctantly supplied to her by *The Washington Post*. Even then he condescendingly directed the woman reporter toward Post Headquarters.

The information she wanted about Gus Gruenwald could be obtained there, but she hoped to get a private interview for the *Post* with Pershing himself, which would be no little feat. Word was about that since the deaths by fire of his wife and three daughters several months earlier, he had become a difficult man to deal with.

Then, too, he was an expert at ridding himself of newspapermen, whom he disliked on principle. War correspondents considered the fifty-six-year-old general a cold, arrogant fish. His stiff-upper-lip attitude wasn't going to deter Roxana. She had dealt with her father too often to let herself be intimidated by the mere male.

She had to get some kind of interview, if only to remind the *Post* she was still an accredited journalist. But, also, she missed her writing. She loved the written word, the infinite variety of rhythm the words made when strung together, the many nuances possessed by a single word. Her fingers itched for a typewriter.

There was a particular odor about all army posts, a combination of army stew, horses, mothballs, garbage, leather, and perspiration. Peaked khaki tents, which had replaced the old white canvas ones, were everywhere, along with drilling soldiers, many of whom missed step at the sight of the young woman with the hourglass figure, strolling down Sheridan Road. The soldiers wore khaki now instead of Old Army blue and some carried holstered .45s instead of carbines and sabers.

Behind the front desk at Post Headquarters she encountered a

brash young man with whitish blond closely shaven hair. Lieutenant George Patton eyed her up and down and snapped, "We're
not an information service. The guard should never have let you
through."

She delivered up a sad smile and lowered her eyes. "Gus
disappeared after—oh, sir, I'm merely trying to find my baby's
father."

The lieutenant softened imperceptibly. "I see." He rose and
rustled through a file cabinet before returning to his desk. "Really
can't tell you much. The army has a contract with Gruenwald
to procure beef for our commissaries at forts Hancock and Bliss
and Camp Furlong. No permanent address is given on the contract."

That was enough. Fort Hancock was fifty miles to the southeast
of Bliss, and Camp Furlong was outside Columbus, New Mexico,
fifty miles to the west—right on the railroad line running to
Tucson. Could there be a tie-in? Satisfied with this newest piece
of information, she thanked the lieutenant and headed for Quarters No. 1.

The two-story brick structure was built along simple, square
lines with a covered wooden porch extending around three sides.
A year before, its resident, General Scott, had entertained Buffalo
Bill as well as a more friendly Villa. Now General John "Black
Jack" Pershing occupied the commander's quarters, along with
his orderly and his sister Mae, who cared for his remaining child,
a son named Warren.

Surprisingly, entree was simple enough. The general himself,
furiously puffing on a cigar, opened the door. The press reported
that the man had started smoking again after the deaths of his
wife and daughters. He was distinguished, with gray in his sandy
hair, but his mouth was tight under the stern mustache. "You're
here to see Mae about the dress fittings?"

"No, sir. I'm a reporter. I want to interview you about your
perspectives on Villa."

His face fossilized, and his tone became brusque. "Then come to the press conferences. My aide hands out the prepared statements."

"And limits the questions to clarifying the prepared statement," she said just as brusquely. "I want an in-depth interview."

"Out of the question," the general snapped and shut the door.

But in that instant before the door closed, she got a glimpse of his private office just off the main hallway and the man slumped unceremoniously on the office's leather sofa: a cowboy with an unshaven face and a battered white soldier-Stetson slouched low on his head.

6

From the end room in Columbus's Commercial Hotel, one could view the motion picture theater that stood on the other side of the dirt street. The marquee announced *Tillie's Punctured Romance* with Marie Dressler. Incredible, that an outpost in the desert beyond El Paso would have a motion picture theater without even electricity. A special carbide generator had to be used.

Down the hotel's hallway, a Victrola scratchily played "The Sheik of Araby." Angelina purred cigarette smoke through her nostrils, and leaned against the window casing, quiet as a cat. She wasn't listening to the song's lyrics; instead, she was reflecting on her success with the man in the rumpled bed behind her. How easily he could be manipulated.

Then, everyone could be manipulated, if a certain finesse was utilized. Her father, especially; her brothers and Marta; Maria Josefa; Gus. But not Enrique, at least not easily.

She could remember exactly the first time she knew she wanted Enrique. Not "loved," for she had loved him from her earliest memory, but "wanted."

It was five years ago. She was twelve. With her mother she had gone up to Cloudcroft in the Sacramento Mountains of New Mexico. Every summer the businessmen of El Paso sent their women and children there to escape the city's dehydrating heat.

An excursion car, with canvas curtains that could be pulled down against sudden showers, huffed and shook and trembled its way up and around the sharp, steep curves. Each bend of the mountain revealed breathtaking vistas of forested peaks and deep rocky canyons that brought "oohs" and "ahhhs" from the passengers. The high S trestle signaled the last mile of ascent to Cloudcroft hill. It was the steepest railroad grade in the United States, and each time the trip was made, Angelina shivered with a special thrill of danger that was unequaled—until that afternoon the train rolled into the tiny Cloudcroft depot and she saw Enrique.

Staying with him at the Bavarian-accented Cloudcroft Lodge were two other men, one a Mexican governor who made little impression on her. The other was Pancho Villa, who even then had created a name for himself, the "Centaur of the North." At that time he was a hero of the Mexican peons, having himself rebelled against the Lopez Negrete family of Durango, for whom his family had labored in feudal servitude. Some said it was because Don Arturo Lopez Negrete's son had raped Villa's sister.

Villa had a real fondness for children; he patted them and talked to them often. She well remembered his wonderful smile, although her mother claimed he was a ruthless man full of hate and she couldn't understand what her nephew was doing with the odious man.

Enrique never did explain to his aunt why he was with Villa, only that he was there in Cloudcroft to buy the mountain produce—carrots, cabbage, and corn—for the family import business.

What Angelina remembered even more that summer than Villa's smile was Enrique's pale brown eyes. At the tennis courts, on the golf link, in the casino's amusement hall and bowling alley she caught them on her. Each time a small tremor of excitement went through her, as if he knew her secret—as if he knew of that determination within her that would stop at nothing until she had what she wanted.

Maybe to everyone else she was just an exquisitely beautiful child to be pampered and petted, but she meant for Enrique to know differently. One afternoon he had ridden horseback with her and her mother. The air was sweet with the scent of giant pines and firs and spruce. In the meadows were wild strawberries and raspberries to be picked, and she could still remember the vivid carmine Indian paintbrush, sunflowers of pure gold, and asters like the purples of heaven.

Even then she had known she was a sensual person, that with each passing year her senses required stronger stimulation. Thwarting a playmate, taunting a servant, persuading her schoolmates at Loretto into smoking and other things that would have horrified the Mother Superior—these things were losing their titillation.

In Enrique she recognized the ultimate stimulant; she recognized his dangerously primitive nature, an essence that he would never acknowledge. For him to do so would make it so.

When they returned to the Lodge's stables and her mother went up to her room to change, Angelina towed her cousin along with her up to the copper-roofed tower, insisting that he must see the view of the limitless white sands fifty miles away in the basin below the Sacramentos. The amused look on his face proclaimed he knew what she was up to.

It was there, in the cupola's sitting room where they were alone, that she took his strong hand and placed it inside her riding habit against the breast that was just beginning to burgeon. There was no shock on his face, but his expression closed over. "You are but a precocious child, Angelina, and the game you are playing is dangerous."

"It's no game," she said quietly, tensely. "My body is readying itself for you, Enrique."

He did not remove his hand. "What you want is wicked, it's incest. Do you understand?"

She nodded, her eyes glowing.

He wedged her small budding nipple in the web of his thumb and forefinger with just enough pressure to make her breath suck in. "There is the seed of destruction in you," he said huskily.

"No, Enrique. There is the deeper taste of life in me. A hunger that is forbidden to the silly people who are weak and afraid."

"And perhaps wise. I will find my source of exhilaration elsewhere."

"We shall see," she said with an assurance that belied her twelve years.

"The liberation of Mexico offers more danger, more excitement, more satisfaction than what you might tempt me with, Angelina."

Impudently her laughing eyes had glanced down at his crotch. "Your better half indicates otherwise, Enrique." Then, seriously, "And you will never be satisfied—nor I—until we have each other."

He had squeezed her hard then, so that her lids briefly closed with the ecstasy. And when they opened, he was leaving.

After that, during the times when he was in El Paso, he regarded her with an almost fraternal amusement that made her even more determined to make him hers. If it was to be a test of wills, so be it.

Then, finally, she was ready to engage in that test. When Enrique last came to their house, the month before, he had deserted her family early that evening after dinner, pleading another engagement.

She slipped into the guest bedroom he used when in town. "Take me with you, Enrique," she said from behind him.

He tucked a Luger into his shoulder holster and adjusted his waistcoat before turning to face her. "The Caballo Blanco is no place for a lady."

She raised one delicately winged brow. "I am no lady."

"Of that I am well aware. But I do not want to have to defend your honor, Angelina." Above the black sweep of the handlebar mustache his eyes mocked her. "Or is there any honor in you?"

"Absolutely none."

He threw back his head and laughed, and she knew she had delighted him. "You are seeing another woman?"

"Gus would resent being called a woman," he said and turned back to the dressing table to insert a torpedo-shaped gold link into the cuff of one sleeve.

The name was enough. It was a simple task to bribe the Chinaman who brought the Academy's laundry to deliver the note to Gus at the Caballo Blanco. Perhaps not that simple, for Gus didn't show for several nights. When he finally did, the Chinaman returned to the Academy the following day with Gus's reply. He would take her to Enrique, wherever he was.

She had bought Gus's services with a turquoise-inlaid silver bracelet she pilfered from Maria Josefa. It was a cheap piece of jewelry, but she knew beforehand that Gus would try to hedge his outlay on the other end with Enrique.

She also knew that Enrique would not hesitate to pack her back to El Paso with Gus. So when she found out the destination was Tucson, she convinced Gus to leave her at one of his stopping points along the way—at Columbus, where her father or his hirelings would never think of looking for her.

Then she performed her coup de grace. She seduced Gus.

She turned now to look at him. His big, strapping body was ensnared in the sheets. Mouth open, he snored loudly enough for an asthmatics convention.

It wasn't the first time for her. The stablehand in Durango— a man of thirty-five or so with a wife and three children—had ultimately given in to her repeated flirtations and bold looks of invitation. Her father's lashing had not drawn a word of explanation from the man's quivering lips, for even to intimate that she had been the initiator would have meant an agonizing death for the stablehand. As far as her father knew, there had only been a kiss.

With Gus, who was built like the Ronquillos' prize breeding

bull, the act had been exciting, then repetitious, and, at the end, boring. Still, it ensured that when he presented her crucifix to Enrique as proof that she was waiting for her cousin, Gus wouldn't be able to resist a small amount of triumphant bragging. She was very wise in the way of men.

Gus's bragging would no doubt ensure his instant death and, best, his silence on the whole affair of her disappearance.

With complete assurance she knew that Enrique would come for her. Yet, a part of her recognized instinctively that while he might become obsessed with her, she could never totally satisfy Enrique. The wild demon that drove him was stronger even than her own private monster.

Tucson's Gay Alley was an area similar to El Paso's Tenderloin District, at least that part visited by the lower- and middle-class customers. In one of the upstairs rooms Don Enrique Ronquillo tipped back his chair and propped the heels of his black patent oxfords on the windowsill. He was dressed more for the drawing rooms and salons of the world's capitals than for the rough district of Gay Alley. Civilization's garb—cream-colored trousers and vest and a brown striped shirt and ivory silk cravat—belied the primal man it clothed.

Against the darkness of night the dusty windowpane reflected his saturnine features: the high sweep of cheekbone, the curling sensuality of the lips beneath the mustache, the slightly brooding slant to eyes as pale brown as a Mexican jaguar's.

What the windowpane could not reflect—and what very few people were ever permitted to see—were the darker hearts of his eyes, where lurked a compassion for the human race. A compassion that warred with disgust. A disgust for the obsequious, for the fearful, for the weak, who anxiously wished to please him.

Perhaps that explained why the son of one of Mexico's wealthiest and most aristocratic families had thrown his lot in with Pancho Villa. Perhaps that was why, despite a surfeit of eager women, he was still infatuated with Angelina. Was it because she feared nothing, not even the promise of Hell? Or because of the taboo of incest, of bedding his cousin? Had she been his sister, he would still have desired her. Nevertheless, some spark of ethics, moral fiber, principle—whatever one called it—had not been entirely destroyed by his privileged life among the landed gentry.

The knock he had been expecting brought him to his feet. He crossed the uneven wooden floor and admitted the man dressed in business suit and bowler. The tall, solid-built German American had pale blond hair and a thick chiseled face with a short flat nose. Gus was a greedy opportunist, ruthless and ambitious. He was also dangerous—and yet he was one of those weak men, because Enrique knew Gus Gruenwald had a price. One day someone would retire Gus early to the cemetery. Enrique shrugged mentally. Gruenwald's character, or lack of it, didn't concern him. What did was Gruenwald's contacts with the Kaiser's ministers.

Enrique twisted his chair away from the window so it faced the rickety table, and Gus Gruenwald took the other. Tequila was poured into glasses, and over their chipped rims the two men examined each other—the one a supply officer for Villa, the other a German agent. "You have the shipment of Mausers?" Enrique asked.

Gus tossed back the raw liquid all at once. "On its way from San Francisco now. The arms'll reach Arizona—and cross the border at Agua Prieta—by this week. It'll cost you five hundred American dollars."

Enrique cocked a brow. His many mysterious trips for the purpose of procuring arms for the Army of the North had inured him to greedy men like Gruenwald. Then, too, he had a deep sense of the fitness of things, which enabled him to slip unobtrusively into other cultures, to assume other values and judgments. That rare gift allowed him to understand the minds of foreigners. He understood Gus exactly. "Five hundred dollars? The German Chancellory made it plain that the Mausers were a gift for Villa."

Gus shrugged. "A Central Power like Germany doesn't realize

that patriotism can't feed an empty belly. Besides, the five hundred is also for this."

His sausagelike fingers thumped out the jet and black-pearled crucifix. "Your little sweetheart said to give this to you."

Enrique flexed his fingers, feeling the tendons in his forearms tense and stretch. "Where is Angelina?"

"I left her at Columbus"—Gus's smile was thin, the mouth lipless and straight, looking exactly like the slot in a piggy bank— "in return for a little pleasure rendered on her part."

Below the table Enrique's hand moved fluidly, and the Luger's big 9-mm bullet slammed squarely into Gruenwald's gut.

Enrique's lids hooded his eyes and their dark hearts of compassion were momentarily obliterated by a glaze of abject viciousness.

7

Using her railroad pass, Roxana caught the midnight train, the so-called "Drummers" or "Drunkards" special, for Columbus. Also aboard was the regimental polo team, returning to Camp Furlong from a game at Fort Bliss. More than half the soldiers were incapacitated by a prolonged session with John Barleycorn. Their melancholy rendition of the old army favorite, "The Girl I Left Behind," was abysmal.

Roxana was dressed in a military jacket and skirt, made fashionable by the war in Europe, and a plumed chapeau with an eye-level veil, all of which served to draw the lonely soldiers' attention. Absently, she smiled at their chivalrous efforts to gain her notice. She was more than a little concerned that her task of tracking down Angelina Asunsolo was taking her away from El Paso, where the action was. What if Villa attacked Juarez while she was away and she missed out on the story? Some Texans even expected him to attack El Paso itself this time, in retribution for Wilson's recognition of his rival Carranza as Mexico's de facto government.

Frigid desert air was blasted into the coach and she glanced up to see a man coming in from the car's platform. The swaying of the coach made his gait unsteady. Either that or he was drunk. Or both. He lurched and staggered down the aisle in a cowboy's loose-jointed way. A sheepskin jacket was slung over one shoulder, and at his waist hung a sheathed knife. An ugly-looking pistol was holstered against one thigh. Recalling her one brush with a gun—the pearl-gripped derringer—she shuddered.

Tumbling into the empty spot beside her, the cowboy only half missed sliding off onto the floor. With the mock pomposity that only the crocked can affect, he touched the brim of his hat, muttering, "My apolo—"

In the harsh glare of the coach's naked light bulb they stared at each other. Their inordinately wide eyes narrowed to equally suspicious slits. "You're following me!" she charged.

"I believe you're following me, ma'am!"

His gin-laden breath washed over her. She turned her head, quaffing deep drafts of breath through her lips, and faced him once more. "I distinctly saw you at General Pershing's house and before that in front of Union Station and before that at the Caballo Blanco."

Her inventory was not insolent, though it was thorough. "Well, I'll be a sonufa—"

"Please!" she reproved stiffly.

"I kept thinking you were familiar. You're the whore that—"

"That is enough, sir!"

"Madam, ishiz cowboy bodderin' jew?" asked a soldier.

"No. No." The last thing she wanted was to be involved in a brawl.

Oblivious to the soldier's threatening glare, the cowboy continued to muse aloud in inebriated wonderment, "So, Gus's spy, no less—"

"Spy?" she echoed incredulously.

"What were you doing at the Caballo Blanco?" he fired back with the formally elaborate speech of a drunk.

"Tailing a man involved in a missing persons case," she said indignantly. "Miss Van Buren, with the Rocky Mountain Detective Agency, sir."

From a face scruffy with three-day-old beard, the blue eyes bore down on her like gunsights. "Well, I'll be damned for a preacher man. If it's not the Miss Prim and Proper Roxana Van Buren."

Her body drew away, and she eyed him warily. "We've met?"

His head tilted backward, and deep sandpapery laughter worked its way up out of his chest.

"I don't see what's so amusing, sir."

When at last he stopped, he turned flinty eyes on her. He doffed his soldier-Stetson with inordinate mockery. His wild sun-streaked hair had been flattened against his forehead by the hat's headband. "Why, I was engaged to your sister, the lovely Rowena, Miss Roxana."

Sam Brady!

She had only seen him maybe half a dozen times, and that was over—how many years ago? Seven or eight. She studied him openly. What had happened to the handsome young man with the intensely blue eyes that had looked out on the world with an integrity and a sweetness that had been his source of power? She saw a face tanned and baked by the elements. The nose looked as if it had been broken. Cynicism pleated either side of his mouth, and sun and wind lines grooved the outer corners of his eyes.

The eyes! Those clear eyes. After what could only have been the result of years of hard drinking, they were—empty. She shivered then, recalling the scandal.

"Don't worry, I won't rape you, ma'am," he slurred, almost intentionally she thought. "My tastes don't run to cold, bloodless spinsters."

She had never thought he was guilty of the charge, but his barbed words prompted her to snap, "As I remember, Lieutenant Brady, you preferred married women—unwilling married women."

"Mister. *Mr.* Brady." Latching on to the back of the seat in front of them, he pulled himself to his feet. "Been a pleasure, ma'am," he drawled, "but I think some more fresh air is in order."

The Golden State Limited chugged into Columbus and halted at the small yellow frame depot to release its passengers. Fortunately, Sam Brady was nowhere to be seen among them. The baggageman, a Mexican youth, pointed her toward the only hotel in town. She declined several offers of escorts from drunken soldiers, and they set off in weaving groups for Camp Furlong, which was no more than a mile south of Columbus and separated from it by the railroad tracks. She was left virtually alone.

Hoping the investigation would require her staying no longer than overnight, she had brought only a grip, and she clutched it to her against the chill breeze as she crossed the tracks and scurried toward the sleeping, darkened town. From its far side she could hear remnants of music, no doubt from some cantina still going strong. That most likely would be Sam Brady's destination.

The Commercial Hotel, a two-story wooden building, was a long, dark empty block away from the tracks. The nightclerk yawned and pushed the register across the counter. Roxana signed her name, scanning the page for that of Gus Gruenwald. Of course, he more than likely would have used an alias. There was also the possibility that he hadn't even stayed overnight but perhaps had gone on to Tucson. Whether Angelina was with him or not, he would know something.

She described both of them to the desk clerk. Yawning again and stretching, he said, "Lady, I work the graveyard shift and don't see nobody."

His yawning made her sleepy. It had to be almost one. She would get some sleep and then ask around the next morning before catching the train back to El Paso.

Popping and cracking and zinging noises made her sleep restlessly, but the explosion brought her instantly awake. She snapped upright. From outside gunfire rattled, and from the hallway came screaming and shouting. She flung back the covers and ran to the door. A woman in her nightshirt and rag curlers ran down through the hallway, illogically clutching a clock to her bosom and yelling. A tremendous babble of noise could be heard down in the lobby. Suddenly from the far end of the hallway tongues of flame leaped along, seeming to devour the floor.

Roxana dashed for the stairwell. A tremendous heat struck her face. She held up her arms to shield it. Fire engulfed the lobby and was sucked into the upper floor. Smaller flames licked at the hem of her nightshirt and scorched her feet. She picked her way down through the flames toward the front door. Gripped by panic, other fleeing guests, most of whom were also in their nightclothes, did the same.

The street was chaos. Black-dressed, big-hatted Mexicans whirled their horses on their haunches and fired their pistols indiscriminately at the scrambling townsfolk. Some tried to flee into the desert; others stood paralyzed with shock, unable to decide what to do. A man lugging a rifle hurried past, stuffing boxes of ammunition into his overcoat.

The baggageboy who had directed her to the hotel grabbed a crying, cotton-headed child and jerked it from the path of the thundering horses. A Villista leveled his pistol on the two and the baggageboy's hat went spinning off, but he continued running, dodging in an erratic zigzag, with the squalling child in tow.

She could think only of making it to the railroad tracks and the comparative safety of the army camp beyond. But then a rifle bullet caught the woman in the rag curlers and she buckled and sprawled on the tin boardwalk; Roxana backed toward the hotel's doors. There was no safety there, not with torches of flame curling out of the windows. The showering cinders forced her back into the street. Behind her the hotel went up in an orange mushroom. With a roar, part of its roof caved in and black smoke billowed into the sky.

In that flash of light a horseman was illuminated, his face

laughing down at the nightshirted woman he supported before him in the saddle. At that instant firelight glinted off the black crucifix lying on the woman's bosom.

It was four in the morning, and Sam sat at the kitchen table across from Major Whittington. The major and he had served at Fort Fillmore when they were shavetails just out of West Point. Whittington had taken an adobe in town for the convenience of his wife and three-month-old baby, who both slept soundly. Sam wished he could. He gulped the cup of coffee that was finishing off the tail end of his soused state.

Having spent several hours reviewing old times, the conversation turned to the Army's immediate problem, Pancho Villa. "We've heard reports before of Villistas camped south of here," Whittington was saying. "A foreman for the Palomas Land and Cattle Company even claimed to have seen Villa himself yesterday. It's my task to sift through these reports. Following S.O.P., I wired Fort Bliss, but they seemed to think that it's El Paso and not us Villa will attack. With fifteen thousand men, maybe more."

Sam sighed, and the cigarette between his lips bobbed, dropping its ash. "A Mexican informant confirms what the foreman told you." He brushed the ash from the oilcloth-covered table. "The Mexican claims Villa's forces are camped some fifteen miles west of Palomas. Villa has maybe five hundred men with him."

Whittington cocked his bristling red head. "Sam, if Headquarters doesn't buy the story, why are you here?"

"Chasing down reports. That's what Pershing hired me for—an intelligence scout."

The job wasn't as highfalutin as it sounded. The general was putting his reliance for intelligence scouts on cowmen, half-breeds, ranch bosses, adventurers, gunfighters—the remnants of the old Indian frontier. A Secret Service of old ghosts, Sam thought dryly. " 'Sides, I'm keeping check on our friend Gus Gruenwald. Headquarters doesn't think he's that dangerous." He shrugged and ground out the cigarette. "Maybe he isn't."

Whittington leaned forward, clasping the now cold coffee cup. "Most of us never did believe the evidence against you at the court-martial."

"Thanks."

The way Sam's face closed over, Whittington didn't press. "It's been seven years. What you been up to?"

"Drifting. Cow-punching up in the Sacramentos and down in Sonora."

"You still bitter with the military?"

The lean lips crimped a parody of a smile. "Naw. The *aguardiente* and gin and mescal are eating away all the bitterness."

"Then why you working for the Army now?"

"I know the lay of the land, its folks, I speak the lingo. The military can use my services. And I can use their pay. Got my eye on a little place in the upper Rio Grande valley."

Most mornings that vision of the little ranch in the valley was the only thing that made him bother to sober up. It was the one piece of sanity worth clinging to: a wreck of a ranchhouse on a mere three-hundred-twenty-acre spread that was only passable grazing land, except for that part where the river abutted it. Some old coot would probably come along and latch on to it someday soon.

"The Old Man speaks highly of you," Whittington was saying. "I don't think Pershing would have searched you out, if he hadn't—"

The rattle of gunfire shattered the desert silence.

Instantly both men knew what was happening. The major grabbed for his boots, usually left at the doorway. "Shit, where are my boots!"

Sam jerked open the door and straightway encountered one of the Mexican raiders. The raider shot at him point-blank—and missed. He was so close the blast from the weapon almost seared Sam's face. That proved to be the attacker's last mistake. Sam killed him with one shot before the Villista could fire again.

Sam could hear the major shout to his wife to get the baby.

Outside, screams of women and children punctuated the continuous crackle of rifle fire. Whittington grabbed his elbow. "Sam, the arms and ammunition are locked in the guardhouse. It's my responsibility to open it. Get Mary and the baby to safety—as a favor to me. Please."

Sam nodded, and Whittington took off toward Camp Furlong in his stocking feet. Sam turned to Mrs. Whittington. She was a dainty little bird of a woman and her lips quivered as she nuzzled the blanketed baby against her shoulder.

"Let me hold the baby, Mrs. Whittington." Wordlessly, she handed her child over to him. His hands swamped the squalling bundle. Any other time he would have been shaking at the tiny scrap of humanity entrusted to him. But now all he could think of was to git.

He set out at a lope, past the buildings and houses, heading for the desert and the cover of the mesquite. Mrs. Whittington was holding onto his belt, and he guessed he fairly tore out her arm socket as he plunged on. He kept close to the shadows of Walker's hardware store and Miller's drugstore. Flames scorched the sky. Behind him he could hear the bugles wailing from Camp Furlong. Other shouts of "Viva Mexico!" split the night air.

In front of the Hoover Hotel half a dozen or more Villistas had dragged out a man in his white underwear and a long coat flapping loose, and his wife, who was bawling like an abandoned calf.

"I don't have any money," the man begged. His bandy legs visibly wobbled. "But here"—he reached inside the coat's pocket. "Here, boys—*muchachos*, I'll write you a check. Each of you. Any amount." Ludicrously, as the man wrote with a flourish, the Mexicans began forming a line.

A cowboy in a felt pot hat galloped by on a frenzied horse, heading north up the dark street that was Deming Road, away from the fight. Next thing, the man was lying on his back, staring up at the sky.

The houses thinned out, and Sam pushed Mrs. Whittington

to her knees. He huddled a protective shoulder over the baby and at the same time skedaddled across the desert like a sandcrab. Cactus thorns tore at his shirt. They hadn't crawled far when a Villista loomed up from the chaparral. Sam thrust the baby toward its mother. From his kneeling position, he barely got off a shot that only winged the marauder. The Mexican flung himself at Sam. They rolled, grappling with each other. The man was old and gray but he had an ornery face. Sam swung and the Villista dropped in a sprawl. Loud groans grumbled up out of the Mexican's throat.

"Mr. Brady!" Mrs. Whittington nudged at his back and pointed.

Several Villistas were riding in their direction, searching for refugees. Sam knew that as long as they crouched low in the tangle of soapweed and mesquite, there was a good chance they wouldn't be seen. But the Mexican's groans grew louder. And then the baby chimed in. The cries of the two were going to give away their hiding place. Sam's pistol was yards away.

Like a wounded buffalo about to be left behind by the herd, the old Mexican started to bellow for his cronies. Sam jerked out his knife and held it to the old man's throat, and the Mexican shut up instantly.

Sam glanced over his shoulder at the wailing baby, and Mrs. Whittington grabbed up the hem of her nightshirt and packed it into the infant's mouth. Its little fists waved wildly in protest.

A short distance away the string of Villistas loped by. They numbered maybe a score or so, looking to their right and left as they rode. Beneath him the old Mexican let out a screech. Sam slammed the knife's hilt against the Mexican's jaw, and the yelp died with the crunch of jawbone. One of the straggling Villistas turned in the saddle, seeking the source of the sound. Sam could feel the sweat of imminent death break out on his upper lip. Seeing nothing, the Villista, satisfied, caught up with the rest of the pack. Then they were gone.

Sam sucked in a long breath and turned back to Mrs. Whittington. "It's all right now."

The baby was limp. Immediately she jerked the nightshirt from its mouth and the infant began reviving, stirring and whimpering again in protest.

Sam felt like he had put on fifteen years during the fifteen minutes since the raid had begun. He didn't take kindly to responsibility for anyone else anymore and here he was saddled with two helpless human beings.

It looked as if he was about to be relieved by the bouncing beams of a touring car's headlights. He recognized the car. In it were an elderly grocery-store owner and his wife, also fleeing. He stood up above the unconscious old Mexican and hailed them. The car looked like it was going to career by until the headlights flashed across Mrs. Whittington and the baby.

Sam propped a boot on the running board. Both the old grocer and his wife looked gray as cold ashes. "Lemuel, take the major's lady here and her baby with you to Deming."

"Get in," Lemuel croaked, "and let's git going!"

The car bucked forward, leaving Sam to hoof it back toward Camp Furlong. As he retrieved his Peacemaker, an anticipation that was almost pure joy welled inside him. He looked forward to a hell of a scrape; he needed badly to give somebody a drubbing. He'd been itching for it ever since that run-in with Rowena's prissy sister.

Jesus, two thousand miles between him and the Van Burens and he had to go and meet up with that militant bluestocking!

There was plenty of chance for fighting by the time he edged his way back into the shadows of Columbus's remaining buildings. The main part of town was an inferno. Along with several people, three horses and a mule lay dead on the street. "Viva Villa!" and *"Muerte a los gringos!"* echoed against the adobes and false front buildings, untouched as yet by the fire. Every so often a scream could be heard that was promptly silenced.

The trade-off of gunfire was heavier now that the sleepy soldiers had tumbled from their beds and groped for their weapons. From the far side of the tracks, over at the camp, came the erratic bark of the Army's complicated Benet-Mercier machine guns which jammed more often than they fired.

The barest pink of dawn, crazily mixed with the hot orange of the burning sky and the searchlight from atop the wooden water tower, illuminated the white form that crawled along the tracks beneath a coal car. More than likely a Villista looking for a good position from which to pick off more victims. Could be Sam's first outlet for his savage need to fight!

He sprinted across the open space between an adobe cantina and the train, his broad back dangerously exposed. From somewhere nearby a bullet zinged alarmingly close. He bellied down beneath the car. The shadow ahead was rapidly humping the railroad ties. Sparks and flashes lit up either side of the tracks. He elbowed his way forward between the coal car's wheels and gained enough to latch on to one bare ankle. A small outcry was followed by the foot's furious kicking. Even as he hauled up over the body, he realized it belonged to a woman.

Worse, it belonged to the Van Buren woman.

"I might have known!" he grunted. He flopped her over onto her back and looked down into the face that, but for the streaks of soot, was as white as her nightshirt, and the mouth that was parted in an O.

"Just what do you think you're doing, Mr. Brady?"

Her indignation pleased his sour mood. He wanted to laugh at her outraged propriety in the midst of a terrorist raid, especially when her mouth began to open and close, working soundlessly like that of a fish out of water.

And he enjoyed feeling her squirm beneath him. But her white nightshirt offered too much of a tempting target for the guerrillas. "Keep crawling, Miss Roxana, until you see the legs of the water tower. And keep your ass—posterior—flat, unless you want to lose it."

Off to the right a gang of Mexicans had pulled up their mounts and were pumping bullets into Ah Moy's Laundry. The Van Buren woman shot ahead, worming low over the ties, and for a moment he was distracted by the sinuous movements of her delightfully curved derriere. Then bullets laced the car just above his head and went singing off, and he collected himself and slinked along faster than a sidewinder.

Surprisingly, the woman kept her head and obeyed him, because when she had scooted even with the water tank, she waited. Of course, crawling out into the open wasn't that appealing either. Still, at that end of the tracks the two of them weren't sitting ducks—at least until the impending daylight exploded over the Las Floridas and Potrillo mountains.

He rolled over the track rail and grabbed for the woman's hand, half dragging her from beneath the car. "Run!" he said, and set off at a lope. In that infernal long nightshirt she couldn't run very well. Close behind them bullets pinged up the dust. At once she was galloping even with him. Her nightshirt was hitched up to her knees. He risked a look at those lovely limbs.

"Where?" she gasped. Her hair was plaited in one long, thick braid that bounced on her back with every stride.

"Almost there."

Stables were close by. Maybe they could chance hiding under the cowhides he knew were piled there. But the raiders might hit the stables, looking for horses, saddles, any kind of loot they could make off with fast. He tossed out that idea.

"Here," he said, jerking her inside a small, confining building.

The stench was god-awful, but it didn't matter. The exhilaration of temporary safety was greater. To celebrate, he pressed the spinster against the splintery wooden door of the clapboard outhouse and kissed her.

It didn't take a Lothario to recognize that the woman had never been kissed. She stiffened, reminding him of a dead body with rigor mortis. Still, he found holding her damned pleasing.

"Mr. Brady!" she mumbled indignantly against his lips.

"Ahh, hell!" He released her shoulders and stepped back. Dawn's light shafting through the quarter-moon aperture fell on her face and he couldn't help laughing at her infuriated expression.

His laughter angered her even more than the kiss. With a violent push, she shoved him backwards. He grabbed out at her to keep his balance. But the filthy floor was slippery, and he toppled back onto the bench's hole.

He sat there, listening to her departing laughter.

Sonafobitch, but the woman was pure trouble!

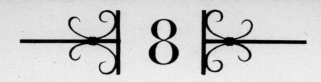

Not a telephone in the town! Roxana wanted to cry. Here she was sitting on the hottest story in a century—"United States Soil Invaded By a Foreign Army"—and she had no means of getting the story to the *Post*.

She paced the concrete floor of the red brick schoolhouse. It was being used as emergency quarters for the homeless women and children, who for the past half hour had been drifting inside in varying states of dazed confusion. Like most of them, she still wore her nightclothes, all that she possessed now.

Her nightshirt was stained with grease and soot and dirt, and its hem reeked of—dear Lord, the horrible way that disreputable cowpuncher had kissed her. And in a convenience!

Angrily, she brushed the back of her hand across her mouth, but she could not rub out the kiss's violation. Roxana, who was always in command of a situation, who always knew exactly what she wanted to do, had been speechless. Her shell of self-confidence had barely hidden her uncertainty and indecision.

For a stunned moment she had clung foolishly to the lean, decisive muscles of his shoulders, feeling oddly short of breath, before the restoration of her sanity had sent her slamming out of the privy.

By that time the guerrilla raiding had subsided, with only sporadic firing within the town proper. The heavier fighting was nearer Camp Furlong where the cavalry, entrenched behind bales of hay, was exchanging gunfire with the Villistas. Overhead the morning sky had been black with roiling smoke from the flames that had consumed the main portion of town. The railroad depot appeared to be one of the few central buildings untouched.

The railroad depot!

Of course. She could send her story out by telegraph. It took less than five minutes to wangle a blue striped smock from an army wife and a pair of huaraches from an old Mexican woman with splayed feet. The women were adamant that they weren't leaving the building until the Villistas were driven off completely.

Roxana's feet were longer and much narrower than the Mexican woman's, but the huaraches would have to do. And the nightshirt would have to serve as a blouse under the smock. With the smock's sashes tied in a neat little bow at the back, she looked almost presentable, except for her disheveled hair. But there was neither comb nor hat to be had in the schoolhouse, and the best she could do was arrange the braid atop her head in a coronet.

By seven, the morning sun had burned off the chill that came with the desert nights and brightly lit the dismal sight before her. Incredibly, the Commercial Hotel, along with several other establishments, was nothing but a heap of hissing, blackened rubble. Cannon and guns were still exploding less than a mile to the south. Here and there people were running. An Oakland touring car wheeled past, crammed with armed, deputized men.

Citizens were already dragging dead Villistas out of the streets and mounding them south of the railroad tracks. Toward Camp Furlong she could make out soldiers behind machine guns surrounded by layered sandbags. As she hurried on to the depot she learned a Major Whittington was leading a patrol that was engaging in a running fight with the retreating Villistas. She made a mental note of the name for her dispatch.

The depot's telegrapher was frantically tapping out Morse sounds. Waiting for a lull, she scribbled out a few lines. She would have to file a longer dispatch by mail. When a break came in the telegraph key's furious clicking, she implored the man to send her story.

From beneath the visor's shade his eyes were red from lack of sleep. "Lady, Camp Furlong has commandeered this telegraph for emergency use. Sorry."

At her dejected expression, he added, "Special trains are on their way now, and you can bet that, besides reporters, they're gonna be packed with soldiers. Maybe then, with the extra equipment and wires they'll be hauling in, you can get your story out."

She couldn't wait that long. By then Rooney would also have the story. And she had information and interviews and stories still to gather. "Look, my publisher, The Washington Post, will make it worth your while to wire out my story as soon as there is a lull in the communiques you're transmitting and receiving."

Her persistence won out. "All right, lady, for fifty dollars, I'll do it."

"The Post will pay you, I assure you."

"But I can't promise how soon I can get to it. It might be another couple of hours or so."

She wanted to kiss his balding head. "Thank you, thank you!" She would like to see Charley Rooney's expression when he learned she had scooped him. Charley's teeth would most likely clamp down on his cigar stub in a fit of antipathy.

Whatever chagrin Charley Rooney may have shown at her scooping him on the Columbus Raid, she wasn't to see, because her time for the next several hours was taken up by interviews with the Raid's survivors. Deming's Safeway store, some thirty miles north of Columbus, had sent down food supplies for the townsfolk, and El Paso was forwarding clothing and personal articles by the same trains that were bringing in more troops and, as the telegrapher had predicted, a gaggle of reporters.

The stories Roxana encountered were conflicting. No, Villa was not involved in the Raid. Bodies of Carranza soldiers were found among the dead—supposedly enemies of Villa. Yes, Villa was there; someone had found his wallet, but then the wallet was mysteriously missing. A few survivors even theorized that the United States government itself had clandestinely arranged for the Raid in order to whip up war sentiment and to use Mexican soil for tactical maneuvers in preparation for entrance in the Great War.

The dispute over the exact time the Raid started was finally settled when it was noticed that a bullet hole stopped the depot clock at 4:11 A.M. Roxana made note of this, then, with the rest of her collected notes, shouldered her way through the press of reporters at the depot's door. Charley Rooney was nowhere in sight. She made her way to the telegrapher, who looked even more harassed than that morning. She touched his shoulder, and he looked up impatiently. "You sent the dispatch?" she asked.

"The *Washington Post* one? You bet. Your partner even gave me another fifty, cash, for sending it before I wired out to the other newspapers."

"My partner?"

The telegrapher looked around at the crowd of men. "Sure, you know, the one with a face like a hatchet."

"Charley Rooney," she said, feeling sick.

"Yeah."

"His name was on the telegram?"

"Figured it didn't matter, as long as the story went out to the *Post* first, right? Look, lady, I gotta get back to work."

So, Charley Rooney had managed to scoop her after all. He was a slick, conniving shyster!

Her balloon of elation deflated, she went mechanically about the town over the following days, gathering information. No one had yet been able to get that interview with Villa and somehow she meant to. This time, she would be the one to scoop Charley Rooney!

A poster distributed by the Columbus Chief of Police offered a five-thousand-dollar reward, dead or alive, for the capture of Francisco (Pancho) Villa. Beneath his photo, inset on the poster, was a smaller caption that offered one thousand dollars for the arrest of three of his lieutenants.

Next to one of the posters Roxana saw a sign that announced ironically:

COLUMBUS LOTS
BUY NOW WHILE THEY LAST.

One afternoon two events occurred for which the entire town seemed to turn out. The first was the cremation, to prevent disease, of the sixty-odd guerrilla dead. It was a macabre bonfire of bodies soaked in kerosene, mixed with creosoted railroad ties, more bodies, and more ties. The air reeked with the sweet, gut-wrenching odor of burnt flesh for days.

The second event was a novelty: the arrival of five aeroplanes. A handful of aero squadron mechanics worked far into the night in a portable machine shop set up in a tent, making bolts, drilling holes, and assembling the completed planes. They appeared little more than crates. At both events people stood around with their little Kodak boxes, snapping pictures.

The reporters, of course, used more sophisticated cameras, capable of clear glass plate negatives, and flashes, for taking night pictures, that exploded with powder. Usually, the reporters swarmed over to the depot, which smelled now of cigar smoke, stale coffee, even whiskey. If the Signal Corps wasn't using the telegraph, the reporters took turns dispatching their various stories.

But there were few facts to file. The Army and Washington were closed tighter than clams with their information. It was anybody's guess what the Army had in mind, and in the absence of fact, the reporters had to content themselves with exciting the readers with sensational vignettes of the Raid itself. Wall Street was in a furor over the Raid, and William Randolph Hearst was demanding protection for his Mexican assets.

Even as Roxana hurried about collecting her stories, the town of Columbus took on new shape. Daily, new arrivals were disengorged by the trains: white-dressed nurses, more reporters, women volunteers wearing arm bands with red crosses. And, of course, the tidal influx of soldiers. Conical Sibley tents with wooden floors ringed the town and troop trains jammed along the sidings.

Horses from stock cars were paraded down hastily constructed unloading ramps. Every day, trains arrived with Jeffery Quads—four-wheel drive vehicles. With them came knocked-down escort wagon bodies with their canvas tops, in lieu of regular truck bodies. The army had farriers, saddlers, and wheelwrights, but no motor mechanics, and Roxana heard many a picturesque curse from the soldiers who tried to assemble the wagon bodies for anchoring to the truck chassis. Finally, the aero mechanics pitched in to help.

Naturally, she was persona non grata among most of the reporters with the metropolitan dailies and the wire services. Whenever she entered the depot where most of the reporters congregated, Charley would triumphantly flash his saber-toothed smile. "Well, if it isn't the woman who wants to play reporter."

The other newspapermen studiously applied their grease pencils to their copy, ignoring her. Several had commandeered typewriters from somewhere, and the keys' pecking increased noticeably at her entrance.

The newspapermen were billeted in the backs of the remaining stores and homes. She was fortunate to find housing in the quarters behind Ah Moy's Laundry. The old Chinese woman, whose hide looked as tough as pigskin, virtually adopted her and plied her with ceremonial tea.

"You just wait," Ah prophesied. "All hell gonna blake loose."

At night the two women would sit on their cots in the small room behind the laundry and drink tea. The little room looked as if it belonged to one of those rich Chinese warlords. Gold and black brocade covered the walls, and green and red tasseled pillows mounded the two narrow cots. A chain-suspended red silken lantern glowed over the low, black-enameled table where quince twigs burned continually in a jade container. A little altar of joss sticks and vermillion candles was wedged into one corner.

Occasionally, Roxana would join Ah in smoking the thin cigarettes the Chinese woman so adeptly rolled. Over tea or during a cigarette they often speculated about what had happened.

The biggest question was why the raid at Columbus. In reprisal for Wilson's recognition of Carranza? El Paso would have been a riper plum. But then Fort Bliss was not an ideal objective for a guerrilla assault. Columbus stood isolated, yet because of the isolation, the town was amply supplied with reserves of food and arms—offering the explanation that Villa had raided for booty.

The shrewd Ah explained her version of the Mexican revolution in a speech that had become anglicized over her sixty-odd years yet was punctuated with occasional and inconsistent slips.

"All this time Villa, he been considered a fliend of the United States. Maybe, he one damn Indian, but he also one smart head boss, lunning his army. U.S., they thinkee so, too. Pershing and Scott, they thinkee he one hot-damn good Mexican patriot. Thinkee he might end the Levolution. They ask him up to dinners at Fort Bliss. Even let the 'melicans sell him weapons and ammunition.

"But then that jackass Plesident of yours, Wilson, he goes and sides with Callanza. Wilson, now he no let Villa have any more weapons. But the Plesident lets Callanza ship trainloads of soldiers and arms from El Paso to Alizona, so Callanza no have to make his men marchee over Mexico's mountains. I watchee those trains go by."

Essentially Ah believed that Villa was extracting double vengeance by provoking the United States onto Mexican soil so that all Mexico might rally to Villa against the American invaders, and leave Carranza without support.

Roxana had her own theory. It was a combination of all the other reasons for attack plus one more. Gradually she had picked up bits of information that puzzled her. On March 9, the day Villa picked for the raid, most of the garrison was off post, only just returning from the polo match at El Paso. Quite a few of the officers, including the commanding officer, were away at a dinner dance at the country club in Deming.

She recalled Sam Brady's strange reference to Gus and spying. Could Gus be an agent provocateur, a saboteur? Could Gus have been involved in planning this attack?

Gus—and Angelina Asunsolo!

In the excitement of the Raid and its aftermath, Roxana had all but forgotten her initial objective and reason for being in Columbus. Was the nightshirted woman with the guerrilla Angelina? The odds were small that there existed two crucifixes of jet and black pearl in a fifty-mile radius of each other.

And the guerrilla: was he Gus? The faces in Arturo Asunsolo's snapshot were blurs in Roxana's memory, but her intuition told her the two she had seen emblazoned against the backdrop of the burning town were Enrique and Angelina.

She had found Angelina only to lose her!

Angelina's trail led into Mexico, but how to follow it? To cross into Mexico's wild badlands where Villistas and Carranzistas battled for supremacy was sheer folly. If thirst and starvation didn't kill the fool, then Carranza's Mexican Federales or the fierce Yaqui Indians or the guerrilla bands of revolutionaries would.

Then Roxana's opportunity came. On the sixth day after the Raid, the Signal Corps posted two dispatches. The first was from Washington to the Commanding General Funston at Fort Sam Houston, Texas:

YOU WILL PROMPTLY ORGANIZE AN ADEQUATE MILITARY FORCE OF TROOPS, UNDER THE COMMAND OF BRIG. GEN. JOHN J. PERSHING, AND WILL DIRECT HIM TO PROCEED PROMPTLY ACROSS THE BORDER IN PURSUIT OF THE MEXICAN BAND WHICH ATTACKED THE TOWN OF COLUMBUS.

The second was a copy of the telegram sent by the Mexican President Carranza to his representative in Washington:

THE DEPARTMENT OF STATE SHOULD UNDERSTAND THAT
THERE IS NO JUSTIFICATION FOR ANY INVASION OF MEXICAN
TERRITORY BY AN ARMED FORCE OF THE UNITED STATES, NOT
EVEN UNDER THE PRETEXT OF PURSUING AND CAPTURING
VILLA.

Everyone was surprised that Carranza was opposing the United
States against warring with his enemy, Villa. Everybody but Ah
Moy. "Callanza makee stiff attitude toward U.S., because he
hope Mexicans will support himself instead of that no hot-damned
Indian Villa as their helo."

Roxana was beside herself with her luck. If she could finagle
her way into the Punitive Expedition, as it was now being called,
she could kill two birds with one stone: track down Angelina
without the risk of great danger, and get an interview with Villa!

What a scoop to be in on his capture! And it would assure her
a position as a staff reporter with the *Post*. That night with Ah
she celebrated her luck over a cup of rice wine that was perfectly
horrendous.

So was her headache the next morning. But her spirits were
exuberant—until she realized she had yet to find a way to accompany the expedition.

Still dressed in the smock and old huaraches, but with a pair
of white gloves gleaned from the clothing doled out from the
schoolhouse, she sought out Pershing's tented headquarters. The
tent had been specially provided with Delco electricity.

The brash Lieutenant Patton from Post Headquarters at Fort
Bliss admitted her to see the general. The story was being told
that, after the Raid, the polo-playing Patton camped out on the
front porch of Quarters No. 1 every day until the general agreed
to take him along on the Punitive Expedition as one of his aides-
de-camp.

Pershing looked up from the paper he was preparing, the large,
bold script—"General Orders, No. 1"—clearly visible to her reporter's curious gaze. "Not you again!" he snapped.

She repressed the nervous urge to tidy her hair before the fierce look. Pershing was known as a man who was a soldier through and through. It was said he was merciless with the inefficient or anybody who did not render a satisfactory performance of duty. The impact of his personality and authority was already felt there at Columbus.

"I have my press credentials, sir, and I want to go along with the expedition to cover the story."

"Out of the question. Reporters get under foot. And a military expedition is no place for a woman!"

"But several reporters are going, sir. Floyd Gibbons of the *Chicago Tribune* and—"

"They are traveling on their own, providing their own way. Lieutenant Patton!"

The aide stepped inside the tent and saluted smartly. "Sir?"

"Show this—this lady reporter out."

That evening Roxana was frantic. The expedition was leaving the following day. Several of the Associated Press contingent had banded together and purchased a wheezing Model T Ford. Charley Rooney and Floyd Gibbons had bought a venerable wreck, so rumor went, by giving payment in check written on a scrap of butcher's wrapping paper. Of course, the *Post* would honor any checks written by their senior war correspondent. Yet the *Post* had clearly told her she was on her own—unless she wanted to count their penurious fifty-dollar advance.

That sneaking four-flusher Rooney was going to beat her to the interview with Villa!

She had to find a way to join the expedition.

It was Ah who came up with the solution. "Quartermaster Sergeant, he come lookee for washwomen to lun Troop lawnry. I no have one hot damn about going on expedition." The old woman extended one bare foot that had been bound when she was a child. It was as gnarled as an ancient tree. "These stumps too old to walk me far. But you go in my place."

From the outside world's clothing donations Roxana obtained

a rather drab black serge gown that buttoned from neckline to hem, with not a frilled cuff or other embellishment to lighten its severity. Dressed as shabbily as her impeccable nature would permit, she approached the quartermaster's office. With the preparation for the march feverishly under way, an ant line of soldiers hastily entered and exited the large tent. Inside were mounds of papers and requisition forms and boxes that bore the legend of their contents by serial numbers.

The quartermaster was a grizzled veteran, a man with a body still young but with the snows of more than twenty years of active service on his head. He looked up with a preoccupied frown from the inventory book in which he was busily scribbling. One hobnailed boot was propped on a pine crate stenciled in great black letters 200 LB. BACON.

When she told him of her visit, he rapped out gruffly, "You got any experience in the laundry business?"

"At the El Paso Laundry." She could only hope there wouldn't be time to check her references.

He thrust a form at her. "List the supplies you'll need and turn it in within the hour. All civilian employees receive the same wages, from the mechanics to the drivers, and will be stationed at a base headquarters in Mexico. Be ready to move out at notice."

The joy of her success was dampened when she collided outside the quartermaster's office with none other than Sam Brady. Soldiers bent on errands streamed about them, preventing her from easily stepping around him. It was the first time she had seen him since that awful moment in the outhouse when he had taken advantage of her fright.

He was wearing a red double-breasted shirt that had seen better days and, as usual, a day's growth of beard shadowed his jaw. Still, a part of her methodical turn of mind couldn't help but think that if he ever shaved and cleaned up and stopped drinking—and on and on—he might be damned good looking.

"What are you doing here?" she demanded.

He pushed his hat back on his forehead. "I might ask the same of you."

"Why, still tailing my missing person."

He raised a skeptical brow. "At Camp Furlong?"

She shrugged. "One never knows."

By the way those long eyes narrowed—what Rowena used to call his devilishly handsome Black Look—it was evident he didn't fully believe her. But he did stand aside and let her pass.

She should have known that nothing good could come from an encounter with the coarse, cocksure man. That night, after she and Ah had gone to bed, they were awakened by the opening of the screen door—a sound that was suspiciously similar to a door being jerked off its hinges. Before either could slide between their bedclothing, the inside door was slammed open. A moment later the curtains to the bedroom were thrust apart to reveal the intruder.

"What the hell you up to, lady?"

"Mr. Brady!"

Ah's lantern took light, and the frayed red silken shade cast an unearthly glow on the hard set of his face. Ah must have thought otherwise. "One hot-damn fine man to see you. That's good!" The stooped old woman slipped away into the front portion of the adobe, leaving Roxana to face Sam's wrath. A peripheral part of her mind noted that he took up a lot of space in the room.

"I don't know what you're talking about," she said indignantly.

"A laundress, my ass!"

"Please!" She jerked the bedcoverings up to her shoulders, although the long-sleeved, high-necked muslin nightshirt more than adequately covered her. "Will you get out!"

He grabbed the one chair in the room and, turning it around, straddled it, his arms propped on its scrolled back. "All right, Miss Roxana, ma'am. You're going to tell me just what you're up to."

"I told you, Mr. Brady! I'm looking for a missing person." She was really getting angry now. What business did he have following her around, breaking into Ah Moy's house, questioning her? She told him as much.

"I'm an intelligence scout for Pershing, and anything unusual is my business. Furthermore, I am now the head guide for the Punitive Expedition. And if you think you're going on the expedition, you better try thinking again."

She wasn't aware that her hands let the coverings slip to her lap. "You wouldn't—you wouldn't say anything—you wouldn't prevent me from going, would you?"

He smiled cheerfully. "I'd take great pleasure in doing just that, ma'am."

"You really are despicable. I can fully understand why Rowena had second thoughts about marrying—" She broke off at the sudden opaque look that emptied the blue eyes.

"Maybe I should let you go after all," he drawled after a long, tense moment. "With five thousand soldiers hungry for a woman, it shouldn't be too long before—"

Her breath sucked in. "Pershing controls the soldiers with an iron hand," she offered uncertainly, "doesn't he?"

There was a smug look on his face. "Maybe his soldiers. But not everyone going answers to Army discipline. There are the reporters, the civilian drivers, and the intelligence scouts, like myself. I'm sure you recall my history of preferring unwilling women."

"You don't frighten me, Mr. Brady. I don't believe the young man I knew was capable of such a deed."

For a fleeting moment his face was naked, revealing old pain and what might have been gratitude. Then a remote mask of indifference quickly covered it. "You're still not going on the expedition."

A reassessment of her position was in order. Her mind did some swift calculations, rifled through a dozen alternatives, and hit on one.

Since there were virtually no maps of northern Mexico, and the few that were available were highly inaccurate, she, like the

Army, was going to need whatever reliable guide she could find. The Army was using American cattlemen, prospectors, Mormons who had homesteaded in Sonora, even old Apache scouts left over from the Geronimo wars that had taken them down into the desert and mountain wilderness that was northern Mexico.

And she had a scout sitting right before her.

"Mr. Brady, I would like to propose what I think is a marvelous plan. I believe the girl I'm trying to find, Angelina Asunsolo, is with Villa's bunch. I'm almost positive I saw her the night of the raid with one of the Villistas. She was wearing a black-pearled crucifix that had belonged to her mother. That's why I need to go on the expedition.

"While I try to find Angelina Asunsolo, I could pose as—well, as your woman." She hurried on before he could interrupt. "We wouldn't have to get married or anything as drastic as that. But believing that I belong to you, the rest of the men would leave me alone."

"I think your plan stinks."

"Please, I haven't finished. Don Arturo Asunsolo has promised me a five-thousand-dollar reward if I find his daughter. Alive, naturally. The reward is yours for—for carrying out the charade I've described. And of course, your help will be necessary in finding her."

There was absolute silence in the room while he mulled over her proposition. "Lady, five thousand dollars and I ain't what you call *compadres* every day of the week."

"You'll take me?"

"Can you ride horseback?"

"English saddle."

"Well, it'll be a Western saddle and the trip is gonna be like riding through Hell. But for five thousand greenbacks, I think we just might manage to overlook our Mutual Abomination Society."

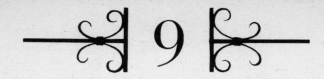

9

This was *El Leon del Norte*, the Lion of the North, the liberator of oppressed peons, who upon capturing Juarez had wisely administered the city for one year, ruling as its lord and master. He had paved its streets, rebuilt its hospitals, raised the salaries of the schoolteachers, kept up its railroads, even sent an entire boxcar of frijoles to Fort Bliss to feed the five thousand Mexicans who had fled the revolution that was devastating their country.

And this was *El Centauro del Norte*, the Centaur of the North, whose overriding passion was for fine horseflesh; so much so that he had negotiated with Butch Cassidy for the prize stud *Principe Tirano*. Astride a good steed, the awkward movement of *El Centauro*'s short bowed legs was never noticed.

And this was Villa, whose weakness was women, and who rode the writhing Mormon girl on the dining table as expertly as he did his fine horseflesh. Her strawberry-blond braids slapped against the table's edge. The girl's father was tied to a chair next to the sewing machine and could only watch and pray. The potted red geranium atop the sewing machine looked out of place amidst the rough, hardened men gathered to watch the deflowering. The anguish on the Saint's face merely excited Villa that much more.

Enrique's expression was one of boredom. After all those years of association, he knew and tolerated Villa's vices as well as his virtues. The mestizo was a primitive man in his emotional makeup. He had a volcanic temper, but he was gifted with a matter-of-fact common sense and a mercurial, nervous temperament that generated great energy, making him a terrific driving force. He was an organizing genius. He struck at Carranza-controlled towns like forked lightning over the desert. Taking the towns by surprise, he extracted his booty and vengeance, then abandoned them to strike elsewhere.

At that moment Enrique was unimpressed with both Villa and the carnal scene being enacted before him and Villa's other officers, who cheered and delivered ribald comments with each pumping thrust Villa delivered to the babbling, incoherent girl.

The officers, all big rangy men of the northern Chihuahua ranch type, lounged against the calico-papered walls, each hungry for the moment when Villa would tire. Afterwards, if they were lucky, he might pass along to them the girl spread-eagled on the red-checkered tablecloth.

They wore flat-brimmed, low-crowned hats with the Villista swashbuckling insignia: a hair-woven narrow hatband of the type made by the Indians along the border, with a little silver buckle. Enrique forewent the hatband insignia but otherwise wore the necessary range wear, including the *botas de ala*, carved leather leggings.

Thumbs hooked in his gunbelt, he strolled to the dining room window framed by crimson worsted curtains and studied the street, empty but for the odd little one-seated buggies. Set in the midst of Mexico's rugged and barren Chihuahuan desert, Colonia Juarez was a tribute to the Mormons' skill with the elements.

Like the other Mormon colonies scattered across the white stretch of adobe desert, Colonia Juarez was a prosperous community of wide oak-shaded streets and two-story brick homes with bougainvillea entangled about their basement windows. No business district existed in such colonies; rather each Mormon family raised or fabricated all it needed and bartered for what it could not. This was what had brought Villa to Colonia Juarez: the need for food and horses to replenish what had been lost at Columbus.

The passive Mormon men with their funny round hats were barred behind their doors, helplessly trying to protect their families. As foreigners, the Mormons were forbidden by the Mexican government to bear arms, not that they would have anyway. Fortunately, that day, by order of Villa their families would go unmolested—but for this one family. Such was the whim of circumstance that the fifteen-year-old girl had appealed to Villa's appreciative eye.

Her beseeching for heavenly intervention at last disgusted Villa. His ejaculation finished, he pushed himself from her and buttoned his trousers. "Bah! Where were the guardian angels when the *hacendado*'s son took my sister, eh?" His voice was rather high-pitched, especially in relation to his fiercely masculine countenance. "Stop your sniveling, girl. You would prefer one of my lieutenants instead?"

Above the kinky, drooping mustache, his close-set eyes passed over the four *Dorados*, the trusted Golden Ones of the Division of the North who would die for him if need be: squat Tomas Urbina; tall, thin Candelario Cervantes; slender-boned Pablo Lopez; and the aristocratic Don Enrique Ronquillo. Villa was never absolutely sure about Enrique, and for that reason he liked him. One day he might have to kill him.

"Hey, Enrique. Take the girl out of here."

Enrique looked back over his shoulder at Villa. Adenoids prevented Villa's lips from closing completely, so that he had a look as if he were always smiling—smiling now even while the girl's father silently wept. "Come here," Enrique told the girl quietly.

Her hair was the color of pale fire. She would have been pretty, but she wore a look of dumb animallike despair. Fear made her lips quiver uncontrollably. What sport Villa found in the cowed, in the weak and the frightened, puzzled Enrique. There was no challenge and, therefore, no pleasure in that which could be had so easily. Perhaps that was why even at that moment Enrique's thoughts turned to Angelina.

His cousin teased and taunted him, but were he to slash aside that taboo that, by honoring it, stamped him as civilized, would he truly possess her? Or would she possess him?

Angelina had known he would come for her that night of the Columbus Raid, and in the days since, her dark eyes watched him, waiting for that weak moment that could only mean his own destruction if he took her.

The Mormon girl stood before him, head downcast, her loose jacket's bodice ripped below one bust seam and the buttons torn away. She smelled of semen. "You will be shunned here, do you understand, girl? No honorable Mormon boy will want to take you as his wife; your friends will avert their eyes. Your parents will be marked with shame. Come along."

Angelina lazed back in the claw-footed tub and watched the water swish about her flaccid nipples. The black-pearled crucifix between her breasts swayed gently with the lap of the water. The sensuousness of the warm water slowly tautened her dusky peaks. Her fingers twined in the tufted hair just below the water's surface, dirty with the sand and dust of many days of hard riding.

Incredible, she mused, lips parted, that one would find a luxurious tub and bedroom inside a reconstructed boxcar. The boxcar was a veteran of several years of warfare. Most of the railroad cars had holes burned through the floors, where the Mexican *soldaderas* had built fires and cooked for their men. Others had no floors, and many had no doors. Villa had rescued that particular boxcar from being demolished for use as tender for the engine. Then he had had it made into a private car for some American reporter in the early years of the revolution, before he had come to hate that breed of journalist.

The inside was partitioned off, one end serving as kitchen and the rest of the car outfitted with bunks and tables. The outside of the car still bore a large faded circle of white paint and in its center was painted in Spanish: THE CHICAGO TRIBUNE—CORRESPONDIENTE ESPECIAL.

Villa's own private train was made up of two cars. One consisted of a kitchen and dining room; the other was outfitted with four brass double beds and other bedroom furnishings, including a partitioned-off water closet that was one of Villa's greatest treasures. He delighted in showing it and pulling the chain three or four times, demonstrating how it worked.

Ah, the four brass beds. In each town he captured, the population would be invited to his special train to greet him. Particularly the women. An aide would then be sent out to pick out the crème de la crème of the pulchritudinous to fill those four shiny beds. If the aide brought back virgins, that was all the better. A night of revelry would ensue, and at daybreak the last "guest" would be kicked out and the train started on its way to other areas to be conquered.

Not this time. This would be the last rendezvous with the private train for a while. With the United States Army on the march against Villa, it would mean a return to guerrilla warfare— or so Enrique explained to her. A matter of dividing into smaller groups; of hitting and running; of hiding in the silence of the desert or in isolated mountain retreats and of striking unexpectedly. It promised the excitement that she thrived on. And it promised her the life with Enrique she wanted.

Angelina's fingers deserted the furry nest to pick up the Yaqui cigarette that lay in the soap dish. She inhaled the haylike weed slowly, delighting in the smooth sensuality of the smoke that expanded in her lungs and cooled the fever in her brain.

The Yaqui Indians understood sensuality and made no pretense about observing taboos. Her mind's eye could see the warriors' mahogany bodies, naked but for the breechcloths, glistening with sweat; their long black tangled hair trailing down their cheeks and swaying with their lithe movements; their eyes dark, fathomless, and primeval.

Enrique would be like that, below that veneer of civilization's education. Yet it was the tantalizing workings of his mind that set him apart from all other men. The two of them were so much alike, wanting all of life and letting nothing keep them from taking it.

She closed her eyes and slowly shook her head, loosening the pinned-up curls to fall about her damp shoulders. Her mouth was parched with the wanting of her cousin. The wanting seared her soul. Her love consumed her with an intensity that was an agony. Her happiness at being with Enrique mocked her with its hollowness, because he could go through life without her if need be. He had the revolution to fill his soul. Nothing could fill her emptiness but Enrique. Enrique, whom she had always wanted beyond all else, but who was beyond her reach.

The boxcar's door opened, and he stood there, even more lethally handsome with the *bandoleros* crisscrossed on his khaki-shirted chest and the twin Lugers riding his hips. Slowly, with some difficulty, her eyes focused on the girl standing partially behind him.

He left the girl at the door and strolled over to the tub to stand looking down at Angelina's lushness. Purposely she did not cover herself, and the desire she saw flicker in his eyes was tempered by the self-contempt that curled the thin lips below the brigand's mustache.

"You've taken a liking to the *marihuana*, Angelina. It can turn on you. *Cuidado.*"

She shrugged—carefulness was not a part of her nature—and jerked her head toward the door. "Who is she?"

He looked back over his shoulder at the young girl. In the same room with Angelina the girl paled by comparison. "Molly Brunsen. She's one of the Saints; her father's the Elder of the Mormon colony."

Angelina's lips pouted mutinously. "What is she doing here?"

Enrique's eyes crinkled. "Villa gave her to me."

10

"I know my daughter quite well, Mr. McClarney," Justice Augustus Van Buren said. "To say the least, Roxana is a very determined woman."

The *Washington Post* editor rubbed his ink-stained hand over the nonexistent hair of his smooth pate. He knew the Supreme Court Justice's daughter, also. Augustus Van Buren didn't have to tell him that his daughter was a very determined woman.

"If Pershing goes into Mexico, Roxana will find a way to accompany him, Mr. McClarney. She will do everything humanly possible to get that interview with Pancho Villa. But this Villa isn't human. He would murder my daughter without compunction."

McClarney realized this was going to be another one of those unpleasant days in the life of a newspaper editor. The same kind of day he had last suffered through when Roxana Van Buren had deigned to visit his office.

Both the father and daughter sat in that chair with the identical manner of royalty. He didn't have to study the dignified features of the old gentleman across from him to guess that the father and daughter shared many of the same character traits, indomitability and determination being two of them.

McClarney sighed. "I couldn't have foreseen that the United States would be sending a military expedition into Mexico."

"Nor that my daughter would find a way to accompany the expedition," Van Buren said, "though I should have expected it. Her letter, little more than a hastily scribbled note mailed from Columbus, confirmed the worst."

The old editor made a half-hearted attempt at placating the justice. "Your daughter's dispatches on the Columbus Raid have been exemplary, sir. You have reason to be quite proud of her."

"Pride is a hollow thing. I want my daughter alive. I want her back with us, in the United States, where people are safe."

"People weren't safe in Columbus, New Mexico."

Augustus Van Buren was through with amenities. He fixed the newspaper editor with an imperious gaze. "I want my daughter back, McClarney. You were responsible for hiring her."

McClarney leaned forward and met the justice's accusing glare with hard-nosed honesty. "Your daughter's a grown woman. I did everything in my power to discourage her. If I hadn't hired her, someone else would have, especially now that she has proven her capability as a reporter."

"I realize that. I would have demanded that you fire her, had I thought it would do any good. But as you pointed out, she would simply have applied at another newspaper. Instead, I have an alternative plan, Mr. McClarney."

There was something about the justice's eagle-eye gaze that made the editor dread asking just what that plan was, but he knew that the influential man would have his way and it would be quicker, wiser, and easier to follow Van Buren's lead. "Do tell me about it, sir."

The pressed lips eased into a slight smile. "With the enormity of the recent events that have transpired in the Southwest and

Mexico, I have come to the conclusion that you could use another reporter to cover the story of the Punitive Expedition."

"We already have another one, besides your daughter, assigned to the story."

"Yes, a Charley Rooney, I believe."

McClarney tried to hide his surprise, and Van Buren continued. "I've checked on the man. I leave nothing to chance, Mr. McClarney."

"I can see that."

"Unfortunately, this Rooney is not the type that will serve my purpose. I need an intellectual-type reporter to accompany my daughter and Rooney. One with sophistication." Van Buren stared above the apex of his clasped fingers, seeing some panorama McClarney could not, then turned that gimlet gaze back to the editor. "A reporter with an Ivy League background should do quite nicely. A handsome young man, mind you."

The editor swiveled the chair away from the justice to give himself a respite from that penetrating stare. "Do I understand your drift," he asked, turning back at last to look the old gentlemen in the eye. "Are you wanting a reporter who possesses those qualities in order to tempt your daughter in returning to the States and civilization?"

Van Buren beamed. "Exactly."

McClarney tried unsuccessfully to keep the incredulity from his face.

"If the situation requires further drastic measures, I would even expect him to woo her and wed her."

"You're not asking for much, Justice," McClarney said dryly.

"Nothing's too much, when my daughter's life is at stake. I think you understand, McClarney?"

The editor did. He realized his job as editor could be at stake. Oh, Justice Van Buren was a fair man. All of Washington acknowledged that. Still, the editor did have to shoulder the culpability for sending a woman on the dangerous mission of obtaining an interview with Villa. With such a faux pas against the editor, the justice could influence public opinion in such a way that the results could be disastrous for McClarney.

"I will find the young man perfectly suitable for the mission you have in mind, Justice Van Buren."

"I was sure you would."

McClarney expected to see a triumphant smile on the justice's face. Instead, he was surprised by the humble set of the justice's lips and the relieved expression that was almost gratitude in the eyes. The formidable Supreme Court Justice possessed the tender feelings of a father, after all.

Augustus Van Buren received the caller in his library. The suavely handsome young man was slightly above average height, with dark brown wavy hair à la the Prince of Wales, and light hazel-green eyes. He was dressed with male sartorial elegance in a fine black double-breasted frock coat with matching waistcoat and trousers.

His features were well defined, with intelligence obvious in the unwavering gaze. The dossier indicated the man was twenty-nine, younger than Roxana. The age difference was slight enough to be of little importance.

McClarney had done his job well.

With the ease and poise of a man accustomed to both lawn tennis and the Assembly Ball, Marcus Sullivan took the over-stuffed leather chair the justice indicated. "You graduated from Harvard, Mr. Sullivan?" August Van Buren asked without preamble.

"Six years ago, Justice Van Buren."

"I understand you entered the private banking house of Hepplewhite and Sons in Pittsburgh."

The eyes, guarded, suspicious, narrowed slightly. "That I did."

"Yet, you did not stay long?"

"I found that I had a love of the written word and departed for other areas of the world—as I imagine the dossier before you indicates."

"Ahh, yes. Singapore, Fiji, Reykjavik, Helsinki. Your articles seem to be a composite of vignettes, a travelogue of the unusual. Well done, from what I can ascertain, although you haven't been that successful in syndicating your work, it would appear." Augustus Van Buren flipped over another sheet. "Your father, one of New York society's illustrious Four Hundred, it's noted here, refuses to support your avocation."

Mark Sullivan's mouth tightened, but the justice noted with satisfaction that the young man controlled his irritation. "*Vocation*. Justice Van Buren, just why did you request my visit? McClarney assured me that it would be to the benefit of my career to see you."

The older man closed the folder and looked up. "McClarney was quite right. I won't mince words, Sullivan. One of McClarney's correspondents, covering the Columbus Raid in New Mexico, is my daughter Roxana. I want her persuaded to return to the safer environs of Washington. By whatever means, even if marrying her is necessary."

Mark's thick brows peaked. For a moment he could not speak. And when he could, he still hesitated, piecing together the parts of the startling conversation. The justice marked this deliberation to the young man's credit.

At last, Mark said, "I've been out of the States for the past two years. For all I know your daughter could look like Medusa. I assume that marriage to her would enable me to pursue my career in the manner I would like?"

"Most certainly, if that marriage assures me that my daughter will reside safely in the United States. Shall we discuss the terms of our agreement further?"

Mark flashed a disarming smile. "Most certainly."

11

Under the dehydrating March sun the First Column of the Punitive Expedition rode south out of Columbus shortly before noon. The general, alternately leading the Second Column in his sturdy Dodge touring car and on horseback, was moving in a parallel line with the First Column; however, he traveled more speedily since his column was not slowed by the supply wagon train that accompanied the First.

His organization of the search for Villistas was essentially the same as that used by Crook and Miles in the hunt for hostile Apaches: small, highly maneuverable forces that could move swiftly out from a base camp and in a pinch live off the barren and wasted country for days. Sam, hired by him as the main guide, rode with a detachment of Apache scouts in advance of both columns.

Photographers from San Francisco, Chicago, and a dozen other metropolitan cities gathered along the apron of barbed wire that marked the international boundary to get pictures of the doughboys going off to war.

The guidons of the First Column snapped smartly in the hot wind. A double file of the Thirteenth Cavalry, headed by Major Whittington, broke into a lively trot that trailed a rooster tail of desert alkaline dust back on the rest of the column. Word was about that the Thirteenth Calvalry, still stinging from the surprise attack on Columbus, was under a Congressional committee investigation.

Behind the Thirteenth jauntily marched the infantry brigade to a rapid "hup, two, ree, four," followed by the field artillery and two companies of Engineers. Lastly came the wagon companies, still using mules: an ambulance company, a field hospital, the field kitchens, and a Signal Corps detachment. A black sergeant from the Tenth had been put in charge of the laundry brigade, berefting Roxana of any hope of having Ah as a female companion.

All the motorized vehicles were to follow later, once a base camp had been set up—if they followed at all. For, in some instances, wrong chassis had been ordered for wrong engines. Civilian drivers, perplexed by the newfangled machinery, pored over technical manuals when the engines quit. Of course, the cavalrymen boasted that the touring cars and trucks couldn't go everywhere that a horse could. What would happen when spare parts were needed?

It was in the Signal Corps' wagon that Roxana rode, with a horse Sam Brady had managed to procure for her tied to the tailgate. Since Pershing was with the Second, Sam had thought it better she ride with the First until base camp was reached. "Then it's just you and me, Miss Roxana," he had told her, his expression glum—whatever that meant.

Charley Rooney, along with Floyd Gibbons and two or three other newspapermen, was traveling with Pershing and the speedier First Column, and she could only chafe at being so far behind. Rooney still had the lead on her!

The one comfort was that she was traveling with the wireless sets and would be apprised of news, either being received or transmitted. However, the black transmitters were as touchy as the proverbial prima donna and at the mercy of the desert elements. The six Signal Corpsmen alternately swore at and stroked the radio tubes.

The Corpsmen treated her with both reserved courtesy and unspoken curiosity, and she had to wonder what Sam Brady had told them that had induced them against army regulations to let her accompany them in the wagon.

Of course, their reserve could partially be due to her outlandish attire. Sam had warned her to come prepared for extremes in weather. From the donation heap she had retrieved a long, scruffy cowhide overcoat, a decent pair of kid-and-cloth high-topped shoes, a yellow frilled parasol, and, lastly, a white pith helmet that most likely had seen action in the Boer Wars of Africa.

In her knapsack she carried a few more personal items. From it she extracted her pencil and field pad to record the march. That first day was uneventful, except for finding beside the dirt road the body of a man, evidently an American. He had been blindfolded, his hands tied behind him, and shot through the back of the head.

Half a century before, the Mexicans were hostile when France installed Maximilian and Carlotta as rulers of Mexico to protect Europe's foreign investments. Apparently the Mexicans still weren't receptive to foreign intervention in a similar attempt to protect foreign investments.

That night she wrote about the horrible scene of the dead American by the light of the kerosene lantern that was suspended from the metal ribs of the canvas-covered wagon. More than even a bath, she wished at that moment for a folding typewriter.

To alleviate the boredom of journeying through the limitless expanse of tawny sand, the six Signal Corpsmen would kneel between the wooden benches along the inside of the wagon and shoot craps. In watching, occasionally asking questions, she gradually put the men at ease. They sometimes talked to her of "back home," and one, who had the habit of sniffing through his nose like a boxer, paid her a dubious compliment: "You ain't so eccentric, after all, Miss."

So as not to draw attention to herself, she remained within the wagon when the First Column camped at night. The days were stifling hot inside it, and the nights were terribly cold, the temperature dropping as much as ninety degrees, and she yearned to warm herself before one of the blazing campfires. She forced herself to drink the "Rio" coffee, which was boiled until all natural flavor was gone.

For months there had been no rain, and the hundreds of animals and men stirred thick clouds of dust that penetrated nostrils and throats, inflamed eyes, and even filtered into the clothing. Even within the protective confines of the wagon, a corrosive dust settled over everything like a blanket of snow.

Then a violent windstorm, common for that time of year, waged war with the column for three days. The Signal Corps wagon rocked with the gale force of the wind, and the Corpsmen battened down the wirelesses, while Roxana clung to the bench to stay upright.

After four miserable days the column arrived a little before dusk outside a veritable oasis that was Colonia Dublan. It was a pretty little Mormon town of broad streets and tall, brick houses that would more likely be found in Washington, D.C., or Georgetown than in the midst of a vast desert.

The Second Column had already set up the base camp in groves of cottonwoods rimming summer cotton fields. Shelter tents had been double staked and stone-weighted against the spring's high winds. Here on the outskirts of Colonia Dublan, General Pershing, his staff, and some units from the Second Column awaited the First.

In particular Pershing awaited her.

A corporal approached the Signal Corps group and summoned her to the general's tent. Prudently she left the helmet and parasol in the wagon and, mechanically tidying her hair, went to confront the general.

On her way she passed one of the hundreds of shelter tents that dotted the area. Before it was the Model T she recognized as Rooney's. From beneath the tin lizzie she could hear the pounding of a tool mixed with his muffled oaths. A handsome young man, wearing a worsted sports jacket with the half-belt at back, knelt on one knee and passed the tools Rooney called for. Rooney's problems with transportation were little consolation, since she had the worse task of facing the general.

She wondered if she might not have been better off facing Villa. Pershing's face was mottled and his jaw muscles twitched. He paced before his makeshift desk of packing crates and snapped his riding quirt against the leg of his khaki trousers. On the desk was a coal oil lamp with a brown manila government envelope to serve as a lamp shade. The lamp's deflected light caught the expression of his aide-de-camp. Patton was making a great deal of effort to press his lips into a stern line.

Pershing was immaculately dressed with the style and dignity of a brigadier general. He wore a campaign hat, boots and britches, a khaki shirt, and a narrow tie—and, of course the ubiquitous .45-caliber automatic pistol holstered on his hip. In comparison, her plain black serge dress was marbled with white dust.

Still standing, she calmly folded her hands before her. "Good evening, General Pershing. You wished to speak with me?"

"My doxy!"

"Pardon me?" she asked with a slight lift of her eyebrows.

"Whatever made you presume to inform the Signal Corps that you were my doxy!"

So that was what Sam had told them. No wonder they were so courteous—and curious. "As I told you, General, I wanted to come along to cover the expedition for *The Washington Post.*"

"You've not been issued an accredited pass from the War Department, Miss Van Buren."

"I know. So Mr. Brady felt it was the best solution—"

"Sam Brady?"

"Yes, General."

"I should have known. Women have a penchant for getting mixed up with that man." He turned to Patton. "Get Sam."

"Sir, he's out on an undisclosed mission."

"Oh, yes, so he is." He swung back on her and shook his quirt at her, like a reprimanding finger. "You're going out on the next truck convoy back to Columbus, do you understand me?"

"General?"

All three of the tent's occupants looked toward the open tent flap. Sam, still dressed in that time-softened red shirt, stood there. His sun-browned face was accented by the white dust that creased the lines of his face. His eyelids were crusted with sand.

Pershing's cropped hair was fairly bristling. "Sam, what the hell is going on here. Is this—this woman—"

"She's mine."

Pershing just looked at him, and Sam took off his hat and beat it against the leathered chaparejo of one thigh. White dust powdered up. Even Sam's hair, a taffy gold, was white with it. "Since I had to cover ground quicklike, Jack, I put her up with the Signal Corps. Figured the soldiers would leave her alone if they thought she was your woman."

"Sam, I could have your court-martialed for pulling a stunt like—"

"Not likely, Jack. I've already been court-martialed."

"You're a soldier, Sam, no matter what that bunch of pompous bastards—pardon me, ma'am—on the bench decided. You know what a lone woman in camp can do to the soldiers' morale. It can destroy all discipline."

"You and I both know that camp followers will be swarming over the base camp in a matter of days, thicker than flies on a dead horse. She won't be the only woman."

"And if I refuse to let her stay with you?"

"Then I'd have to hang up the scouting job. Besides, I've already agreed to help her on the side. She's looking for someone."

"Yes. So are we, I might remind you. Villa."

Sam went over to the crate that served as a table and pulled the large map around to face him. The map was laid over with celluloid and marked with crayon. "I've got a fix on him, I think. There, at Las Cruces," his finger jutted at a spot, "some fifty or sixty miles south of here. Sergeant Chicken swears he's picked up a set of hoofprints that match Villa's mount, *Siete Leguas*."

The general bent over the map. "What do you think the S.O.B.'s up to?"

"He's always running low on supplies. I reckon he's commandeering horses and food and drafting the locals into his ranks."

"Or adobe-walling them—executing them—if they don't join," Patton snorted behind the two men.

Pershing began rapping out orders to his aide. "I want three fast-moving cavalry columns to march on roughly parallel routes, so that Villa can be intercepted if he moves either toward the railroad or the Sonoran border. The seventh ought to do it. Sam, you ride as advance scout. We'll bivouac a few miles outside Las Cruces. Reconnoiter the town and then rejoin us."

Sam cocked a brow in Roxana's direction, and Pershing sighed. "All right, she goes with you.

"But Miss Van Buren, you and the other reporters, including the other civilians, are subject to the same mail censorship as the soldiers—namely, I want no location mentioned. 'Somewhere in Mexico' will do just fine. Also, no military information of any kind nor discussion of possible future plans. In my absence my aide here is to censor the news stories you send back. If you violate these regulations, you will be subject to arrest. Is that clear?"

Her lips twitched with a repressed smile. "Perfectly, General."

He scowled down at her. "You're not afraid of me, are you?"

"No, I'm not."

"Neither was my wife, Frances." He strode abruptly past her and out of the tent, barking orders to the right and left of him.

She followed Sam Brady out of the tent, having to lengthen

her steps to keep up with his longer stride. He didn't even bother to look at her. "Get your gear together," he ground out. "We're starting out at dawn. And don't dawdle. We gotta move out ahead of the column."

Not watching her steps, she stumbled on a tent's pegged rope, and Sam had to catch her. He steadied her and stepped back as if she were contaminated. He shook his head impatiently. "I've got a feeling I'm going to earn every penny of that five thousand bucks."

They stood between two tents that were banked by crates of supplies. Behind the tents two soldier boys with shovels and scrapers were hacking out a latrine by the dim light of dusk. From within a nearby tent came the lonesome sound of a harmonica. If Sam was regretting his agreement to help her find Angelina, what would happen when he found out she also wanted an interview with Villa? Well, she'd worry about that when the time came to tell him.

"You don't like being saddled with me, do you?" she asked.

He started off again but tossed over his shoulder, "No, but I like the idea of five thousand dollars."

"We've got to find her alive first!" she called out. But she wasn't certain if he heard her.

12

By the dawn's cold, unearthly light, they both stared at each other. Sam was outfitted in a great canvas duster that made him look much taller and even more formidable. From beneath the battered Stetson, which was now more of an off-white, he eyed her dumbly. "My God," he got out, "what is that—that getup?" His hand made a vague sweeping motion toward her.

"The coat and gloves are for protection against the cold," she said practically, "and the the parasol and cork helmet are for—"

He closed his eyes. "Don't bother explaining further." From his duster's inside pocket he whipped a red flannel bandana that was identical to the one loosely knotted about his throat and looped it around her neck. "It'll come in useful."

It was a strange experience, having a man stand so near to her, tending to her as if she were a child. At such close range she studied his face. His jaw was badly shaved, and he wore that same impatient frown that gathered the black slash of brows over the bridge of his nose. But the long dark lashes somewhat softened his grimace.

When he finished knotting the bandana, he glanced up at her. And though that glance was purely disassociated, she found she could not hold it, and her lids lowered like that of some shy maiden. "Well, shall we go?" she asked crisply.

But he was already striding off toward the two tethered horses, muttering to himself, "I hope we find that Asunsolo woman quick."

He brought her mount around from the wagon's tailgate, a deep-chested dapple gray gelding that looked as if it had plenty of Kentucky breeding. It was a lively prancing piece of horseflesh. His own mount was a rangy skewbald stallion that stood a full sixteen hands high. It had a roomy chest, open flanks, and wide nostrils.

"Your gelding cost me a good piece," he told her as he saddled the horse for her, jerking the latigo and slapping down the stirrup leathers.

"You'll be reimbursed by the Rocky Mountain Detective Agency," she said stiffly. Obviously he wasn't going to make an effort at cordiality during the course of their business relationship.

They rode out about an hour ahead of the cavalry column. The sun had barely crested the bleak horizon and was already dispersing the night's chill. They both stopped to shed their overcoats; she tucked hers into her valise which Sam had strapped along with a bedroll to the rear of her saddle.

The intense sunlight exposed the desert's vastness with only the intermittent, dusty olive-green tufts to break the pale landscape. Here and there rose the taller saguaro cacti, lifting their fluted arms and headless necks in eternal vigilance over their empty domain. Far to the southwest, mountain ranges sailed the desert floor like giant ships of granite.

Sam didn't bother to speak, so neither did she. Finally, she couldn't stand the grating silence. "We're not traveling very fast. Aren't you afraid Villa and his men will get away?"

His head, which had been slowly but constantly rotating in a semi-circle, turned toward her briefly before he fastened his squinted gaze on the horizon again. "When you march a horse at a high speed—a sustained trot or a long gallop—you cost the horse and yourself a loss of a lot of sweat. With reduced water rations, it's dangerous. Villa knows this, too. So you can bet he isn't going anywhere any faster than we are."

"Oh."

But the day seemed unending. A bouncing tumbleweed was the only moving thing on the horizon. She even welcomed the repetitive crunch of the horses' hooves against the sand to interrupt the eerie silence. Hot sand, hot wind, hot sun. Fierce color-killing sunlight. With all that sky, there simply wasn't any air in it. Sweat rolled down the valley between her breasts and puddled the shirtwaist under her armpits. She unfurled the yellow parasol. Still, the air was so hot and dry that her tongue went rough under the roof of her mouth.

The day's monotony was broken abruptly a couple of hours later by the sight of a man who had been hanged from one of the tall telegraph poles that paralleled a set of railroad tracks. The man's head rested on his shoulder, almost peacefully it seemed. But the vultures hanging on the telegraph line like laundry looked ready to swoop.

At that moment the Springfield scabbarded alongside his saddle and the .45 Peacemaker strapped to Sam's thigh were vastly reassuring to Roxana. As was the knowledge that the cavalry couldn't be many hours behind.

The mauve haze of mountains continued their capricious retreat from her. At noon they passed the little town of El Rucio. The few tilled fields lay wasted, as if a swarm of locusts had devastated them, and the stick and wire pens and corrals were empty of goats or cows. The whole region had obviously been blasted by war.

She was hoping fervently that they could dismount and rest in that treeless little pueblo of adobes that banked the railroad track. But Sam, leaning on the saddle's pommel, paused only long enough to chat amiably with a man in a dirty white apron, the local *carnicero*. Occasionally the butcher stared curiously at her, and she realized again how peculiar she looked, wearing the white helmet and carrying a yellow parasol. She mentally shrugged. A lady had to be protective of her skin.

While Sam and the butcher talked, the horses dipped their heads to quaff noisily the muddy water in the trough. The sight of the flies swarming about the beef strung from the *carnicería*'s timbers killed any hunger Roxana might have had.

Once outside the huddle of tin-roofed adobes, Sam hauled up under an old wooden windmill that creaked with the intermittent hot breeze. He offered her some hard biscuits and cold bacon, but she weakly shook her head. He shrugged and washed down the food with a swig of water from the canvas-covered canteen, before he refilled it from the tin tank.

When he passed it to her, she looked at it blankly. He expected her to drink after him. The memory of his lips against hers crowded in on her. She had been outraged—but not repulsed. Wordlessly she took the canteen and tilted it to her lips. The water had a dull, metallic taste; still, it momentarily refreshed her.

"Why didn't we stop to eat back at the pueblo?" she asked, passing him the canteen.

"The anti-Villistas hate Americans more than they hate Villa, and Chihuahua is mostly pro-Villa. So, we won't take any more risks than are necessary."

She thought about the American shot beside the road and said nothing else.

The grueling pace resumed. The insides of Roxana's thighs began to chafe, and every motion of the gelding only rubbed them that much more raw. The steam from the horse's flanks didn't help. She was determined she would not complain. Whatever a man could endure, so must she if she ever hoped to prove that she was as capable as a man at obtaining a story.

"What did the man back there—the butcher—have to say?" she asked, hoping conversation would take her mind off the discomfort her body was enduring.

"That he's been butchering deers that bark."

For a moment what he meant didn't register. "They've no other food?" she forced herself to ask.

"Sure. An occasional rabbit or armadillo—the pork of the desert."

"Oh?" she managed, gulping back the sudden increase of saliva. "Did he know anything about Villa?"

"Yeah, the Carranza garrison at El Valle, a pueblo west of San Miguel, was badly beaten by Villa a couple days before. Also, the butcher doesn't think Villa's at Las Cruces."

"What are we going to do, then?"

"Check out Las Cruces anyway. Negative information is often just as revealing and useful as positive intelligence. Discovering where the enemy is not helps point to where he is."

She wanted to ask how much farther to Las Cruces, but good breeding and her feminine pride wouldn't let her. So she silently suffered the heat that lay over the baked adobe and dull sagebrush. Beneath the pith helmet her head began to ache dully.

Much later, she began to miss the heat. They were following a narrow and steep rocky trail that wound through the Sierra de las Tunas foothills. The foothills blotted out the warmth of the setting sun, and she was getting chilly. Down came her parasol. Her feet were numb, and her nose was running.

Finally Sam halted. "We'll break out the overcoats again," he told her.

When she dismounted, her legs wobbled, then crumpled beneath her. Sam grabbed for her and levered her down to sit on a low, rocky outcrop. His brows furrowed into one long questioning line.

She was abashed by her weakness. "My limbs are numb and"— her hand awkwardly indicated the area of her thighs— "the skin is rubbed raw."

He nodded his head, grimaced, shifted his weight to one leg, looked off at nothing, then stooped and lifted her dress's hem to the level of the top of her kid boots. She gasped at the unexpected action. Her hands pushed ineffectually at his.

"Don't get your dander up, Miss Roxana," he growled. "I'm gonna get your limbs to working again." He squinted up at her. "That is, unless you want to give up your search."

"No."

His hands began a rapid massage of each stocking-covered calf. Tingling sensations ran through her legs, and she wasn't at all certain if it was a result only of the restored feeling or something more.

He withdrew his bandana from about his neck and handed it to her, saying, "Take this one and yours and wrap them about the inside of your limbs. The material will help buffer the friction."

It was an indelicate situation, but she had known to expect just such a problem. She believed in him and was grateful for the care and protection he was giving her.

With sober tact, he withdrew some distance away and busied himself with rearranging and tightening the saddlebags and rolls. When he drew out a brown-colored bottle that could only be gin and unscrewed the tin cap to take a long swallow, she hoisted her skirt high and gingerly wrapped a bandana about each tender thigh.

After she straightened her skirts, she looked up. He was silhouetted against the dying sunlight, a man as lean and hard as the land. She put the disturbing image from her mind and said briskly, "I'm ready to ride."

He offered her the bottle. "Want a stoke to warm you against the cold?"

"No, thank you," she said, her voice caustic with disapproval. There was a certain dignity in animosity.

He shrugged and remounted. She was left to mount up the best she could.

The bandanas did help, but her body was weary from the continual jouncing. After hours of riding, every bone in her rattled like an old Model T. When they at last topped a rise and the distant lights of a pueblo twinkled in the dusk, she asked hopefully, "Is that Las Cruces?"

"San Miguel. A hotbed of Villista sympathy that we'll bypass. And we won't reach Las Cruces tonight."

She stifled a grumble of disappointment. The only thing that kept her from toppling out of the saddle was the knowledge that Rooney was stuck in back with Pershing and that she was going to get to Villa ahead of him. But first they had to find that Wraith of the Desert.

The stars came out, seeming so close that they practically balanced on the foothills. In Washington the stars nearer to the horizon would have been obscured by either the many buildings or the city's bright lights or both.

Sam said, "We'll bed down here."

She sat up straighter in the saddle and looked around. They were in the midst of nowhere. Just undulating hill after hill crowded together. "Here?" she squeaked.

"You were expecting the Waldorf?"

She dismounted and untied the bedroll, unfolding it well away from his. She sat on the bedroll and watched as he moved about, momentarily disappearing from view in one of the gullies that divided the hills. Apparently, he was doing the same thing she needed to do. She moved off behind a clump of beargrass and carefully squatted. Warnings of fat, hairy tarantulas, deadly rattlers, and prehistoric-looking vinegarroons hurried her about her business.

When Sam appeared again, he carried an armload of dried agave trunks. He mounded the chunks of shriveled cacti and set fire to them. They burned briskly, and she leaned forward, holding her palms up to the warmth.

Within a few minutes he efficiently produced more hardtack, but at least the bacon had been reheated. In addition, there were the issue canned peaches. "Coffee?" she inquired tentatively.

"There isn't any," he said. "I picked up the habit of afternoon tea in the Philippines and haven't drunk coffee since."

"Tea!" She brightened. "I'd love some."

He sat back on his haunches and looked directly at her. "There isn't any of that either," he said flatly.

The burning agave cast a clear light on his face. Curiosity was mirrored in its hard lines. "A lady like you doesn't take off from home and head out for a frontier town like El Paso just for a lark."

"You make me sound awfully stuffy," she mamaged between dainty bites of bacon.

He shook his head slowly. "I haven't made up my mind yet, but there's more to your story than what you're dishing out."

Now was as good a time as any. "You're right, Mr. Brady, I haven't been completely forthright." Fastidiously she licked the peach syrup from her fingertips and continued. "You see, all my life, ever since I could read, I've wanted to be a journalist. I've always been fascinated with the power of the printed word—the way it can transport the reader anywhere, the images it conveys, the effect it has on changing viewpoints. . . ."

She didn't know why she was telling him all this. Perhaps because he was a good listener. He sat there, propped against his saddle, and watched her expression as she talked. He didn't interrupt. Drawing occasionally on his cigarette, he seemed to listen intently—to the tone in her voice, the pace of her words, maybe even her choice of words. His absorption made her uneasy, and she came to the point quickly, without having eased into it.

". . . so in order to get the position as staff reporter for the *Post*, I have to bring back an interview with Pancho Villa."

"Good God!" he muttered and arced his cigarette off into the darkness. "I've hired out to a lunatic."

She raised a placating hand. "All I'm asking is to be there when Pershing captures Villa."

"Dammit, lady!" he exploded. "I didn't agree to that." He

leaned forward and tugged another bottle from his saddlebag. "That could take months."

"So could finding Angelina Asunsolo," she pointed out with what she thought was reasonable logic, and searched for one of her own cigarettes.

He tilted the bottle, then wiped the gin from his mouth with the back of his sleeve. "Not likely. The Villistas dump the women they carry off as soon as they tire of them."

"I don't think Angelina Asunsolo was carried off against her will, Mr. Brady. I think she knew the man she rode off with. I think he was her cousin, Enrique Ronquillo."

"Heard of the man. A supply agent for Villa." He tossed down another long swallow of the gin. "Last winter Ronquillo successfully intercepted a shipment of arms bound for the Carranzistas and diverted it to Villa. Neither the Secret Service nor the State Department was too thrilled about that incident."

She smiled. "I don't suppose so. Enrique Ronquillo sounds to me like a romantic character out of one of Robert Louis Stevenson's novels."

Sam took another drink and, staring into the fire, said, "Did you know, the genius Stevenson always wore a velvet coat and liked to be looked at?"

"No, I didn't."

The swift transition to another subject was unexpected, as was the source. She had to remind herself that Sam Brady was educated. She recalled portions of his letters that Rowena had read aloud, his references to the museums and art galleries of London and Paris; once he had quoted Kipling. She remembered the moment clearly.

The news of the charges against him had broken in the *Post*. Rowena had expected some explanation in his forthcoming letter. There was none. Furious, Rowena had read aloud the one-line postscript; then, wadding the letter, had hurled it into the fireplace.

Unintentionally Roxana murmured now that one line, " 'If

you can bear to hear the truth you've spoken, twisted by knaves to make a trap for fools . . .' "

" '. . . Or watch the things you gave your life to, broken,' " Sam finished where her voice had dropped off, then said no more. In the silence coyotes yipped outside the firelight's perimeter.

He tilted the bottle to his mouth again, and she was afraid he would wax morose at the memory the poem conjured up. Instead, he began to talk of Montesquieu's theories and of Lewis Carroll.

She brought up Victor Hugo and old Omar.

When Sam dramatically began to recite the *Rubaiyat*, accompanied by grandiloquent gestures, she started laughing. Abruptly she sobered. It occurred to her that the power to make a woman laugh was a strong aphrodisiac. She found herself staring across the fire at this man and recalling once again the urgent and thorough way he had moved his mouth over hers when he had kissed her.

At her sudden silence, he canted his head, one brow cocked quizzically.

"I think I'll try to sleep now," she said lamely, grinding out her cigarette. She turned away from his sharp gaze to bury herself deeply in the fur-lined bedroll.

13

The fierce *malpais*, the badlands of the alkali tablelands, was left behind as Sam led Roxana higher into the steppes of the Sierras. The vegetation altered subtly. The cactus patches of nopal and the scraggly clumps of mesquite and ocotillo yielded to small groves of manzanitas and even cottonwoods in the canyons.

The weather did not yield. Roxana estimated that the temperature had to be at least 120°. At any moment she thought she might collapse in a puddle of her own sweat. Without the parasol and cork helmet her skin and scalp would have been a mass of fried blisters.

After a full bottle of gin the night before, Sam Brady was his usual taciturn, grumpy self. How often did he replenish his saddlebag's supply of bottles?

Toward midmorning they passed a solitary peon in a spring wagon loaded with lump sugar. Beneath the floppy sombrero his brown face was screwed up with near joy that they weren't *bandidos*, and he readily offered up sugar lumps to Sam. Like a schoolboy, Sam popped a lump inside his cheek and passed one to her.

Her cheek swollen like a squirrel's, she sucked on the sugar lump until it finally dissolved a half hour later. Now she was thirsty. "What happens when the canteen is empty?" she asked of Sam's back.

The broad shoulders shrugged. "Where there's cactus and trees, you can find something to drink."

"And if there aren't any?" she persisted. The image of the cool, blue-green Potomac River flowing beneath mammoth, leafy shade trees haunted her.

"There are other ways." He pointed to the west, where clouds were fisting up over the jagged peaks. "You learn to watch for the rain. You know where to place small rocks and how to pack them with loose earth to make rims for catching the rainwater, at the ends of runnels in the sloping sides of mesas and hills."

Her lips pursed. "But it's muddy water."

"Hunh-unh. In a few hours the sediment settles, and the water is pure and clear."

"The clouds boiling up over there, are they rain clouds?"

"Nope. But we've got a hell of a windstorm coming up. Raise your bandana over your nose. Now."

Within minutes, as if summoned by his prediction, the wind arose. She was still fidgeting with her neck scarf. The yellow parasol began to bob uncontrollably, and she had to stop and fight the wind to retract it.

"Forget the damn parasol!" Sam shouted.

"No!"

But even as she fought the wind a thick cloud of corrosive dust blotted the horizon. The grit filled her ears and mouth and nostrils and abraided her exposed flesh like sandpaper.

Sam grabbed at her mount's reins and spurred his horse forward. Her gray balked, then broke into a sharp trot that sent Roxana bouncing. She grabbed for the pommel, and her precious parasol sailed off and up and away. "Nooo!" she cried out. Her voice was lost in the wind's roar.

Soon tears were drawn forth by the searing wind and harsh, driving dust, and mud caked about her eyes. She had to lean forward, her chin tucked against her throat, merely to stay in the saddle. As crazy as it seemed to Roxana, all she could think about was the poor horses.

Then Sam was tugging her down from the saddle. "A dog hole, in the cliff of an arroyo," he shouted at her ear. Taking the saddlebags, he left the horses to fend for themselves. One hand wrapped about her upper arm, he steered her toward the small concavity of rock and wedged her down beside him.

Wearily, she removed the neck scarf and began wiping the scabs of sand and dust from her face. When she looked up, Sam was removing a bottle from the saddlebag's pouch. "Have a drink of gin, Miss Roxana?"

She frowned. "That's something you don't leave behind, is it?"

One end of his mouth crooked in a grin. "You must admit it comes in handy."

"I'll take some water, thank you."

He unscrewed the canteen and passed it to her. The brackish water never tasted so good. "Marvelous," she said.

He tilted the bottle to his lips and took a long swallow. "I concur."

"Don't you think you drink too much?"

He smiled down at her, but his voice was hard and clipped. "I may be congenitally poverty-stricken and for five thousand dollars do something lunatic like hauling an old maid around with me, but, by damn, I'll drink whenever I want to!"

"I might point out . . ." she began in a practical voice.

"Please don't spoil the beautiful day."

". . . that any given pleasure, like drinking, should be considered thus: Does the pleasure of it outweigh the pain, or the pain the pleasure? If the latter is the case, the man who drinks is simply a fool. He is not getting pleasure at all, but in the sum total, pain."

"Miss Roxana, you are a pain in the . . . neck."

Primly, she removed her gloves and took out a cigarette, prepared to wait out the remainder of the windstorm in silence.

By midafternoon the storm abated. Sam located their mounts, which had not strayed far, and the journey was resumed. Any thoughts she might have had of reaching Las Cruces soon were dispelled a couple of hours later when they rounded a bend in the trail and came upon a mine shaft. Sam sawed back on the reins.

"What is it?" she asked.

A faint plume of smoke corkscrewed from the timbered shaft. "The odor."

She smelled nothing.

"Death. It's the smell of death. I'd bet my last bottle of gin the Yaquis have paid a visit."

Then she smelled it. The same sickening sweet odor that had hung in the air for days after the bodies had been cremated at Columbus. A pinion jay emerged from the junipers in a flash of blue feathers, and she jerked in the saddle with a smothered gasp.

Sam edged his horse forward. "God Almighty. God Almighty," he said.

"What is it?" she whispered this time, the rigor of her spine telling her she didn't really want to know.

He dismounted. "Wait here."

But of course, her journalist's natural curiosity got the better of her, and she eased up behind Sam to peak around his shoulder. Between the tent and a wooden gondola lay the nude body of a man. An object was stuffed in his mouth. Too late, she saw what it was and made the connection between it and the lower portion of his mutilated torso.

She turned away and began vomiting beside a scraggly creosote bush. Sam came up behind her and passed his neck scarf over her shoulder to her. "What if—if the Yaquis are still about?" she asked in a low, taut voice.

"Not likely. The blood is black, and the vultures have picked at the flesh. The Yaquis have probably been gone for some time now."

"Sam, please!" She felt another clot rising in her throat.

A groan from somewhere within the shaft spun them both around. Just inside the shaft's portal was another man, an old one. He was barefooted and barechested. The dusty particles of sunlight showed that the fletching of an arrow protruded from between his bony shoulder blades.

Sam knelt and turned him over. The miner's lids fluttered opened, and Sam said, "The Yaquis—did they strike alone or were there Villistas with them?"

"No, just the injuns," the miner rasped. "After they first attacked, I hid . . . deep in the mine. They had their fun with Elam . . . and didn't bother to come after me."

Sam rose, saying, "I'll get some water."

The miner's hand raised to stay Sam, but he was already moving away. She knelt beside the old man and tried to comfort him. She wished Sam would hurry back. She was terribly uneasy. No, just plain frightened. Never could she remember feeling so vulnerable. Even facing her father's wrath, she still could exercise her power of the barbed word.

"You're going to be all right." She didn't know what else to say to the old man.

"No. I'm going to die. Git my boots, gal. A man . . . always dies . . . with his boots on."

His prominent ribs rose and fell with his labored breathing, and she knew he was right, he was going to die.

"Where are they?"

"The tent . . ."

The tent was a shambles. It looked like the Yaquis had held an orgy of destruction within it. She plowed through the jumble of mining tools and books and bottles and cooking utensils. The Yaquis must have taken the boots. Then something pale blue caught her eye. It was a man's house slipper. She burrowed through the remnants of clothing and found its mate.

When she returned to the mine's shaft, Sam was already beside the man, tipping the canteen to the seamed lips. "I, I found your boots," she told the miner, holding the houseshoes just out of his sight. "I'm going to put them on for you."

The old miner managed a weak, near-toothless smile. "God bless ye, gal."

When she finished, she looked up to find Sam watching her, an oblique light in his eyes. "There," she told the old man, "You've got your—"

The old man was dead.

By the time Sam buried the two men it was late afternoon and Roxana was in a hurry to leave the accursed place. Apparently he felt the same, for he wasted no words but mounted up immediately.

She couldn't get to Las Cruces soon enough. What seemed like eons later, the white plaster twin towers of Las Cruces's little mission came into view. Sam squatted on a knoll above the pueblo, peering through a pair of field glasses. "Villa and his men aren't there."

A little groan escaped her. "Now what do we do?"

Sam rose. "I'm going down to find out just where he is. And you're going to wait here."

She seated herself on a brace of rocks, prepared to wait. The sun was going down, and she began getting numb with the cold. What if Angelina was down below? Would Sam even think to inquire for her? What if Sam was in trouble? Worse, what if Yaquis were still lurking about?

Las Cruces was a low dome of green trees, and at the end of every street was a vista of the mountains. Warily, she guided her gelding toward what had to be the plaza. Iron grills were set over windows carved out of pale pink plaster walls. Strings of red chiles hung out to dry festooned the doorways, and big yellow pumpkins adorned some of the flat dirt roofs.

As Sam had done, she swiveled her eyes from right to left. Knots of Mexicans in pajamalike clothing and straw hats slouched against the adobe walls and watched her. The men looked like *pistoleros* who would cut an American's throat with real pleasure.

The mission, with its twin towers, occupied one side of the plaza, and a local command post the plaza's opposite side. She halted before a two-story adobe with a clapboard front. A sign suspended from the grilled balcony announced in arabesque, CABARET LA REINA BLANCO. Drunken laughter spilled from the slatted doors. Sam would be there. The skewbald tied to the hitching post confirmed it.

She drew a deep, steadying breath and, tying the gelding next to Sam's stallion, entered the cantina through its swinging doors. Suddenly the rousing laughter was cut short at the sight of the woman in the cowhide coat and white cork helmet.

It was so dark inside that at first she couldn't make out anything. Then she saw Sam, sitting alone before a round table. And he saw her. Shock registered on his unshaven face, followed by an incredibly adoring smile. He rose unsteadily to his feet and, arms thrown wide, shouted in a slurred voice, "*Querida!*"

She should have expected his natural state of intoxication. She stalked between the tables. "Sam Brady, I hired you to—"

His hand manacled about her arm, and jerking her down in the chair next ot him, he planted a hearty kiss on her lips. "Ohhh!" She pulled back and met the hard, cold ice cubes that were his blue eyes.

"Dammit," he snapped low in what was anything but a slurred voice, "do you realize the trouble you could be getting us into?"

Before she could respond, an aproned boy appeared at the table, apparently to take her order.

Sam said something in Spanish and, tossing a handful of Mexican silver pesos on the table, nodded toward two Mexican soldiers lounging at the bar. One officer had a beer-keg torso, the other was taller, with the great hooked nose of the Hispanics. The two wore the Rural Federales' mustard-colored uniforms. Menacing-looking pistols hung from the holstered belts about their thick waists. Since the saner Americans in Mexico had deserted its

Latin hospitality months earlier, both of the officers watched Sam and her with suspicious glints in their peach-pit eyes.

"A *sus ordenes*," the boy said with alacrity.

"I've invited the officers over there to dine with us," Sam told her when the boy went off on his mission. "Breaking a little bread with them might save our necks—and maybe get some information out of them in the bargain."

The silver coins must have been the open sesame. Food and more liquor appeared as if by magic, as well as the two officers, who formally seated themselves on either side of Sam and herself. One round of the Dos Equis beer, and the officers' cool restraint warmed with the beer. While Sam and the two Mexicans talked convivially in a mixture of English and Spanish, she stared warily but hungrily at the pink tamales.

At last hunger got the better of her, and she began eating. The tamales were surprisingly sweet, especially when followed by cautious sips of the bitter beer that really wasn't that bad when one drank enough of it. It even took away the terrible taste of the memories of earlier that afternoon—and the bloody aftermath of the Yaqui raid. She wanted desperately to forget it, or else how would she have the courage to continue in that god-forsaken spot of earth?

Villa's name was mentioned often. Once, Sam said something about the American Steel and Refinery plant at Chihuahua, and the rotund officer jovially slapped the table's edge. "Ahhh, *si!* A.S.&R.—American Steal and Rob. We know the company." He laughed as if he'd made a great joke. So did Sam. Why hadn't she noticed his percolated, rich, throaty laughter?

Her bottle was empty and another magically appeared before her. But after only a few swallows from it, Sam swooped it from her and downed the contents himself. At that moment the big-nosed officer gestured toward her and spoke rapidly, excitedly.

Sam swallowed and shook his head.

The officer continued his drunken harangue. The other officer pounded Sam on the shoulders with an emphatic, "We go, eh!"

Puzzled, she glanced at Sam. His head seemed to shift at different angles atop his neck. "What's going on?" her suddenly fuzzy tongue managed to mumble.

"I explained to them why we were in Mexico: because you were my *novia*, my betrothed. And that we'd run off from Texas to get married."

"You did what?"

He was still smiling at her, but his eyes had narrowed, looking terribly unfriendly, and they were sliding around on his granite face. "Would you have rather entertained the gentlemen here in one of the upstairs bedrooms?"

She gave it great thought. "Nooooo," slid smoothly from between her lips. "I don't think so."

"Well now, sweetheart, they think we should celebrate the evening by getting married. They don't just think, they insist."

Instantly she sobered. She shot to her feet. The table tilted at a thirty-degree angle. So did the room. "Earthquake," she said. That's what it was. A huge, hushed earthquake.

Sam caught her arm to steady her. His appealingly boyish grin was just a quiver away from being a grimace.

"*Vamos a la boda*," said the soldier on her left, Officer Big Nose, taking her other arm.

Darkness had already settled over the pueblo, and the cold wind whistled down the empty streets as the soldiers escorted Sam and her to the mission. It was a hub for the most important events in a Mexican's life—baptism, confirmation, first communion, marriage, and death.

Marriage! "Do something," she hissed at Sam.

"I am. I'm going along with the farce and saving our lives. Do you have any other suggestion?"

"You get married. I donwanta."

With much pummeling on the massive, hand-carved doors, the officers were able to arouse the tonsured padre and convey their wishes of a wedding ceremony.

"We have an old Spanish wedding, no?" the officer still holding her declared.

"No!" she responded, but he was merrily tugging Sam and her toward the clay-walled sanctuary.

The little black-robed padre, looking very uncertain, went to stand before the altar's large tin retablo. The ivory tones of San Juan Nepomuceno, patron saint of the pueblo, glowed warmly from the brass nicho in the west crucero. The heavyset officer gently nudged at hers and Sam's shoulders, indicating to them to go down on their knees.

"*Un rosario*, padre?" questioned Officer Big Nose.

The padre shook his head, and Roxana looked questioningly at Sam. "A rosary," he whispered at her ear. "Tradition calls for it to be looped over the shoulders of the engaged couple."

"Maybe they won't be able . . . to find one . . . and we won't haffa go through with—"

"*Mira*," called the heavyset soldier, returning from the back of the chapel. He was holding up two long *ristras* of red chiles. "*Un rosario!*" Knotting the ends together, he trundled forward and lassoed her and Sam's shoulders with the circlet of chiles. "*Perfecto!*"

The whole thing didn't seem real to her: the padre intoning a Latin ritual she didn't understand; Sam's and her consenting replies, prompted by gentle, reminding pokes on their shoulders; and finally the paper cigar band produced by one of the officers and slid onto her ring finger by Sam.

Her mouth and nose screwed up with disappointment. "A cigar band!"

"Best that they can do, sweetheart," Sam said, that silly oaken smile slipping all over his face.

She had hoped the horrendous affair was over, but she and Sam were hustled back to the cantina, where they were unharmoniously serenaded by a guitar and a dilapidated accordion. The cantina's patrons took turns dancing her around the area that had been cleared of tables. Sam sat and glumly watched and drank. So did she, between dances. It was one evening she wanted to blot out of her mind. She drank some more.

Abruptly Sam stood up. He exchanged parting pleasantries with the two officers that involved a broad wink on his part, and then wrapped a companionable arm about her shoulder.

"Where we going?" she got out, when he headed her toward the stairs at the back of the room.

"To bed."

Her face jerked up toward his. "What? So early?"

"It's beddy-bye time."

He propelled her up the stairs and down a seedy-looking hallway. Suddenly the idea of a bed sounded heavenly, and she practically floated through the door he held open for her.

Somehow, she was on the sagging mattress, and he was unlacing her kid and cloth boots. Gingerly she raised her head and looked down toward the direction of her feet and Sam. "WatabouVilla?"

"He's gone. So will I be in five minutes. I'm going to report back to Pershing. Don't open the door for anyone but me. You got that?"

"You can't leave me!" She felt like crying, thinking that her partner would desert her. She sniffled.

"You're in no condition to ride with me. You're better off here in the bordello. Naturally, they'll think you and I are going to be intimately engaged the rest of the—"

"Bordello!" she squeaked, the heinous word obliterating the rest of his explanation. She tried to sit up and fell back on the bed. The room was shifting with another earthquake tremor.

He dropped her boots on the floor and bent over and kissed her parted lips. "I think I like you better drunk, Roxy, old girl."

14

Sam braced himself against the doorjamb and knocked twice. He was laid low by lack of sleep, the bitter cold that had frozen icicles to his sideburns, and mostly by the glorious warmth of the gin.

"Who is it?" came Roxana's calm voice from within.

"Sam."

"Just a moment."

Still fully clothed in black serge with all those buttons, she opened the door. One arm was upraised in an effort to skewer atop her head the mass of hair, as rich brown as a good Havana cigar. At the thought of a cigar, his gaze sought out her left hand. The cigar band was no longer on her ring finger. He felt great relief. Good, she hadn't taken the ceremony any more seriously than he had. Still, if anyone ever checked the church records . . .

"You're drunk," she accused.

"That I am."

"Is that any way to come here after—after last night?"

"It's the only way."

"Please, don't shout!" Her hands gingerly touched her temples.

So, she recalled the wedding. Obviously, she wasn't feeling up to snuff this morning either. Mauve shadows formed half moons on the firm flesh beneath her eyes. She would be one of those lucky women who aged gracefully. Did she remember his kissing her, also? A really idiotic thing to do, to mix business with pleasure.

Funny, before he would not have considered kissing Roxana Van Buren a pleasure.

Her insane plan of chasing down the villainous Villa for an interview and trying to find one woman in a thousand square miles of Mexican desert and mountains—the spinster had to be a little eccentric, a little crazy, and a little—no, a lot attractive. Or had he been without a woman too long? Maybe he was the crazy one.

Still, the thought of all those tiny buttons running from her chin to her ankle piqued his imagination.

He handed her the preposterous wisp of a parasol.

Her usually controlled expression vanished, and her face lit up momentarily. Ten years ago she had just escaped being handsome, her features composed of hard, angular lines. Age had softened them, and she was suddenly blooming. "Why, thank you, Sam!"

He didn't want her to misconstrue the gesture. "Thank the gentleman who found and rescued it for you. He's waiting outside."

Her eyebrows arched with puzzlement. "What gentleman?"

"A Marcus Sullivan. A reporter for *The Washington Post*."

"A reporter!"

"Please, don't shout," he mimicked her. He peeled himself off the frame. Cold sunlight blasted through the room's windows, and he managed to cross the narrow width of the room and draw the *petate*, the woven straw mat, against the ungodly glare. "When I reached camp this morning, Sullivan was closeted with Pershing himself. Claims *The Washington Post* insisted on his accompanying you."

When he turned to face her, her mouth was pinched. "I won't have it!"

"You talk to him, then. He seems as determined to accompany you as you are to get the story, and Pershing backs him up."

"I'll do just that."

He collected her valise, her cowhide overcoat, and the pith helmet.

"Well?" she asked crossly. "Where do we go now?"

"In case you didn't understand the gist of last night's congenial conversation, Villa was reportedly badly wounded in a battle with the Carranzistas, south of here, at Namaquipa."

"What rotten luck! The desert rat might die before I get that interview." She took the helmet and fastened the leather strap about her chin. "Let's go after him."

"It won't be that easy. With about two hundred or so of his most trusted Dorados, he escaped Namaquipa. The rest of the Villista bands scattered like quail."

He started out the door. There wasn't a lot of time to waste. "I backtracked to Pershing with the news," he threw over his shoulder. "Some of the Seventh's mounts are stove in. Lame and footsore and low in the flesh. While the cavalry rests in bivouac, we have to find Villa. Pershing has arranged for two of the Apache scouts to help."

Trailing down the stairs behind him, she asked, "Did you find out if one of those Dorados is Enrique Ronquillo?"

"No one at the bar last night seemed to recall any names but that of Villa's. But if Villa and this Ronquillo split up, it's gonna be tough as a steer's hide trying to corral the both of 'em."

Outside the two Apache scouts waited, their mounts turned tail end to the cold, dry wind that blasted the dusty street. He could understand why Roxana's eyes would widen at the sight of the Apaches. Both of them had guided the expedition against Geronimo and were now elderly but spry and enthusiastic. The most reliable was First Sergeant Chicken, who was serving his seventh hitch with the Army.

It was the aged Hell Yet-Suey, hereditary chief of the White

Mountain Apaches, who was the most frightening. With his shoulder-length tangled gray hair and wearing his ominous-looking dust goggles, Hell Yet-Suey was especially good at interrogating prisoners. Bandoliers crisscrossed the old blue woolen Army shirt along with a multiplicity of medals, one a "Vote for Teddy" campaign button. He carried a multi-caliber rifle in his hand and a machete strapped to his side. The Mexicans would almost die of fright at his approach.

Like an old warhorse, he glared down at Roxana. The wind was playing havoc with her parasol. "You bring this woman on trail?" he asked of Sam.

Sam tapped his forefinger at his temple. "It must be the firewater, Hell Yet-Suey. I've done gone and lost my mind."

"*Huli!* Damnfine shame."

Roxana ignored Sam's barb. She stepped closer to look up at Hell Yet-Suey's ferocious countenance. Sam held his breath. Roxana was too strong-willed to actually faint, but he hadn't the slightest expectation what she would do. "Goggles!" she said, with delight marbling her voice. "What a marvelous idea!"

Hell Yet-Suey bared his large, yellow teeth in what was a semblance of a smile. "Good for eyes!" he grunted with obvious pride.

Sam relaxed but glanced around, puzzled. The three Villistas that he and the Apache scouts had found hiding in a silver mine earlier that morning were nowhere in sight. "Where are the three prisoners we captured?"

"He took heap sick. All dead."

Sam sighed. For Hell Yet-Suey the only good Mexican was a dead Mexican. "Where are their bodies?"

The Indian's gnarled finger pointed to the long water trough before the *tienda* across the street. Red water trickled over the trough's sides. The owner of the little store stood before the trough and twisted his hands like rosary beads.

Only then did Sam remember the reporter. His gaze flicked back to the cabaret's portico. Mark Sullivan leaned against the stucco wall, watching the scene. There was something about the man that just didn't add up. And for the life of him, Sam couldn't put his finger on it.

Mark stepped forward and removed the tweed hat. His features were perfect. Too damned perfect. Sam noted he even managed to control his surprise at the eccentricity of Roxana's getup. "Miss Van Buren?"

Roxana turned. Her mouth flattened as she awaited his approach. There was the look of anticipated battle in her face. When he stood before her, hat in hand, she said, "I understand the *Post* has sent you to accompany me. If you think to scoop me on Villa, you are making a mistake, Mr. Sullivan."

While she was talking, the reporter's gaze roamed over her face and throat, and Sam knew damned well what he was thinking. Sullivan smiled, and against the smile's brilliance the sun might as well have folded its tent and slunk away into the night.

"Miss Van Buren, the *Post* is depending on either you or Rooney to get that interview. They're depending on me to do what I do best. Write features on the local color. Soften the negative—the poverty, the war's affects, the anti-American feelings—and play up the positive; the romantic señoritas, the gay caballeros, the land of moonlight and guitars, bougainvillea and fabulous bargains. I'm to appeal to the section read by dowager matrons and wealthy old codgers who have reached that state where dreaming is about all they'll ever be able to do."

"Why accompany me? Why not Rooney?"

"Because Rooney's traveling with Pershing. A military entourage offers little appeal to the type of people who read my columns."

A silent moment ensued, then Roxana's expression softened into what might have been a Mona Lisa smile. It was hard to tell. "In that case, you're welcome to ride with us."

Sullivan's smoothly handsome features altered instantly, though Sam was at a loss of words to describe just how. Maybe like a rancher taking stock of a heifer that initially appeared too stringy to breed a prize-winning calf.

"That is, if Sam agrees," she amended.

Sam shrugged. "Pershing seems all in favor of it." Privately, he wondered how in hell the Old Man expected him and the scouts to sneak up on Villa and his *compadres* with two greenhorns tagging along.

With the two Apache scouts, Sam, Roxana, and Sullivan began the steep climb up the eastern side of the Sierra Madres, the knots of gnarled mountains that brooded over the dry plains below. When conversation was possible, Sullivan engaged Roxana in an amiable exchange of their mutual acquaintances back East. The direction of the two colleague's conversation eventually went on to a more profound discussion of the joys and tribulations of being a reporter.

The verbal exchange was limited by the terrain. Often the trail was nothing more than a narrow switchback winding up and down the rocky slopes. Sometimes it was necessary to dismount and lead single file, a measure that also conserved the waning strength of the underfed and overworked animals.

Toward late afternoon a gale seemed to come directly from the North Pole. Sam knew that by dawn even the water in their canteens would be frozen solid. Sullivan had at least had the foresight to pack along a heavy Ulster overcoat.

For a few short hours of rest they made an uncomfortable camp in a canyon. A fire was built, and they huddled around its warmth, wrapped in their canvas and fur-backed sleeping bags, and poked at the beans and bacon that swam together in the tin plates. The Apaches' lids never closed, but Sullivan snored softly and Roxana's head drooped to her upraised knees.

Sam considered the two tenderfoots he was saddled with. Both from a society as foreign to the immediate surroundings as the earth to the moon. Did Roxana miss the rich hum of intellectual conversation muffled by velvet draperies and thick Turkish carpets, the bedroom fireplaces lit by a chambermaid, the soirées where tables sagged beneath delicacies that made the mouth water?

Incredibly, she never complained. He recognized that she possessed the aristocrat's innate knack for assuming that matters of inconvenience should be dismissed.

Yet he saw the deep blush of embarrassment that flooded her pale cheeks when she tried to subtly indicate her need to take a piss. Despite her incongruous trappings and the wild setting, she was still the proper lady, very much inhibited and straitlaced. Each time he took out one of his store of gin bottles and peeled the lead foil off its mouth, her lips tightened with that familiar expression of disapproval.

He swallowed a snort now that heated all the way down to his chilly toes and considered in the firelight Roxana's new companion. He had to admit that Sullivan had fallen in easily with the scouting party. Like Roxana, he didn't complain, even seemed to make himself right at home. But then, the reporter was accustomed to roughing it in out of the ordinary locations. Roxana and Sullivan . . . two of a kind? Sam's mouth tightened at what he had gotten himself into, and he capped the bottle and snuggled down in the furry warmth of the bag.

The hardships of the journey were forgotten when the next morning the tired group arrived in a little valley. What grass there was for cattle, a rabbit could have cleaned in a day. The northern line camp of the Babicora ranch, owned by William Randolph Hearst, wasn't much: a small cabin of pines hewn from the surrounding mountain forests and rimmed by corrals and outbuildings, a carriage seat under the cabin's ramada, and hide stretched over the cabin's windows and oiled to let light through.

The little foreman, Patricio, proved hospitable. He supplied fodder for the animals, corn and hay to fill their bellies. And there were tortillas and frijoles and greasy barbecued *cabrito* for the four guests, with goat's milk or acrid coffee to wash it down.

They sat stolidly at the rough-hewn table and devoured the meal prepared by Patricio's rotund wife. Being a Mexican, Patricio naturally was a little wary of the two Apaches. Sullivan, in an attempt at cordiality, asked Sergeant Chicken, "Heap big clouds come. Bring much rain, snow?"

Sergeant Chicken brushed the grease from his corrugated lips with the back of his hand. "I doubt it. The wind'll blow the clouds south first."

At the Indian's articulate speech, Sullivan's mouth dropped open. Roxana's eyes widened, for old Sergeant Chicken had not spoken during the entire journey. Sam kept his expression deadpan. It happened often enough, city folks expecting a display of primitive intellect from Sergeant Chicken.

To Sullivan's credit, he apologized. "Needless to say, I feel utterly foolish."

Roxana eased the embarrassment. "I haven't thanked you for rescuing my parasol, Mark."

Mark now, was it?

The hazel-gold eyes smiled with boyish appeal. "I have to confess that a private spotted the parasol first and identified it as yours. Since I was on my way to join you, I requested the honor of restoring it to you."

Roxana skillfully turned the conversation from herself, expressing her surprise that the *cabrito* she ate was goat meat. Mark looked a little greenish.

Personally Sam thought it tasted a hell of a lot better than some of the dishes her mother's cook had served up—the tiny little fishes that left the mouth salty and the belly still growling, and the pasty liver that glued his tongue to the roof of his mouth.

Patricio related that a Carranzista officer had come by the ranch the day before and reported that Villa had suffered a leg wound at Namaquipa and was headed farther south for Bachiniva. After lunch, Sam sent Sergeant Chicken back to Pershing's encampment with this latest bit of news.

Though time was an important factor, Sam knew Villa wasn't going to be traveling fast either, not with a leg wound. An hour or so more could be well spent in resting. Sullivan retired to the comfort of a cornhusk bed for a nap. Sam suspected that the *cabrito* had not agreed with the reporter's stomach. Roxana settled herself in a rawhide chair to scribble some catch-up notations.

Sam had other plans for himself and her: instructing her in shooting a firearm. With Villistas nested in canyons and caves and pueblitos, it would be better if she knew how to protect herself.

At his suggestion, she responded, "Marvelous! I'd feel much better, Sam, if I knew how to handle one of those dangerous weapons."

When she smiled like that, her eyes crinkling at the corners, the dimples softening the hollow beneath her lofty cheekbones, she was a downright good-looking woman. So were her ladylike haunches when she sashayed away from him.

As Sergent Chicken had forecast, the wind had blown the storm clouds southward. The day was sunny and warm, with the resinous scent of the nearby mountain pines. With a belt of cartridges looped over one shoulder, he took her out behind the ranch house. An old moss-horned steer followed them. He puffed and bellowed and tossed his shaggy head at the three goats who raised their heads to watch the procession. Roxana laughed with delight.

The bleating of a motherless calf, the lowing of a milk-heavy cow, reminded Sam of a pastoral scene from his Kansas childhood. From long-born habit, he dispassionately shut the lid on the past.

He put the Peacemaker's grip in Roxana's slender hands and aimed the barrel at the corral's top rail where two of his empty gin bottles were balanced.

Like Patton, who had represented the United States in the shooting competition in the 1912 Olympic Games in Stockholm, Sam believed the .45-caliber Colt Peacemaker revolver was a better pistol than the modern automatic. Besides, the automatic sometimes jammed when it was dirty.

Sam put his arms about her shoulders, his head aligned next to hers, and told her to look down the sight. Then he went through the act of raising her arm and bringing the weapon down in a strong steady arc. He talked to her about the correct pressure on the trigger, loading and unloading, and caring for the pistol when it was not in use.

She listened carefully, watching him with that steady gaze of hers, and nodded or sometimes asked a question—a good question.

With the spring sun warming them, he was powerfully aware of her. The faint scent of jasmine clung to her hair. Willful tendrils curled about the creamy column of her neck. Unload; load; aim; fire. He continued until she was thoroughly familiar with the weapon.

At the end of the hour she still had not hit either bottle, but she did know how to use the Peacemaker. Dare he instruct how to use it if the Yaqui Indians reached her first? No, she would know what to do. Yet the idea brought him little comfort.

His brain must have been eaten half away by the gin for him to agree to such an insane scheme as she had proposed. But the image of the little ranch nestled in the lovely upper Rio Grande valley reassured him.

15

The march was resumed at noon, with Hell Yet-Suey departing westward toward the Mexico Northwestern Railroad on the possibility that the report of Villa heading southward for Bachiniva was a ruse. Sam continued southward with Roxana and Sullivan, hoping to reach Bachiniva before dusk and the onset of the night's cold.

When they finally did come upon it, smoke rolled from the scattered clapboard establishments and the adobe homes were stitched with bullet holes. A dazed mother with a sleeping infant bundled on her back wandered aimlessly down the street. At her side trotted a little critter, naked from the waist down so he wouldn't dirty his pants. The plaza's black iron fence leaned crazily into the street. A ragamuffin boy with dusty bare feet sat on a cast-iron bench, crying and patting the dead mongrel in his lap. The cur had been saber-cut.

"This Villa must be worse than all of Attila's horde together!" Roxana burst out. "A despicable monster!" Beneath the shadow of the pith helmet her mouth was grim. She looked exhausted.

Mark looked worse. A green shade tinged his face.

Sam shrugged. "The attack could have been made by any one of his roaming bands. Maybe even this Ronquillo you're looking for."

"I think . . ." Mark began, then slid from his horse and dashed to the rear of the nearest adobe.

Roxana looked from the disappearing figure to Sam. "Whatever—?"

The wretched bodily noises issuing from the adobe's direction told the story. "Aztec Trot," Sam said grimly. "Montezuma's Revenge."

"Diarrhea?" Roxana breathed.

"And vomiting. Apparently your Sullivan didn't have the opportunity to acclimate himself, as you did in El Paso."

"He's not *my* Sullivan. And what can we do for him? It can get serious, can't it?"

"Deadly serious. It can turn into dehydration." Sam wheeled the horse about. "You wait here for him."

Roxana looked about her nervously, but the town's decimated population was more intent on assuaging its grief than committing mayhem. "Where are you going?"

"For a *curandera*. Every village has a local 'self-taught' doctor. The *curanderas* often cure ailments that medical-college graduates can't."

Sam found the *curandera's* house filled with victims of Villa's raid. The floor was strewn with bodies, and the old woman moved on her knees amidst them, administering strange potions from her bag of tools—protective charms, including religious medals, red ribbon, and little sacks containing herb mixtures to be worn around the neck.

Her iron-gray hair was pulled stringently back into a *chonga* at her sun-cooked nape. The elements had wrinkled her skin like a mummy's, but her old eyes mirrored the soul's inordinate dignity and the mind's innate intelligence.

Sam explained Sullivan's problem as she rubbed a man's bloated stomach with a fresh egg in a symbol of the sign of the cross. When Sam finished, she recited the Apostles' Creed three times over the sick man and rose to her feet. She was short, almost a dwarf, standing next to Sam.

"Bring your friend. I will treat him with lavender and manzanilla. Tomorrow morning you may come for him. He will be well."

Sam believed her. Sullivan wasn't too thrilled to be spending the night in the crowded, primitive *jacal*, but he was too ill to protest. Roxana looked skeptical but said nothing.

Reluctantly, she left the gray-faced Sullivan and followed Sam out the *curandera*'s door. Sam plodded the skewbald toward a blacksmith shop that was still standing, though doubtlessly it would be bereft of any horses stabled there. In front of the shop pigs were rooting in the sun-baked earth.

Inside, the short, muscle-bound man was wiping his tear-stained face with his leather apron. The Villistas, he told Sam brokenly, had inducted his thirteen-year-old son into their ragtag army and rode off with him. *"Por Dios,* he was a good boy," he wept, "an altar boy."

Sam questioned the Mexican further about the direction the marauders had taken and contained his impatience at the Latin habit of circumlocution.

At last he determined that Villa was headed for Guerrero, on the other side of the Continental Divide. Sam could only hope that the dispatch he had sent with Sergeant Chicken would bring Pershing and the Seventh Cavalry pronto.

In the meantime, the blacksmith's stable would have to serve as their inn for the night. It was musty with the odor of leather, manure, and the little bit of fresh hay that the blacksmith had thoughtfully provided. Sam unsaddled their mounts and led them into the empty stalls. Next he lit the kerosene lamp against the encroaching darkness and set it up on the soot-blackened forge. The lamp cast its smoky yellow light over the blacksmith's shop and stable.

He propped himself against the stall's knotholed wall and Roxana sat opposite him while they ate the meal of leftovers that Patricio's wife had packed. "Want a cigarette?" Roxana asked when she had finished. She removed a package from the leather pouch at her belt.

"Un-uhh. I roll my own."

"I suppose I shall have to learn how when the last of this package is gone."

He hunkered down before her and drew out the tin of papers and the small bag of tobacco. "It's easy enough." He showed her how to hold the thin rice paper between her fingers. "You shake out a plug of the tobacco, just so, and then seal it. Try it."

He watched her slender fingers go through the motions of spilling out the rich-scented black Mexican tobacco, but when she put the rolled paper to her lips and her tongue stole out daintily to lick the paper's edge, he almost lunged forward to help her.

He had to keep himself from planking her right then and there. Living the wild, vagabond life he had for the last seven or so years had reduced him to operating on animal instincts. Certainly not the civilized manner his mother had sought to instill within him. But then she was dead and could not bemoan her son's degeneration.

He thought of the disciplined soldier he had been. His mind's eye recalled those inspections that every soldier nervously prepared for. With one white glove turned inside out, he would buff the brass sabers on his collar and each one of the brass buttons that marched down his shirt in double ranks. Next he would breathe on his sleeve buttons and rub them against the blanket of his cot.

He took a deep drag of the cigarette. Well, he could hardly be called disciplined anymore.

Roxana tilted her head back against the pineboard wall and slowly exhaled, the smoke eddying from her lips. Wisps of wild chestnut hair fell about her square face, softening its contours. "Are you still in love with her, Sam—Rowena?"

He felt the black bile churn in him like a morass. He didn't want to talk about Rowena, nor of the past. His suffering belonged to him alone, and he was almost jealous of protecting it. "No."

"Good."

He had to hand it to Roxana. At least she didn't prattle on like most women, until they drove a man loco. But when she had something on her mind, she certainly said it. Abstractedly, he noted that her gaunt face was made powerful by the strength of her character. It would take a hell of a man not to buckle beneath that strength. He was suddenly glad that he wasn't the one in love with her.

"Why haven't you married, Roxy?"

She laughed shortly. "I did. Several nights ago."

He frowned. "I'm not talking about some forced farce of a ceremony."

She shrugged and stubbed out the cigarette in a clearing of straw. "The men who came calling didn't want to settle for anything less than the best, after meeting Rowena."

He was tired and wanted to turn in, but he said, "It must have galled you."

Her laughter was bright, almost too spontaneous. It died abruptly. "On the contrary, Sam." She looked him square in the eyes and he felt as if her words were a judgment against him when she said, "If they were so blind as to decide on external qualities alone, then I wouldn't have wanted any of them anyway."

She was harmfully honest; and right, of course. He was both chagrined by her forthrightness and made drowsy by the stable's consuming warmth, so he made no reply. The cigarette drooped from his upper lip and his eyelids drooped along with it as his wandering gaze strayed to Roxana's badly worn kid boots up the row of the old dress's myriad buttons. He became aware that she was waiting, as if expecting something of him.

Startled, he raised his eyes to hers. And he knew. "You're lonely anyway, aren't you, Roxy?"

"Yes."

So was he.

Most likely it had all been inevitable. Urged on by all their circumstances—their solitude, their close proximity, the dangers they had mastered—they eased toward each other, eyes locked, till they met on their knees in the center of the stall. Each was breathing harder than usual, as though experiencing a physical strain. Sam's alter ego knew that neither of them was thinking clearly, that the turmoil of the previous days had muddled their thoughts.

Roxana's prudery was vanquished during those days, by living in close contact with a man. It was that prudery that had constituted one of the main barriers between them. There was no room for either false modesty or physical shame when life hung by a thread, and Roxana was learning that life was sweetest when it was most uncertain.

Their union, stamped with so many uncertainties, was sweeter than they could ever have expected.

Roxana was simply made for love. She may have been ashamed or frightened when his fingers fumbled with the row of infinite buttons; she might have averted her eyes from his when he tugged off the chemise and unhooked the corset of steel stays to reveal her nakedness from the waist up. Nevertheless, with her bountiful breasts free and bare, she could not maintain her inhibitions amidst the savage, barren beauty of Mexico. Its very desolation stripped away her prim facade.

When her bodice was unbuttoned at last, Sam beheld the incredible beauty of her body. For a moment he could not even touch her, so astounded was he by a loveliness he had never suspected. A wasp waist was natural, unaided by the restricting corset.

"Sam." Her utterance of his name was more like a gasp.

"Put your arms around my shoulders, Roxy."

"My arms feel as heavy as cast iron, Sam," she said in a voice hushed with wonderment.

He kissed her mouth, softly, wanting to prolong her pleasure, to initiate her gently, then drew back. He waited a moment to see if she wanted to change her mind. When she did as he ordered, slipping her arms up about his shoulders, he kissed her again, but this time his tongue darted between her lips to find its complement.

Her hand cupped his neck and she answered his kiss. Knee to knee, they pressed against each other, instinctively seeking that which makes one of two. They were breathing heavily and Sam was surprised at the headiness that swept over him. He hadn't felt that virginal thrill with a woman since he was a cadet. And the young woman had been Roxana's sister.

They drew back, still holding one another. Roxana's face was flushed and her skin pinked by his raspy beard. Her pupils were dilated, her lips parted in expectation. "Sam, touch me. Please, all over. Hurry, before I change my mind."

The milk-white breasts with the faint blue veins were almost too heavy for her wisp of a body but not for his hands. He weighted one in his palm, and bent his head. The warm scent of her flesh enveloped him.

She surprised him. Her hands alongside his face led his mouth to the dusky tip of one breast. Her head lolled back when his cheeks flexed lightly to coax her nipple into hardness. His mouth oscillated between her breasts, as if unable to decide which was the more succulent.

With a shuddering sigh, she lifted the soft globes to make them more accessible to his lips. "Oh, Sam, I didn't know I could ache like this with the wanting."

He raised his head, his fingers reclaiming what had so recently filled his mouth. Confusion swept over her expression as he lifted the inside of her left wrist to his mouth and, very lightly, kissed the pale blue veins that led to her palm. He thought to reassure her, but that wasn't exactly what he wanted to do, though he could find no better word for it. Whatever "it" was, though, "it" was close at hand.

"Relieving that ache is the most natural, most beautiful thing in the world, Roxy," he whispered into the hollow of her palm.

There was something appealingly childlike about her dazed smile. Shyly, she tunneled her fingers through his hair. Then, more boldly, she pulled his face down to match her lips to his. Her mouth was sweet and hot, and he had the urgent need to find out what she was like if she let herself go.

Beneath his hands he could feel her shoulders begin to tremble, ever so slightly. When her whole torso quivered against the length of his, he drew away. Her dark liquid eyes peered intensely into his. "Sam, I'm nearly thirty-one years old, and I need to know what it is to be a woman," she breathed in a barely audible whisper.

His hands loosened the heavy skein of curling hair, the wire pins scattering in the straw. "Lovely, lovely." How utterly soft and feminine she looked with the tousled mane falling softly about her shoulders and breasts.

He passed her back into the straw, his fingers working awkwardly at the buttons remaining below her waist. Her arms lay in a position of abandon above her head, her lids closed, her lips parted in expectation. When at last he spread open her skirt, he unveiled long, slender, perfectly formed legs encased in white merino stockings. Above her garters, the legs met in an enticing carpet of luxuriant curls—curls that were just a shade darker than the soft fluff of her armpits.

He rapidly shucked his red shirt and dungarees and knelt over her, half afraid to consummate what they both so desperately wanted. He had been well endowed by nature, so much so that some of the women he had known had tightened that entry ring of muscle in fear at the sight of him and, at least initially, had suffered needless discomfort.

Not Roxana. Her lids slitted to watch him, the corners of her lips tucked with a smile, she marveled, "Sam, old man, you make Michelangelo's *David* look like an overcooked noodle."

He erupted in unrestrained chuckling and she joined him. Their shared laughter broke down the last barrier of her reserve, so that when he eased into her their coupling was the most natural thing in the world. His throbbing power moved within her welcoming vulnerability in a long, steady stroke that increased in tempo as her hands caressed the back of his neck, his shoulders and spine, then slipped hesitantly downward to explore his hairmatted thighs.

Then something hot and elemental, a more primal impulse, took over. Their arms and legs interlocked in an animated puzzle. His masculine instinct perceived that she wanted to give, and to give again, and to go on giving.

"Sam, dearest—I must be either a saint or a glutton for punishment—but please don't stop. Not ever."

It was her nature that she accepted him fully, with no reticence. When her hands encircled his buttocks and pressed him deeper into her, he lost all control of his measured lovemaking.

She was murmuring incoherent words now, but he was too far gone to try to discern their import as he did his will—her will—upon her. Faster; harder; deeper. Beneath him he felt her go rigid, her fingers anchoring into his buttocks; then her body gave a deep, shuddering spasm and went lax. And he was coming and coming and coming.

Afterwards, he lay on his side, still buck naked, his head propped on his hand. Near his thigh the straw was splotched with her maiden blood, and his brain tried to sort out the wonder of this woman. He wanted to ask if he had hurt her, but, surprisingly, he found that he was shyly reluctant. He had never bedded a virgin. He felt oddly happy and companionable and, at the same time, wary. He was a little bit surprised that he had been the one she turned to for the easing of the body and soul's relief. Sullivan would have been the natural choice. But then, Sullivan was ill. Also, what had just occurred was a spontaneous act, unplanned, he was certain, by either of them.

Sam's ego deflated like a beached jellyfish.

He watched her as she painstakingly but ineptly rolled a cigarette for each of them. She was wearing only his old red shirt, but it covered all but her lower thighs and calves, and her dark hair tumbled riotously down the back. She looked like a little girl, and the sensation of intimacy with her, combatting piquantly with her modesty, was extraordinarily pleasant. As for her, well, she was aglow with life.

She lay back down beside him on her back. His forefinger touched the sweet pulse at her throat with something akin to amazement. "Roxy, old girl, you're one hell of a woman."

A pencil-thin column of blue smoke slipped from between her lips. "Coming from a misogynist, that's quite a compliment," she said matter-of-factly.

He frowned. "I never have considered myself a woman-hater. In fact, I love them."

"I'm sure you do."

He scrutinized her face to see if she was being sarcastic, but her eyes in the mellow lamplight were quite candid. "Loving women, Sam, may well be the thing you do best. But, obviously, other than by force, the only way you'll end up before an altar is in a casket."

This was dangerous ground, talk of marriage. He took a long drag on the cigarette, thinking hard. Five thousand bucks lay on the line. Better to get the subject out in the open and clarified now, because he didn't want any problems when he walked away with that money. "You're right about marriage. I'm not really a very sociable animal. And you? Is marriage in your plans, one day?"

"Hardly. I won't make compromises. I want to be a journalist. The best journalist I can be. And a woman can't compete in the man's world and also be a wife and mother—at least not to the husband's satisfaction."

Cigarette smoke rolled from his lips behind his sigh of relief.

"Sam, what will you do with the reward money?"

"There's a little ranch I have in mind, north of El Paso. It reminds me some of the ranch I grew up on; only my home wasn't quite so pretty as the countryside is around the Rio Grande valley. I could settle down there and drift into El Paso whenever the urge for socializing hit me."

She nodded, and they shared a companionable silence, wrapped in their own thoughts. Sam's admiring gaze focused slowly on the shapely calf before him, covered in the finest, almost invisible down.

In response his penis sprang to life in an instant.

16

Boss of the richest mines and *patrón* of vast cattle ranches, dictator of Juarez, reputedly a millionaire, *bandido* extraordinary and yet contrastingly appealing, Francisco Villa ruled Chihuahua like a feudal state.

According to the tale, when leaving the state of Sonora, Pancho the Puma stopped at tiny San Pedro de La Cueva to massacre seventy-two old men and young boys. He lined up the hapless group and, since he was short on ammunition, shot them endwise. He placed his rifle against the chest of the first and perforated as many as possible. As the killed and wounded fell, he fired again.

With his grisly sense of humor, he was notorious as a torturer, maiming men the length and breadth of Mexico with the "Mark of Villa": a clipped ear, a missing nose, a disfigured face, a crippled foot.

Yet some still saw him as the idol of the poor. True, he plundered and robbed the wealthy, but they said he was a humanitarian and that he distributed the loot to the impoverished.

People lined up in long queues and he gave them money and food. Naturally, the poor heaped paeans of praise on this modern-day Robin Hood.

Once, on a raid at the Cusi Mine, he ordered a miner shot. The man, dressed in a well-tailored suit, acted unruly. Villa commanded him to remove his suit and give it to a ragged soldier; instead, the condemned miner became enraged and hurled the coat in Villa's face. Pancho so admired his show of daring that he set the miner free and later made him a captain in his army.

This sullen mountain cat with the genius of Stonewall Jackson was also known for showing great concern for *las familias* when taking a town. "Tell the families to stay indoors. Have the families water? Did the families suffer much?"

Enrique had long recognized these sometimes conflicting facets of Villa. He found the dichotomy at the same time challenging and revolting—and he sensed that only a paper-thin veneer of civilization kept him from being a monster, too.

He wondered how long it would take, living with the dregs of humanity, before those baser qualities he repressed would ooze to the surface. What had happened to the men of ideals, the men who had wanted to save Mexico from herself? Juarez, Pino, Madero—all were dead.

For several days now, Villa's Dorados had done nothing but loaf in the little town that lay at the bottom of the Guerrero River valley. They would make no effort to hold the town, just as they had relinquished all the other cities they had captured. Villa's campaign was a series of "hit and run" raids to keep the Carranzistas off balance and to obtain arms, munitions, funds, and recruits—even if they had to impress the men.

This rabble of five or six hundred who had taken Guerrero included *soldaderas* with their ragged children and squalling infants. The entire band lived a directionless, nomadic existence. Often before, they had swarmed like bees, a multitude of fifteen thousand souls, women and ripe girls and children, *peónes* and Indians and Dorados, encamped in the open, in little canyons nestling in the hills, or even in small tents erected atop traveling railroad boxcars. These had made up that glorious Division of the North, *Los Insurgentes*.

But along the banks of the Papigochic River only a small band of women scrubbed clothes on the rocks or cooked frijoles in iron pots hung over the open fires. That evening the *peónes* irrigated their dust-filled throats with *sotol*, and the fierce Yaquis waxed dreamy on their loco weed and threw fits or danced wildly about a fire of dried *agave* trunks. The more gentle Tarahumaras, known for their stamina at long-distance running, played their reed flutes.

When the red bars of sunlight had all but faded from the western sky, Enrique deserted the solitude afforded by the catclaw bosque at the bend in the river and made his way up the grass-worn hill to Guerrero's colonnaded plaza. A block from the plaza stood the baroque Casa de Alcalde, the mayor's house, which Villa had commandeered as his headquarters. Enrique knew that whatever virgins the town might have held before Villa's arrival would be experienced women by next morning.

A Dorado posted outside the *alcalde's* house opened the tile-faced door for him. Inside, piled amidst expensive European furniture, were saddles, kegs of ammunition, even baking powder cans that had been filled with explosives for sabotaging the rail-roads.

Half a dozen Dorado officers were gathered around a huge, ornate dining table, studying an outspread square map on torn and tattered paper. Villa noted Enrique's approach and scowled. "Only an hour ago a Yaqui scout reported an American cavalry column was on the move in this direction."

For several seconds Enrique surveyed the area that Pancho pointed out. Finally, he said, "So, Pershing is building a cage for you."

Villa struck the ragged map with his fist. His festering wounded knee made him even more volatile than usual.

General Cardenas, commander of Villa's bodyguard, spoke up. "This Pershing has only a peacetime army with no experience in countering our guerrilla warfare or in fighting on our terrain or elsewhere. We have little to worry about."

Enrique said nothing.

"And what think you, *mi amigo?*" asked Villa. Pain glittered in his bloodshot and weary eyes.

"That peacetime army is being led by experienced scouts. And Pershing is no amateur. He is a military genius in his own right. Do you know how he subdued the Moros in the Philippines?"

"The Moros?" another officer asked.

Enrique paused, uncertain if the story would be worth the telling. All of the men gathered about the table were illiterate and probably knew nothing about places and events outside of Mexico. Yet, at least Villa, Enrique hoped, would draw a conclusion from the story.

"The Moros are fierce Filipinos who are followers of Mohammedanism, a religion that has a fighting creed. For centuries the Islamic Moro pirates reaped a rich harvest of booty. Their island served as a thieves' market, at which the men they captured were sold into slavery and the women were parceled out to the various Moro harems.

"When the Moro sultan refused to sign a treaty, Pershing summoned two orderlies. One carried a dead pig, the other a bucket of pig's blood. More than anything else, the Moros feared contamination by a pig, which would bar them from the Mohammedan heaven. Pershing scooped up a dipper of the blood, enough to spatter the assembled sultan and his chieftains, then pointed to the treaty. One by one they stepped forward and agreed to the treaty."

The room was silent. Villa ran a forefinger along his shaggy mustache. "What would you propose, Enrique?"

"We must separate into even smaller groups. Hide in the mountain canyons and pueblitos and caves."

Villa's pugnacious chin jutted above his black bandana. "I do not hide."

Enrique shrugged. "Then you will not live to lead your people out of repression."

The faces of the other Dorado officers were expressionless, but their dark eyes were watchful, waiting for Villa's reaction to Ronquillo's challenge.

After a dangerous and mercurial moment, Villa nodded his head, doubling his already fleshy chin. "We are all tired. We ride out tomorrow morning."

Enrique made an ankle-threatening stroll up the cobbled street toward the fortress-monastery of San Nicolas. He scarcely noticed the shapely young woman, balancing a basket on her head, who flirted with him. He was absorbed with thoughts of another woman; in fact, two women.

The rosy-cheeked Molly was a bane to Angelina. Purposely, he courted the Mormon girl in order to delay that ultimate moment of confrontation with Angelina. His cousin. The Devil Woman. Angelina, who cast a wicked spell, which he did not even know if he wanted to resist anymore.

Both Molly and Angelina waited for him in the church's cloister. Prudently, he had installed the two young women in separate rooms—nicely furnished apartments on the whole, which the good plump padres had abandoned at his menacing persuasion. The building was old, built nearly four hundred years earlier, with treads that were worn to a diagonal at their edges by the passage of millions of feet.

Enrique found it amusing that the architecture of the Christian sanctuary was of Moorish design. Its stone block walls were several feet thick and kept the inside rooms cool even during the oppressive heat of the day. Water spilled melodiously from a tiled fountain. The rooms were numerous and cavernous, but instead of appearing gloomy, they projected an Old World aura that Enrique missed.

The monastery offered nicer accommodations even than the *alcalde*'s house, but Villa would not go near a church ever since those days when he had worked as a peon for the Negrete family and had been forced under penalty of the whip to attend Sunday masses.

Enrique went directly to Molly's room. She was sitting on the narrow bed, one leg folded beneath her long skirts, the other dangling over the edge so the upper buttons of her scuffed high-top boot were visible. The armpits of her gray merino dress were stained and perspiration darkened the wool between her large breasts. Strands of reddish-blond hair, turned brown now from exposure to dust and dirt and camp smoke, hung in greasy hanks about her face. In the past week of forced marches, she had lost the dimples in her cheeks and at her elbows. Nevertheless, she still had that softness about her, a placid vulnerability that would be easy to pierce—and so offered him no thrill at all.

At his entrance, her head jerked erect. Her eyes widened, like those of a startled animal. He inspected her with a male's predatory eye. The pulse in her throat beat frantically. "Have you eaten yet, Molly?"

Her lips trembled, but she managed to say, "Tonio brought me a tray."

He tried to place that name and recalled the thirteen-year-old boy inducted by the Villistas at Namaquipa. He was just as frightened as the Mormon girl and was too young to be an effective soldier. Tonio had managed to stop his sniveling only the day before, when Enrique had given him to Molly and Angelina.

He grasped Molly's rounded chin and lifted it, forcing her shamed gaze to meet his. In the acrid sputtering of the candle's tallow light his teeth gleamed white and strong below the black sweep of mustache. "Had you remained a virgin, Molly, you would have been one wife among many at Colonia Dublan, all belonging to one husband. Can it be any worse, belonging to me?"

Uncertainty and fear drained her cheeks of their natural color. Her soft shoulders shook in great spasms. Tears spiked pale lashes that were abruptly lowered. "Oh, God, why me?" she sobbed brokenly.

He gestured emptily to the tin *retablo* of the Virgin Mary above the rope bed. "Why anyone? Why the unfairness and suffering and pain? One takes what life deals and tries to overcome it."

"Oh, God, have pity!"

He lost patience in trying to reason with her. He took her hand and worked loose the clenched fingers whose nails cut half moons into the flesh-padded palm. "Come now. I can hurt you no worse than what Villa did."

But he did. That desperate need to rid himself of his demonic want for Angelina drove him to take the young girl without any preliminaries. Yet the mere voiding of his seed did nothing to lessen the horrified fascination he had for Angelina, no matter how many times that night he plundered the hapless Mormon girl.

With each driving thrust his cousin's name pounded against the back of his brain. Angelina. Angelina. Angelina.

Angel. That very name was a mockery of all that was holy. Something even more powerful and even more elemental than the bond of blood had locked them in a struggle that was more than simply forbidden passion. When two powerful wills collided, it was inevitable that one must subjugate or destroy the other.

Her ethereally beautiful face with the laughing eyes and beckoning lush lips was emblazoned on the back of his eyelids. The face of a saint, maybe, but burning with diabolic fires predestined to consume the most resolute sanctity—or was it merely that of an angel yearning earthward, doomed to fall?

When he threw his head back and groaned out his agony at that excruciating and exquisite moment of ejaculation, it was Angelina who held him to her breast.

Below him Molly lay crying. He could feel only impatience for the girl; at least she did not suffer that greater torment of the soul. Still, he tried to contain the savagery that possessed him the third time he forced his way between her still plump thighs. By dawn, when he finally collapsed on top of her, he felt crusted, hot, and flayed. He still had not found the release he sought.

The stale, cold smell of morning terminated the long night for Angelina. She had spent its dark, endless hours pacing the adobe room's tiled floor, because the tentacles of pain that writhed about her lungs, her heart, her very being, were too constricting to bear inactivity.

The *marihuana* cigarette she puffed did nothing to soothe her lacerated nerves. She wanted another draw of that finely powdered heroin given to her by one of the Dorados serving under Enrique. She tugged the pink rebozo closer about her shoulders. She was cold. And empty.

Without having seen or heard what had happened in the other room, her instincts nevertheless had known what had taken place during the night—exactly what had taken place, so that three times in the length of that agonizing night, her body had clamped rigid, her face the frozen rictus of a death mask, and a long, keening wail had reverberated within the room's walls. The Dorados assigned to guard the monastery had looked from one to another at the sound of the eerie howling, thinking it was some distant drove of wolves.

Sometime around dawn a knock brought Angelina whirling toward the door in anticipation, her long peasant skirts swishing about her ankles. But it was only Tonio with a breakfast tray of *pozole* and a cup of steaming, cinnamon-spiced Mexican chocolate.

The boy stood mute before her, his dark brown puppy's eyes worshipful. Of all the *soldaderas*, this beautiful one had treated him the kindest. No foul words on her soft lips or swift lash of the hand from her when he faltered in following a command. The lieutenant's other woman, she was not so pretty, always crying, and, those few times she did talk, she spoke in the *Norte Americano*'s harsh gutteral language.

Even after a tormented, sleepless night Angelina was as lovely as those flowers that unfold their petals to greet the dawn. She burned with an inner fire that made her countenance almost luminescent. Her delicate hand reached out and brushed the sugar-brown hair from the boy's forehead. She smiled, showing her sharp little teeth. "Tonio, how sweet of you to think of me."

His tongue was in a knot, and he could only look down at his dusty feet. Uncomfortable before this madonna, his toes wriggled on the cool stones.

"Ahh, I embarrass you," Angelina said. She touched the boy's beardless cheek, still soft as baby's. The consuming rage within her knew it had found its outlet. She took the tray from him and set it on the *tocador*, a lovely hand-carved chest.

"Come here, Tonio." Obediently he stepped into the room to stand humbly before her. She took his small hand and held it between her breasts, over the black pearl crucifix. "I know your loneliness, that you miss your mother."

He bit his lower lip to keep from betraying how close to tears he was. His own mama would have wanted him to act like a man. "*Sí*, madonna. I want to go back home."

"Until you can, I shall love you as my own son, Tonio." She released his hand and gently clasped his head against her breasts. "*Mi hijo, mi querido*—my son, my love," she murmured consolingly as she stroked his hair.

Tonio stood in her embrace, feeling near to paradise, that this grand lady should care for him. When the madonna drew away slightly, he felt a sense of panic at losing this small vestige of tenderness and refuge in a world that had gone terribly awry for him. As an altar boy he had been taught that the angels watched over him. When the Villistas had dragged him away from his father's blacksmith shop, he thought that perhaps the angels had foresaken him. But now, now the lieutenant's own special angel, the madonna Angelina, would care for him.

"Do not worry," she reassured him softly, as her fingers unbuttoned her bodice, "I only want to feel you close to me, as a mother feels the infant that suckles at her breast."

At first he didn't fully understand, and he offered no resistance when once more she clasped him to her. He could smell the drenching sweetness of her naked flesh and feel the softness of her breasts against his cheek, as soft and cushiony as his mother's large breasts had felt. The madonna continued to stroke his cheeks, his hair, the back of his neck. When she drew his face over to one nipple, he felt only the slightest alarm. Something in the back of his mind warned that it was wrong.

But how could it be wrong, the kindness that she was offering him? And his mouth, after that first uncertain moment, worked hungrily at the nipple, desperately seeking sustenance.

Somehow she had enfolded him against her on the bed, murmuring soft words of encouragement. A terrible urgency that was new and confusing claimed him. Her hand, slipping beneath his loose cotton *calzones*, found him. And with swift, stroking motions, she made him hers forever.

Afterward the madonna reassured him that what had happened—the befouling of his trousers with the white, sticky substance—was right, that he was becoming a man. He felt a new joy and knew a great sense of indebtedness to her, so that he would do anything for her. And when she asked him to find her a pistol, he gladly obeyed her request. He would protect her, serve her, love her. It would be his mission in life.

Within an hour Tonio had returned with a firearm, an old .36-caliber pistol. Angelina knew the day would come when she would need it, but she had not expected she would have the opportunity quite so soon. About eight-thirty that morning the town of Guerrero erupted with shouts, gunshots, and screams.

She ran from her room into the courtyard. Enrique was already at the grilled gate, stuffing his nightshirt into his breeches and talking in rapid-fire syllables to a soldier. Behind him, the Mormon girl stood in the doorway, her complexion pale and wan, her hair disheveled, fright etched into her features.

Angelina ran to his side. "What is it?" she demanded, shouting to make herself heard above the sudden din.

He pointed to the high wooded bluffs that banked the east and west sides of the river valley. A continuous stream of mounted American soldiers could be seen scrambling down two steep trails. "Pershing!"

He snapped another order to the soldier and turned back to her. "I've ordered a buggy brought around to the gate. Bring Molly with you and meet me before the Casa de Alcalde as quick as you can."

Her eyes captured his, and she asked him in a low monotone, "And if I choose not to flee with you, Enrique?"

"Then I will find you and kill you, before I will give you back."

It was a simple statement. She knew that he meant it and she was thrilled by the intensity of passion beneath his candid words. She nodded. "I shall be ready."

He was already strapping his Lugers to his hips and loping from the tree-shaded courtyard, when she turned back to Molly. The girl's eyes clung to the departing Enrique with a desperate need that only a love slave can come to feel for her captor.

Angelina crossed the flagstones until she stood before the girl. From the folds of her peasant skirt, Angelina raised the pistol. Molly's eyes widened, her mouth opened, but no sound could emerge. She was paralyzed with shock and terror. Calmly, Angelina rested the barrel between the girl's rounded breasts and pulled the trigger. Gunpowder left a black doughnut around the crimson puncture.

17

The stolid Hell Yet-Suey and a wan-looking Mark stood on either side of Roxana while she watched from the bluff as the American Regulars descended on Guerrero, which was walled east and west by high forested escarpments. The last two weeks had taken their toll on her, and the mere act of standing required more energy than she thought she had left. Mark had little more strength than she. He had no comment to make on whatever rites the *curandera* performed, but his affliction seemed to have been cured.

All Roxana's hopes and plans hung on the battle beginning below. If Villa was captured . . . if she could get that first interview . . .

The town looked like an antbed, and it was difficult to distinguish what was going on or which side was winning. Pinpoints of firing erupted all over the town, sending up what looked like puffs of smoke signals. Where was Sam in all that melee? Of course, she was concerned for him. With all they had experienced together, from the dangers of the desert to the hilarity of a gunpoint wedding, he had become a friend. Friend—rubbish! He was her lover.

Ha! That was just the problem. Not only did she feel no shame, but she knew a deep sense of gratitude to Sam Brady for having saved her from being a dried-up old maid. Yet her stubborn pride reared its ugly head at experiencing such a feeling of gratitude. Where was her self-esteem? it demanded angrily.

The anger was directed at herself and only indirectly at Sam, which she knew was unfair. She found it difficult to be civil with him, which, of course, mattered little to him. She had to wonder why, at her age, she was letting her pride mar that glorious feeling she had experienced—the knowledge of what it was to be wholly and sublimely a woman. He had made her acutely aware of her breasts, of their soft, free sway beneath her dress whenever she moved. Why in the world did women bind what made them so expressly women?

Even as she stood watching the skirmish, her body throbbed at the memory of those rifle-hardened hands caressing her intimately.

As the battle progressed, it was even more difficult to tell what was happening. An indigo pall of mingled gunpowder and smoke billowed into the Chihuahuan sky. Somewhere in the pandemonium below her were Villa and Angelina Asunsolo, and it was all Roxana could do to keep from mounting her gray gelding and charging into the town.

Beside her, Hell Yet-Suey grunted and shook his head, his long white hair swishing about his blue wool blouse. "Heap Mexican. Shoot 'em all." His teeth bared savagely. "Damnfine fight not going good."

What was she standing there for, watching the Punitive Expedition's first encounter with Villa's forces, when she should be covering the story firsthand?

She mounted her gray. Hell Yet-Suey looked up with surprise wrinkling his old face. "What the hell woman thinks she doing?"

She was ignoring Sam's order to wait out of the range of battle with Mark and the old Indian, who had just returned from his scouting mission. "To cover the battle," she said tersely.

"Are you out of your mind, Miss Van Buren?" Mark demanded. He crossed to her and put a restraining hand on the saddle's pommel. His face was richly handsome, and she wondered that she had not fallen in love with him. "You can't file a story," he gritted, "if you're lying dead on some dusty street."

"Are you two going with me or staying here?"

Naturally, they followed her. Mark in grim silence, and Hell Yet-Suey mumbling rabidly. Experience and old age had taught him that the white woman, when riled, could be just as fiercesome to tangle with as her red sister. Still, as the three horses picked their way down the trail toward the embattled town, the old Apache grumbled loudly about crazy white women.

The battle of Guerrero was a repeat of Columbus and Bachiniva. There were scenes of tragedy and unutterable pathos. Sporadic firing was being exchanged from doorways and narrow alleys, but the heavier bursts of gunfire were some blocks away from her, on the town's south side. Bodies lay sprawled in the streets; some, mere children.

While Hell Yet-Suey held their reins, she and Mark moved among the dead. He counted them, identifying their sex and approximate age, while she recorded the numbers on her field pad.

"This no good," Hell Yet-Suey would mutter, standing over her protectively.

She tried to console the bereaved inhabitants of Guerrero, unfortunate bystanders—an old mother, weeping over her son; a wife bemoaning the loss of her husband; a little girl sobbing over the death of her brother.

An American trooper was propped against the blood-splattered, stuccoed wall of a *panadería*, whose display window had been robbed of its cakes and rolls. When he saw her, he weakly beckoned her and Mark over. "One of you wouldn't have a cigarette, would you?" he asked.

The dark stain on his khaki shirt was slowly, steadily enlarging. Powder burns about the wound told her he had been shot at close range and that there was nothing that could be done for him.

"Sorry, old fellow, I don't smoke," Mark managed to say evenly.

Roxana could feel the same sickening sorrow tearing at her lungs that she saw in Mark's face. It was no longer smoothly handsome, but there was something in its mobile lines that appealed to her even more.

She pulled the cigarette package from the purse suspended from her waist. There was one left. She lit it and placed it between the soldier's lips. When he had taken a puff, she removed the cigarette. "What's your name, Private?" she asked gently.

"Bartholomew—Bart," he got out. He nodded toward her pad. "Say, would you write home . . . to my family in New Jersey. Tell them you saw me?"

She gave him another puff. Then, while the battle still raged about the pueblo, she took down the letter he dictated with great effort. He died before the letter was finished, so she signed it, "Your loving Bart." The postscript, detailing his death, she would pen later.

She and Mark, with a scowling Hell Yet-Suey hulking behind, came upon another American soldier, face up in the doorway of a home. The lower portion of his right jaw was gone, exposing the torn interior of his mouth. His eyes were open, unseeing. Tenderly she pressed her fingers against his lids. She recorded his name from the dog tags suspended about his neck.

As she finished, she realized a middle-aged woman and her three small children had cautiously emerged from a darkened corner of the room to huddle about her like chicks. They were all barefoot. The woman tentatively held out a palm. "You have American dollar?"

Mark took several one-dollar bills from his trousers pocket and dropped them into the woman's red-chaffed hand. The woman thanked him profusely and scurried away with her children in tow.

"Hardly 'color locale' material for your column, is it?" she asked him.

He turned to her. His brows met in a frown, and his mouth pressed into a tight line. "You don't have to do this, Miss Van Buren. You don't have to risk your life to prove you're a capable journalist."

She shook her head, a slight almost imperceptive movement. "You're wrong, Mark. A woman has to go as far as a man, then one step farther, to prove herself in the business realm."

He grabbed her shoulders. Hell Yet-Suey growled menacingly, but Mark didn't release her. "For the love of God, Roxana, this isn't the 'business realm.' It's a battleground. It's insanity!"

She looked up into the long-lashed eyes. Their green-gold depths were darkened by anger and something else. Peripherally she noted that he called her by her given name. "Let me go, Mark. I have a revolution to cover."

The anger eased from his lips, softening their contours. For an incredible moment she thought he was going to kiss her. Then he stepped back, and she was free again.

The rounds of the battle scenes took Roxana steadily closer to the plaza, where the bell from the centuries-old church was pealing madly. She hoped to find Villa in the plaza in the midst of the heavier fighting.

What of Angelina? Would she be fighting with the *soldaderas*?

After almost four hours of fighting, which side was winning? What if Villa and his bloodthirsty Dorados prevailed? Suddenly, even with Hell Yet-Suey and Mark as bodyguards, Roxana did not feel so safe.

There was total chaos. Even as the battle raged, vandals were breaking into the shops and stealing the wares. They rushed past her, their arms full of stolen goods—blankets, bottles of liquor, saddles, clothing. A rotund woman waddled by Roxana, dropping a man's shiny leather shoe from her mound of booty.

Nearer the plaza more here-and-there fires were blooming, spewing flames and gray smoke above the red-tiled roofs. Once, when she and Mark paused in the street to record more statistics, he had to yank her from the path of a runaway team of horses, the carriage careening wildly.

By the time she reached the plaza, she was disappointed to find that the Villistas were retreating out of the city. Only a few remained, barricaded behind machine-gun emplacements. From a shop's doorway she scanned the plaza, scribbling notes furiously in her notepad. Fleeing Villistas, mounted and afoot, headed for the concealing brush that surrounded the pueblo. By noon it was apparent that they had split into such small fragments that the band was disrupted beyond the possibility of immediate reassembly.

Hell Yet-Suey's shouted warning "Woman!" brought her writing to a halt, and she looked up to see a *soldadera* bearing down on her astraddle a big piebald.

In that instant Roxana marked the hatred contorting the woman's flat Indian face—and the American saber she slashed out with. Then Hell Yet-Suey's rifle fired, and the saber went sailing harmlessly through the air. The *soldadera* wobbled for a second on her mount, regained her hold, and clattered on down the cobblestone street.

Roxana sagged against the wall, weakened by fright. She had the urge to feel her arms, her neck, her head to see if she were truly unscathed. She had come so close to death. Her heart was beating as fast as a tiny animal's, like that of a timid mouse!

After Mark had reassured himself she was all right, her fright dissolved into righteous fury. Why, when the contingent of male correspondents was safely holed up with Pershing back at Rancho San Geronimo, did she have to risk her life in order to prove herself worthy of a position as a front-page reporter?

Mark was right. This was insanity.

A half hour later, Sam, astride his skewbald, found her interviewing a soldier of the Seventh Cavalry. At Sam's glare the soldier quickly finished telling his story and went about his duty of collecting the weapons spoils. "Roxy, I told you to stay put!"

He scowled down at her from his position in the saddle. His furious glance fell on Hell Yet-Suey and Mark. "Couldn't either of you stop a mere woman?"

"She's no *mere* woman," Mark snapped back.

Roxana looked from one man to the other, not understanding either the two men or their unreasonable animosity toward one another. "What about Villa?" she demanded anxiously, ignoring their ill temper.

Sam's news was depressing. The Punitive Expedition had flushed the Dorados at last, only to find the wily, will-o'-the-wisp Villa had somehow escaped.

His face streaked with blood and dust, Sam leaned wearily on the pommel and related the rest. "Sergeant Chicken thinks Villa could be hiding in one of the caves around here. Field units are going out now to scour the bluffs and woods."

"But you don't think he is, do you?" she asked.

He shrugged. "The pueblo's mayor says that, because of his knee wound, Villa fled in a black buggy, accompanied by only a handful of his followers."

"Do you think Ronquillo fled with him?"

Sam doffed his hat and wiped the back of his arm across his forehead. "With Ronquillo's education and savvy, I'd reckon Villa would want him with him."

She was back where she had started from—with neither her interview nor her missing person. She sagged against the mud-brick building, and Hell Yet-Suey caught her elbow to support her. "Damnfine tired woman!"

"I'm all right." She pushed back the swath of hair that had escaped from under the helmet to curl over one eye, and looked up at Sam. She felt rather than saw in the shadow of his hat brim those keen, searching eyes with their intense look. "What about the captured Villistas?" she asked. "Could Angelina Asunsolo be among them?"

He shook his tawny head. "We took no captives."

At least, Roxana told herself, she could still scoop the story of the first battle between the Punitive Expedition and Villa. "Where can I find the telegraph office?"

"It won't do you any good, Roxy. Villa had the foresight to cut all the wires. I'm carrying the battle report back to Pershing. You and Mark rest up here, while Hell Yet-Suey and the others comb the hills. When I get back, we can start hunting the Asunsolo woman again."

All right, she couldn't use the telegraph, but Pershing's Signal Corps just might be her means to file her dispatch. "I'm going with you."

"Like hell you are. You won't make it over the Continental Divide before you fall off your horse."

She proved him wrong, but the return was something she never wanted to live through again, a trip of thirty miles in seventeen hours. A freak storm blew in, and the raging mountain wind drove the snow and sand and sleet with stinging force.

Mark managed to be phlegmatic about the ordeal. He leaned in the saddle toward her and shouted to make himself heard above the wind's roar, "Reminds me of a trip by horseback up to the Labrang Lamasery in Tibet. Only it wasn't half this cold!"

In addition to the cowhide coat, she wrapped an army blanket about her. She wondered if Sam in his great duster and Mark in his fur-lined Mackintosh were any warmer. Her legs and arms were stiff and cramped from the agonizing cold. Despite her gloves, her fingers would periodically freeze in their clutched position on the reins, and she would have to flex her hands to restore the circulation.

Sam called halts at one-hour intervals, allowing five-minute rests. The blizzard made it impossible to light a fire, but he and Mark huddled her between them, pressing her against their lengths. She found it disconcerting and slightly amusing. She, who rarely had been in the company of a male, other than her father, was pressed on both sides by men. Handsome men, who briskly rubbed her shoulders and arms and hands.

Sam peeled away the icy-wet bandana that covered her nose and mouth. "It's doing more harm than good now."

"Now I know how Hannibal must have felt crossing the Alps," she groaned.

The horses were no better off. They were blowing wind-puffs up and down their forelegs. Toward dawn, her gelding was dying from exhaustion. She turned her back while Sam disposed of the animal. Mercifully, the wind was loud enough so she just barely heard the pistol's sharp report. Now the big skewbald stallion had to pack both her and Sam, while Mark brought up the rear.

By next morning the storm had blown past, though the wind was still chilly. When the three of them reached Rancho San Geronimo her lips were actually bleeding, and her face and hands were chapped and raw.

She had envisioned the establishment of an advance base at Rancho San Geronimo with the general warmly ensconced in a ranch house, a blazing fire in the hearth, a group of cavalry officers standing about toasting their hands. The image of hot tongues of flame leaping in a fireplace was a vision that had kept her going through the bitter night.

What she saw was something totally different. The rancho was a cluster of crumbling adobe buildings along an alkaline stream that was thinly iced over. The soldiers had slept tentless that night. Sunup found them sitting on their bedrolls, pulling on boots and washing their faces in collapsible canvas buckets that looked like horse feedbags.

In the warming spring sunlight, Pershing sat on a slatted tomato can box, looking every inch the brigadier of cavalry and the commander-in-chief that he was. His hand wielded a grease pencil over the sheet attached to a clipboard, and she knew he was no doubt acting as press censor for the newspapermen's releases that had been prepared on the battle. The journalists were only awaiting confirmed word as to its outcome and resulting statistics before dispatching their stories.

That vulture Charley Rooney sat narby on a gas can with his mess kit balanced on his knees. But for the straw boater, she almost didn't recognize him without the wet stub of a cigar perched between his lips. At the sight of her, he dumped the tin plate and came to his feet. Indeed, it seemed everyone—Pershing's staff, the war correspondents, the loitering Mexicans—was converging on her and Sam at once, wanting word of the battle.

When she dismounted, she fell into Sam's arms. "Damn't, Roxy, if you aren't a stubborn old maid."

But concern was pinched into the corner of his eyes, and his tone held something akin to affection. Surprising her, he scooped her into the cradle of his arms. Mark shouldered the way through the press of men for her and Sam.

Pershing rose to meet them. His narrowed eyes took in her condition. "Sullivan," he said, "there's coffee over at the campfire. Get one of my staff to help you."

Sam said, "Gin'll do me just fine, Jack."

Pershing frowned his disapproval but only said, "Follow me." He led the way to his touring car, its khaki top dusted with snow. From one fender waved the Stars and Stripes, from the other one star on a red field.

Gratefully, Roxana sank into the rear seat, while Sam and Pershing climbed in the front. The general let down the isinglass curtains to keep out the chilly wind, and Sam bent his rangy frame over the seat and began to remove her kid boots. It was so mortifying to have to acknowledge that Sam was in fitter condition than she; mortifying to be prostrated and subject to Sam's ministrations. But she could only lie there as he withdrew each boot, revealing the wet merino stockings that now had holes worn in them.

A week's growth of beard hid his features that she knew years before had been handsome. What would he look like, cleaned up and completely sober? For that matter, what would she look like cleaned up? The unforgiving weather, that night of Sam's ravishing lovemaking—surely they had left their mark on her. Was it obvious to Mark and the others?

"Well?" Pershing asked.

Sam's face was as expressionless as the general's. "We routed them, Jack. Thirty dead and two machine guns captured. But Villa escaped us."

For a moment Pershing sat looking out of the snow-flecked windshield. To go farther south meant to risk the severance of regular communication with the War Department. To remain where he was would preclude his personally directing the forces closing in on Villa.

"Well," he said finally, "our orders were specifically to pursue the marauders who attacked Columbus, not to bring Villa back dead or alive. We'll continue to pursue. But Villa is no fool. It may be that this campaign has just begun."

"As I figure it, Jack," Sam said, "we've got Villa entirely surrounded—on one side."

"The problem is that none of his countrymen are inclined to betray his hiding place, either out of loyalty or just from fear of reprisal. And the Mexicans, Carranzistas and Villistas alike, are all hostile toward the Northern Invader. The best we can hope for is to box Villa in somewhere. What would you do, Sam?"

"I'd regroup the troops that are scattered from here to kingdom come and reassign districts for each."

Roxana could restrain herself no longer, and she propped herself up on one elbow. Still, forcing the words past her throat at that moment took a great deal of effort. Her voice came out a raspy whisper. "General, is there any line of communication out of San Geronimo—a wireless set or something?"

He shook his grizzled head. "I'm afraid not, Miss Van Buren. The Signal Corps has run field buzzers to the nearest telegraph lines, but we haven't been able to rouse headquarters at Colonia Dublan yet."

"I've got to file my story as soon as possible."

"Jack," Sam said, "couldn't she catch a ride back on the next supply truck in from Dublan and file her story from there?"

"I suppose it could be arranged. My aide at Dublan, Patton, will see that she's taken care of. In the meantime, Sam, I have another mission for you."

Roxana struggled to sit upright, but her head clanged as if soldiers were shooting craps inside it. "I won't go back to Colonia Dublan. I've got a war to cover, and I'm going to do it. I'll just send my story back with the truck convoy and have the story wired out of Colonia Dublan."

"You're going back to Dublan, Roxy," Sam said. From the front seat he glared at her with that uncompromising frown, tilting his jaw down and peering out from beneath the dark sweep of thick brows. "There's no way I'm gonna lug you over the desert and mountains in the condition you're in—or the one I'm in, for that matter."

"Well, I tell you I'm not."

At that moment a staff officer opened the car door, and a draft of wind chilled the car's interior. Mark leaned inside and held a tin cup of steaming coffee toward Roxana. Snow flecked his dark brown hair and the lashes that bordered eyes dark with concern. He looked at Sam. "Is she going to be all right?"

"She will be if she returns to Dublan," he said flatly.

"You can forget that," she said, and took a swallow of the coffee. It burned the roof of her mouth, but nothing had ever tasted better. "You and I made a deal, Sam Brady, and you're going to keep your part of it! We're going after Villa and Angelina Asunsolo together!"

"For once, I have to agree with Brady here," Mark said. "A lone grave in the midst of the Chihuahuan desert will be little consolation to your father."

"That's enough." Pershing's voice was low and clipped and brooked no argument. "I think this discussion can be continued after you three have rested."

It appeared that their disagreement would be one of those Mexican stand-offs. But appearances were deceiving. That afternoon, as she awaited the truck convoy, she collapsed into the sleep of exhaustion. She awoke en route to Colonia Dublan with Mark cradling her head on his shoulder—and Sam long gone.

That four-flusher was going after Angelina and the five thousand without her.

18

Roxana fixed Mark with an accusing glare. "You knew I didn't want to go to Colonia Dublan."

"I knew you wouldn't make it if you didn't." He ignored the soldier on the other side of her, who was driving the truck. "Roxana, I want you to come back with me."

She tilted her head to the side. "Back where?"

"Back where you belong. Back to Washington."

The driver, one of those leather-tough soldiers, never took his eyes from the empty terrain, but she could almost feel his ears perk up. "What about your 'local color' story, Mark?"

He averted his gaze from her upturned face to the blinding white sand that stretched to the perimeter of mountains on the far horizons. "I'm more . . . concerned about you."

Something niggled the back of her mind, but she couldn't bring it into focus. "I'm a big girl, Mark. I can take care of myself."

His hand closed over hers. His fingers were slender and supple and tanned by exposure to the sun and wind. The palms, however, were not callused like Sam's. "I'd like to take care of you, Roxana." He glanced over at the driver, then, nudging her head into the hollow of his shoulder, saying, "We'll talk about it after we've rested and eaten."

"And filed my story on the battle with Villa," she reminded him.

In two weeks a lot of changes had taken place at Colonia Dublan. On the outskirts of the Mormon town more soldiers than Roxana could have ever counted streamed in day after day to stake out tent towns around the Expedition's headquarters. Interspersed were truck parks, stables, gasoline dumps, and barbed-wire enclosures filled with crates of supplies. In an open field the Army had even hewn out a landing place for the air machines.

The soldier who returned her and Mark to Colonia Dublan left them outside the commanding officer's tent and drove off to have his truck's tank refilled before making the trip north to the base station at Columbus.

Mark had his own trip to make, for the intestinal disorder that had made him so ill at Bachiniva was back again. It was embarrassing for him, and she wisely said nothing but reported alone to headquarters.

Instead of Patton a pinched, bony-nosed Captain Morley sat behind the desk. In back of him another officer was filling his tin cup from the water cooler. With ten thousand soldiers to administer, Roxana supposed that the mix-up that followed was understandable.

"Lieutenant Patton's out on patrol," Morley told her. "Now either report back to the compound or take a hike."

Her cracked lips hurt when she spoke. "I don't understand. I'm a newspaper reporter and General Pershing told me to see Lieutenant Patton about—"

"Sure, and the Old Man told me he'd make me a one-star general next week. Now what's it to be: the compound, or a long hike back to the States?"

Roxana braced her palms on the desk and leaned forward. Her voice sounded shrill in her ears. "Now you listen to me, Captain! I don't know anything about a compound, but I do know that—"

But Morley was already summoning a soldier to remove her bodily from his tent. "And tell her to get herself cleaned up, if she expects any business!" the captain instructed as the soldier forcibly dragged her away.

Indignantly she shoved at his shoulder. "Get your hands off of me! I've got to file my story!"

He was a young man with peach fuzz still on his acne-blotched cheeks. No doubt she was almost twice his age. "Look, ma'am," he said apologetically, "I'm just obeying orders. Don't make it any more difficult for me."

She gave up struggling, but not because of his request. Instead, across the railroad tracks she saw the swarm of civilians at the depot and recognized some of the reporters, one of them Damon Runyon. The news of the Guerrero battle was already out, leaked quite likely by the truck driver who had brought her from Rancho San Geronimo. The telegraph wire was probably already humming with the report of Villa's escape.

Her shoulders sagged dispiritedly at losing out on the scoop again, and she let the young soldier lead her away. Until Mark returned to straighten out the mess, there was nothing she could do.

The young soldier halted before the gates of another barbed-wire stockade. Inside were maybe two dozen one-room adobe shells roofed with canvas tent tops. Each adobe hut couldn't have been more than about ten by fifteen feet.

A beefy sergeant wearing the insignia of the Provost Marshal on his collar—in effect the military police—asked, "Another 'Source of Delight,' eh, Dreyfus?"

The young soldier nodded. "Looks like it."

The sergeant fastened gimlet eyes on the gaunt, blistered face framed by hair that look like an eggbeater had attacked it. His stare took in the white pith helmet dangling from one hand, the cowhide overcoat slung over her arm, and the tattered yellow parasol. "Miss, you look ready for the field hospital. You can't be counting on getting much business. Put her in Number twenty-one," he told the soldier and waved them on past.

That first half hour, she sat on the adobe's cot in a stupor, trying to make some sense of what was happening—what had happened. But for a folding chair and a washstand with a chamber pot below, the room was bare, without even windows. A kerosene lantern was hung from a nail on the tent's ridgepole.

"Dear Lord," she murmured, her gaze fixing on the small black creature suspended next to the lantern. A bat!

The squeaking of the screen door, followed by a knock at the slatted door, jerked her to her feet. Mark! He was getting her out of this mess.

A head of frazzled hennaed hair poked itself inside. The wide mouth paused from snapping its cud of chewing gum to smile. "Just the Welcoming Committee, dearie."

Roxana stared at her stupidly, and the woman said, "Sally's the name. Sally Henson—Number twenty."

Roxana pointed toward the bat. "Do you share Number twenty with one of those . . . creatures?"

Sally breezily waved a fan with pink flowers painted on one side and a funeral parlor advertisement on the other. "Oh, they don't bother you none, dearie. When the weather's warm the swarming flies are a hell of lot more bothersome."

"I hope I won't be here to find out. Is this a field hospital of some sorts?"

Sally's outburst of kewpie doll laughter startled her. "I've heard a whorehouse called a lot of things, but that's a new one. A field hospital, imagine!"

If that first half hour had been a blur, she felt like the dawning of a nightmare was beginning. "Whore—whorehouse?"

"You mean you don't know?"

Feeling foolish, Roxana shook her head.

Sally stepped inside and shut the door behind her. "Look, kid. This is a compound that the general was good enough to set up for us . . . us camp followers. You don't think those sanctimonious LDS's are gonna let us set up practice over there, do you?"

"LDS?" Roxana asked, feeling that a net of unreality had closed over her brain.

"Latter Day Saints. You know, the Mormons over at Colonia Dublan." She leaned against the mud brick wall and her mouth resumed its work on the chewing gum.

Roxana tried to appear bright. "I wasn't exactly aware that *that* was the purpose of this compound."

"Sure. Ten thousand soldiers stuck out in the desert gotta do something to occupy their time. And baseball games and boxing matches just don't satisfy all their—uhh, boredom."

Roxana stood up. She was going to kill Sam Brady. She was going to wrap a horseshoe around his neck to begin with and then—"I have to get out of here!"

"Where you going, dearie? Back to the States? Look, kid, you can earn more in one night here in the cribs than in three weeks back in the States. Where else those doughboys gonna spend their pay? Not a saloon in fifty miles, and even then the cantinas aren't exactly hospitable to American troops."

Where, indeed, was she going? She had an interview to get and a young woman to find. Within a couple of hours Patton would be back, and Mark would straighten out the mix-up. Until then she might as well rest, because she meant to be on the next convoy back to Rancho San Geronimo.

She sat back down on the cot. "Do you have a cigarette I could borrow?"

"Sure." The woman withdrew a Mexican brand package from between tightly packed breasts and offered Roxana one. "You've never plied this trade before, have you, kid?"

Kid? Roxana was as old or older than the redhead before her. "No."

Sally went back to fanning herself in tempo with the snapping of her gum. "It's not so bad. 'Specially here. The doughboys might mill around the compound like wasps, but they get only thirty minutes a whack, or the Provost Marshal comes and drags them out. He also sets the prices. But best, you don't have to worry about the claps."

Roxana knew she probably shouldn't ask. But she did. "Claps?"

"Gonorrhea. Syphilis. The Provost Marshal issues prophylactics to every gent who passes through that gate. Pershing's orders—that and the gents have to bathe twice weekly. Can you believe that? The Old Man's a stickler for cleanliness."

Prophylactics. At least Roxana understood the word, thanks to a lecture on birth control by the Suffragette Emma Goldman. Still, to hide her blush, she lowered her face to the match's flame and inhaled deeply on her cigarette.

"Say, I really like that parasol of yours," Sally said. "A few stitches here and there, and you got yourself a new one."

Roxana eyed it grimly. The parasol was representative of herself. It had been through a lot of wear in the last several weeks, and all for nothing. "Would you like it?"

"Gee, would I!" Sally picked up the parasol and stroked the frayed material with almost loving fingers. "Look, kid, a couple of us are going over to Dublan for an early dinner. Some Chinaman has put in a restaurant over there by the railroad tracks—don't have to tell ya that the Saints ain't too jolly about a commercial establishment. Wanna come along?"

"I think I'll . . . just rest." She didn't plan on being there that long.

After Sally left, Roxana passed the time consoling herself with the fact that later she would be able to get a story out of this experience. She saw the lurid headlines in bold red print. "Trapped in a Bordello." No, "Trapped in a Brothel." No, "Trapped in a Bagnio." Yes, much more refined.

When darkness fell, she began to worry. Where was Mark?

Outside she could hear soldiers prowling the stockades, singularly and in groups, laughing, whistling. Then began the surreptitious knocks. From Sally's adobe came a soldier's off-key serenade.

"I do not know, and I do not care . . . For the things that are or the things that were . . . For half my heart lies buried there . . . In Texas, down by the Rio Grande."

Sally's high-pitched laughter abruptly ended the soldier's song. Imagining what was happening next, Roxana shivered. When the knock came at her door, she backed against the far wall—which wasn't very far. Mark!

"It's me, ma'am. Johnny Dreyfus." The young soldier who had brought her to the stockade!

"Go away!"

"I—I just wanted to see if you were settled in, and all."

She could hear the loneliness in his voice. She opened the door a couple of inches and peeked out. He stood in the cold, twisting his peaked campaign hat brim between nervous hands. "Listen, Johnny," she began uncertainly, "I'm not a—there's been a mistake. I don't belong here. I'm just waiting for Lieutenant Patton to return and straighten out this misunderstanding."

Uncertainty played over his narrow face. "I'm telling the truth!" she said desperately.

His expression was one of comical relief. "Could I just come in for a few minutes then, ma'am?"

When he stepped into the room's light, she couldn't help but close her eyes. The boy was a walking erection. Apparently realizing his condition, he quickly sat on the folding chair and clapped his hat over his lap. He was a gangly youth with ears that stuck out. His painfully sensitive gaze moved about the room and at last, reluctantly, stopped at Roxana.

"Could you tell me anything about Mr. Sullivan?"

The young soldier's brow wrinkled, then smoothed out. "The civie who came in with you?"

"Yes, he's the one."

"Oh, ma'am, he's laid low over at the field hospital with the runs—er, diarrhea."

"I—I see."

At her blush, he blushed also, his cauliflower ears turning scarlet. "I didn't think you were like those other women, ma'am." His big hands mangled the campaign hat. "I just wanted to talk until—"

Until he could work up his courage to approach one of the prostitutes.

And so, he talked: of his family's little farm in New Jersey and how he missed the trees and the green grass and the family but how, when he was mustered out, he was going out to Hollywood, California, where it was said a guy could make money working in those moving pictures and, gee, he felt better talking to her, and he'd pass the word along to his buddies that she was off-limits and just as soon as Patton returned from patrol he'd see to it that the lieutenant corrected this awful mistake.

After he left, she lay on the cot, her hands clasped behind her head. Apparently the bat was making its own nocturnal forages. Her thoughts drifted to Sam—how, like Johnny Dreyfus, he had been such an earnest young man, so full of hope and love and innocence. Life had its way with people. No one escaped unscathed.

Sam, that skinflint son of a bitch!

She was irritated and feeling slightly sorry for herself, and the outburst of unladylike profanity made her feel a little better, albeit slightly shocked at herself. But then, since leaving Washington, she had certainly undergone an astonishing metamorphosis. Life in the Southwest was exciting: it held a fine edge that the effete East lacked.

So she lay awake, listening the rest of the night to the groaning of the truck convoys and clanking caissons and to the creaking of the horse columns passing through the town. Surely Patton was among one of those interminable processions.

The next morning did not bring Patton, but it did bring a flying machine sweeping in to land in an oat field for the benefit of the news reporters and photographers who had not been selected to accompany Pershing. With Sally, she went out to watch the white-scarved aviator pose with arms crossed in front of his Curtiss before he took off again.

It was a gorgeous spring day. For once the wind wasn't blowing. In the drench of April's sunshine the cacti bloomed with riotously colored flowers. Some of the cactus fruit, Sally claimed, had aphrodisiac properties. She rustled up some of the ubiquitous tortillas and bacon along with tin mugs of thick black coffee from the field kitchen, and the two of them sat before Roxana's adobe and ate. Fuzzy fluffs from the cottonwoods drifted through the air to catch on the screen doors of the adobes.

Between bites, Sally mundanely related the tricks of her trade. "See, Roxana, if you'll just lay an oilcoth across the foot of the bed for the customers who don't have time to shed their boots, then you don't have to change the sheets so often."

And there were the more eye-opening items about avoiding conception: The French Secret (Roxana didn't ask what that was), vaginal tents of eelskin, and douches of alum, pearlash, or sulphate of zinc. Brooding over Patton's continued absence, Roxana mechanically filed Sally's tidbits of information away in the back of her mind for a later story.

That afternoon, she went over to the field hospital. Beneath the large canvas tent the heat was stifling, and the sides had been rolled up to permit circulation of air, which was virtually nonexistent. The field hospital housed approximately a dozen cots, most of which were empty. When she explained she wanted to see Mark, the soldier on duty, who wore a white band with a red cross around his khaki sleeve, led her to the far cot.

Looking down at Mark's perspiring face, she wished she had Sally's funeral parlor fan. He held out his hand, taking hers in a weak clasp. His smile was rueful. "This really is an ignominious position for a man to be in."

At that moment she liked him immensely. She smiled and, still holding his hand, sat on the empty cot next to his. "It happens to the best of us."

"Roxana."

"Yes?"

"You are . . . very beautiful."

She laughed. "That's not really true. I imagine I am what some call a handsome woman. Healthy, nice to look at. But I'm not beautiful at all. And it's foolish of you to say so."

At his look of silent suffering, she smiled to soften her reproval.

He didn't return her smile. "Roxana, when I'm over this—this inconvenience, I want to take you back East. I want to marry you."

Her first marriage proposal, and here she was middle-aged. A spinster by all counts. She was a little amused and a little flattered, but not enough to play the coy maiden. She had to wonder what Mark's reaction would be, coming from the same highly proper, conventional background as she, if he were to discover she was quartered in a compound for prostitutes.

"At the risk of sounding trite, Mark, isn't this a little sudden?"

"You don't plan a timetable for love, dear. How was I to know I would meet an attractive woman with courage and warmth and intelligence? We have a lot in common. Both of us are from the East, raised in society's upper echelon. Both of us are highly educated with the same interests, even the same profession: journalism. If you'll give me the opportunity, I know I can make you happy."

"But, Mark, I am happy." Until she said it, she hadn't realized it was true.

Mark scoffed with a growling "Hrummph!" He turned his face from her and looked unseeingly up at the canvas top. "You call wandering over an empty desert, half-starved, half-frozen, half-baked—you call that happiness? With all that's happened, I think you still don't realize that it might just as easily be your body lying out there being picked over by vultures. Sam Brady could give two cents about your survival, but I love you and—"

She wasn't listening to what he was saying. His mention of the possible reality of her death recalled another statement he had made—something about a lone desert grave giving no consolation to her father. Her father, not her "mother and father" or her family. That was the little item that had been worrying her subconscious.

"Mark."

She waited for him to look at her. "You haven't been listening to me, have you?" he charged.

"Mark, my father sent you to bring me back, didn't he? I want the truth."

Mark had the good grace to keep silent, his lips flat against his teeth. After a moment, he said, "I won't deny it. I was to bring you back, even if it meant marrying you." His fingers tightened about hers. "But I swear, Roxana, falling in love with you was not part of the bargain."

"What did my father offer you for this service?" she asked tonelessly.

"The financial assurance that I could continue to pursue my journalism career."

She fought to control her bitterness, and her tears. "But he didn't want to let me pursue mine."

"He loves and worries about you, Roxana. You must believe me. I love you, too. We don't have to go back East. I won't take your father's money. We could somehow manage to live on what I earn until I make it to the top of my profession."

She released his hand. "I may be a foolish old maid, Mark, but I believe you. I believe you really feel something for me. Maybe what you call love. But I can't mate in captivity."

Mark's mouth fell open, and she laughed. "There, I've shocked you, haven't I?" She rose and bent to kiss his forehead. "I'll check in on you later, my dear."

19

With his Stetson clasped behind him, Sam stood looking at the wall of books. The justice probably had read every one of them. Did he read Roxana's columns?

No doubt he did. No doubt that was why he transacted for instructions to reach Pershing to order his head scout sent to Washington. Justice Augustus Van Buren carried a lot of influence, influence that reached all the way to the War Department.

Of course, Sam didn't have to obey the summons. He could have turned in his scout's job to Pershing right there and then at Rancho San Geronimo. After all, he still had an opportunity to make five thousand. But curiosity persuaded him to take the two-week leave and check it out. Curiosity—and the remark by Pershing:

"When you get back from Washington, I have another little mission for you. But we'll discuss that later. First, I want you to hightail it to the capital and confront Van Buren. Sam, for all the injustice done you by the Military Court, and others, you're a cashiered officer still carrying a lot of bitterness with you. Go back and dump it where it belongs before it eats your guts out."

The Old Man arranged for him to catch a ride out on one of the reconnaissance planes bound for Fort Sam Houston at San Antonio. From there, it was only a three-day trip by train to Washington. With luck, he'd be back in Mexico with Roxana before a week was gone. The general even promised he'd keep Roxana pinned down until he could get back.

Sam's mouth twitched. Roxana—and Sullivan. The reporter was hankering after her like a lovesick puppy. And Roxana? What did she feel for Sullivan? Unconsciously, Sam's broad shoulders shrugged. What was it to him? He certainly wasn't the marrying kind.

"Sam."

He turned. Rowena stood framed in the doorway. Leisurely and appreciatively his gaze ran over her, noting that was the response she wanted from him. The black taffeta dress set off the golden hair that was piled atop her head in a mass of curls that he supposed was the newest fashion. How many years since he had last seen her? Ten? She was still as beautiful.

She crossed the room to him and held out her hands, saying softly, "Sam, I thought I'd never have the opportunity to see you again."

He let her take his hands. Closer, he could see the faint tracing of a line on either side of her mouth; not lines of laughter but of discontent. So, she had not been deliriously happy with her father's choice of husbands. A doctor, wasn't it?

"Well," she asked, smiling now, "aren't you going to say anything?"

He said what he thought she'd want to hear. "You're as lovely as ever, Rowena."

"You've always known how to set a female's heart aflutter, Sam Brady."

"Your husband doesn't?" He couldn't help himself.

Her face paled. Her gaze met his unflinchingly. "My husband's dead, Sam."

She dropped his hands to withdraw a lace handkerchief from her sleeve, but she didn't dab at her eyes; rather, she twisted it between her fingers. "He died three weeks ago, of a heart attack. His practice became too much of a strain for him. Rutherford wasn't exactly a young man. He was past forty."

"My condolences," Sam said. He certainly wasn't going to say he was sorry to hear that, because he didn't even know the man.

Rowena moved past the palmetto in the cachepot to take a seat on the comb-crested sofa. She patted a spot beside her. "Come sit with me, Sam. It's been a long time, and we've a lot of catching up to do."

He tossed his hat atop one of the palmetto's fronds and bit back a grin at the consternation that flickered in those lovely eyes. Taking a seat, he stretched out his long legs and said, "I suppose you know why your father wanted to see me?"

"I'm sure it has something to do with Roxana. She's always been rather mulish and—oh, Sam, we really are worried about her. What she's doing is so dangerous!"

"No one's forcing her."

Rowena placed a hand on his thigh. "It seems like some quirk of fate . . . that you'd become involved again with our family."

He didn't move her hand. "You might say that." Or that the old gods were having a hell of a good time playing with peoples' lives.

"Our family hasn't changed. Mother's involved in a dozen charitable organizations, Wally's been appointed Attorney General of Virginia, and, believe it or not, I'm president of our local Women's Suffrage Society."

Sam grinned. "Shades of Roxana!"

"I suppose I'm more like my sister than I realized. But she left home, didn't she. And I've returned. After Rutherford died . . . we never had any children . . . the big house seemed so empty . . ."

"So you've become a crusader for women's rights."

The lines about her mouth tightened. "I have to do something to fill my time." She met his gaze, and those incredible blue eyes were filled with a plea for understanding. "Sam, despite everything that happened in the Philippines, despite the nasty gossip here in Washington, I never thought you . . . took advantage . . . of that awful woman, that officer's wife."

"Like you said, Rowena, it's been a long time. A lot has happened since then."

The look in her eyes was pure agony. "Oh, don't you see that I had to do what I had to do? Just as you did. For me to continue with the farce of our engagement—it would have labeled me as a woman desperate for marriage, under any conditions."

He wanted to take her shoulders and shake her, to tell her that she *should* have been desperate for him under any conditions. As he had been for her.

Nonetheless, there was something in what she said. A person had to do what he thought best. Had he not been aware all along of the immense pressures that her familiy and friends brought to bear on her? And he hadn't been here to erase those pressures, to reassure her that he loved her, that what happened had meant nothing to him beyond a brief moment of physical relief.

The odd part of it—the irony of it all—was that he believed, in spite of her straitlaced upbringing, that she *had* understood and had not looked upon what had happened as a betrayal.

"Sam, kiss me."

Her lips were parted slightly, her eyes filled with both sadness and longing. He knew he was getting in over his head, but he put his arm about her waist and drew her to him. Her breath was warm, and her mouth opened hungrily to admit his tongue. Her hands roamed wildly over his shoulders and neck, her fingers tangled in his hair. He could hear her heavy breathing, mixed with his, feeling her breasts heaving against his chest.

When he at last released her, she said, "Sam, Sam, don't leave. Ever." Her hands still clung to his shoulders, and her lips trembled. "I've learned that it doesn't matter what society's wagging tongues whisper. I want to escape the confines of decorum. I want to be free, Sam!"

He lifted one brow. "You didn't mourn your husband very long, Rowena."

"I've wasted years kowtowing to him and the dictates of others. I'll not waste another minute!"

He laughed. He couldn't help himself.

Her eyes widened with shock, and a flush that betokened her demoralization spread up her neck to pinken her cheeks and even her dainty earlobes which were studded with a single expensive pearl in each.

His deep laughter ebbed, and he said, "Pershing was right."

Her shock faded to puzzlement. "Why, Sam, whatever are you talking about?"

He took her hands and lifted them from his shoulders. Kissing the soft hollow of each palm, he returned them to her lap. Her handkerchief lay crumpled on the floor next to her skirts, and he retrieved it.

She took it and rose. Looking down at him, her face had a haunting, sad beauty. "Things have changed—irrevocably, haven't they?"

Not really. She was still the same. He was the one who had changed. Events had changed his life. Maybe the bitterness was still there; but, thank God, at least he was over Rowena Van Buren.

He could, however, still play the gallant. He stood and gave her one of the bows from the cadet days, the bow of an officer and a gentleman. "Rowena, you're too good for me. I've become a shiftless desperado, and you deserve better. But if you should change your mind, I got me a little hovel down Mexico way. A few chickens and pigs scratch and root in the front yard, but it's all mine."

She laughed gaily, and she was the former Rowena. Beautiful—and brittle. "Sam Brady, you don't fool me for a moment." Her smile sobered. "But thank you anyway for allowing me my dignity."

And with that Rowena Van Buren swept from the room and his life.

There was still the formidable Supreme Court Justice to face, and Sam looked forward to this even more. He reasoned that this time Augustus Van Buren was going to do battle for his other daughter.

As though their exit and entrance were timed, the justice appeared a few minutes later. With a monogrammed handkerchief he dabbed at the perspiration sheening his temples. Silver hair winged about the handsome face, similar in bone structure to Roxana's.

"Sorry to detain you, Brady, but I was finishing up a game of handball."

Clad in white duck trousers and shirt and canvas shoes, the justice was still as debonair as ever. Sam thought ruefully that at least his Pendleton shirt was clean, though his Stetson was as disreputable as ever. Like Rowena, Van Buren eyed the Stetson's perch atop the palmetto.

However, he said nothing but offered Sam a cigar from the pewter humidor. Sam took one and rolled its length beneath his nose. The aroma indicated the cigar was of the best quality. Naturally.

"The last time you were in this library, Sam, you were asking for Rowena's hand in marriage," Van Buren said, holding out a match to light Sam's cigar.

Sam inhaled on the cigar appreciatively. He eased the smoke up out of his lungs, letting it expand from between his lips into a helix. "As I recall, Justice, you weren't exactly in favor of the marriage."

Van Buren lit his cigar. "No, I wasn't, Sam. I didn't think you and Rowena were well matched. I didn't think you were right for each other. Do you think I was wrong?"

Sam met the justice's inquiring gaze. "No. The marriage would have been disastrous."

The tension in the room dissipated, and the rigid lines about the justice's mouth visibly eased. "I don't need to tell you how concerned I am about my daughter, about Roxana. I want her back out of Mexico at any costs."

"That why you sent that reporter down there to bring her back?"

The justice's white brows shot up. "Sullivan told you about it?"

"No. Just a hunch, Van Buren."

"My efforts aren't working, and the situation down there is becoming more dangerous by the day—if Roxana's columns are anything to go by."

Sam smiled. "Her columns are understated."

"That's what I imagined. I can't wait any longer for Sullivan to persuade her to come back."

"You know, the young buck has fallen for her," Sam drawled.

Van Buren shook his head. "Knowing my elder daughter, she didn't reciprocate."

"She hasn't agreed yet to marry him, if that's what you mean. But the jury's still out." He felt a sudden rash of impatience to be gone from the stifling room, to hightail it back to Mexico. What the hell was Roxana up to right now? He crushed his impatience and tapped the cigar's ashes into the palmetto's pot.

Van Buren frowned but withheld verbally expressing his disapproval. "She won't marry Sullivan, or anyone, for that matter. She's dedicated to a journalistic career." He sighed, then said, "I'm having Sullivan recalled. There's a need for him to cover the war raging in Europe."

"And Roxy?"

"*Roxana* will return to Washington, when she no longer has a guide to help her track down this Pancho Villa."

"So that's what you wanted of me."

The justice leaned forward, his face drawn. "You appealed to me once for my daughter's hand. I'm appealing to you now. You hold the life of my other daughter, Roxana's life, in your hands. I want you to abandon whatever deal you've made with her."

Sam drew thoughtfully on the cigar. "Why would I want to do that?"

"Because, Sam, I can have your dishonorable discharge corrected. Hell, I can even have you reinstated as a lieutenant."

Sam rose and crossed to the large desk to ground out the cigar in the marble ashtray. "It's a little too late for that, Van Buren. As Rowena said, certain things have been irrevocably changed. Me, for instance."

He retrieved his Stetson from its perch on the palmetto's fronds, and the justice said, "Wait."

Sam turned. His eyes watched the justice, caught in his dilemma. Sam felt a reluctant sympathy for the man.

"If it's money you want, I can—"

Sam shook his head. "All the money on this green earth can't buy back your daughter, Van Buren. If I don't help Roxy find Villa, she'll damned rootin' tootin' find someone who will. You, of all people, should know she's a resourceful woman. Takes after you."

The justice's skin faded to a pasty gray, and he slumped back in the leather chair. "For once," he murmured, "it would seem I have been defeated. By my own daughter. I really thought, hoped, she'd come back on her own. As you said, I should have known better."

"If it'll make you feel any better, Justice, I'll do my damnedest to protect Roxy."

He clamped his hat low over his forehead and turned to go, but Van Buren rose quickly, saying, "Sam, wait!" He crossed to him. "I want you to know I always held you in high esteem. You can't blame me for wanting what was best for Rowena. You two would have destroyed each other. You admitted as much. I want what is best for Roxana, also. If reporting is what she's determined to do . . ."

With another sigh, the justice held out his hand. "Take good care of her, Sam."

Sam lopped a smile and shook the man's hand. "That I'll do. I have a stake in this also. My life to begin with. And a small ranch up in the Rio Grande valley if I bring it all off."

"You have my blessing—and my gratitude, son."

When another week came and went and Patton still had not returned, Roxana began to despair. She felt alone and deserted.

First by Sam, then by Mark. Once he was over his latest bout of illness, orders came from the *Post* dispatching Mark to cover the battlefront in Europe. Mark was surprised at the orders. She wasn't. The tactics were doubtless the work of her father.

When Patton did arrive, she meant to give him a piece of her mind. For almost two weeks she had been detained in a compound for—for prostitutes!

Propping the chair before the door, her usual nightly procedure, she lay down in the flannel nightshift and men's woolen socks Sally had thoughtfully provided. Even with spring's warm days, the desert nights were chilly.

She was prepared to spend another uneasy night, listening to the coming and going of the soldiers within the stockade and to the nocturnal movements of artillery and convoys and cavalry farther away. But lack of sleep the night before weighted her lids.

She awoke to the clattering collapse of the chair. In the darkness she could make out nothing. With her sharply drawn breath she detected the odor of gin. She came up out of the snarl of sheets yelling like a scalded cat. "Sam Brady, you low-down, worthless, sneaking—"

"Easy now, Roxy." The cot gave beneath his weight. "It seems I'm always finding you in some cathouse."

He tried to kiss her, but she snapped her face away and pushed against his shoulders, trying to dislodge him. His beard-stubbled jaw rasped her neck, and she tried to tuck her chin into her shoulder. His mouth found hers anyway. Her anger evaporated as his warm lips moved over hers and his roughened hand gently stroked her neck.

"And just where have you been?"

"With your father." He nuzzled her neck. "Ahh, Roxy, sweetheart, I've missed you like hell."

He was powerfully masculine and she needed that maleness. But she didn't like that weak side of her and she feared that her very need for that maleness could become as insidious a habit as morphine-taking.

Then her next indrawn breath brought another scent—a woman's cheap perfume! She wrenched her mouth from his. "You've been with another woman!" she hissed and struck out in the dark with the palm of her hand.

"Damn't, Roxy!" His hands grabbed her upper arms, and he shook her with a kind of rough patience. The wobbling of her head momentarily disoriented her, and he took advantage of it to wedge himself between her knees and ease her back down with his torso. "The woman was in the line of duty," he explained, his mouth capturing her sputtering lips, his hot breath seeping into her mouth to mingle with her own.

"Line of duty!" she sobbed out. She twisted her face away and fastened her teeth into the muscled column of his neck.

He grunted from the unexpected pain and blindly batted her head away with the heel of his hand. For a moment she lay stunned, gulping deep drafts of air. His mouth kissed her temple almost solicitously. "The woman was a German in Parral, married to a Mexican, Roxy." Her nightshift buttons snapped open one after the other. "She turned the crowd in the plaza against our troop and there was a near riot." He kissed her breasts softly, harshly, tenderly. "Pershing wanted to know if the incident happened out of loyalty to her husband's countrymen"—the nightshift was drawn off—"or if she was a plant for the Germans."

She didn't care what he was saying. Only what he was doing. Oh, God, if only she had never discovered that exquisite pleasure at the hands of this man.

Now she was naked, all except for her woolen socks. He shucked out of his shirt and denims and slid down her, the thick, silky fur rubbing across her breasts, her belly, the insides of her thighs. Something different was happening. She bucked her hips to dislodge him, but succeeded only in offering herself up to him. He anchored his elbows between her thighs and, with his forearms, spread her thighs wide. She held herself stiff as his mouth closed over that other mouth and outraged her body, his breath hot and searing against the tender, furred flesh.

She tried propping herself on her elbows to plant the soles of her feet on the cot, to shrink away from his voracious mouth.

But all she accomplished was raising her buttocks a few inches off the bed, making herself even more accessible. His hands clasped each buttock's cheek and drew her toward him. The tip of his tongue parted the taut folds and followed upward to where they joined, and she fell back weakly, gasping, while his tongue flicked something small but hard. She could feel her own sudden lubrication mingling with his saliva. Her head tilted backwards, pushing into the pillow, her hands cupping his head, both afraid of what was to come and afraid it wouldn't.

Helplessness and rage mixed with her explosive need of him. She fought an inner battle that was eons away from the sounds of his sucking and licking and nibbling, yet she lost the battle. He had been with another woman, yet here she was suddenly begging, urging, "Sam, please, please, take me. Come inside!"

He entered her, with surprising ease, filling her completely, and slid up into her as far as he could reach. He wrapped his arms about her and pumped slowly, then eased out until the head of his organ rubbed with deliberation against her entrance, then plowed along her furrow with tantalizing slowness. Wild now with wanting, she wrapped her legs about his waist, the wet open mouth of her vagina seeking his shaft. Unconscious little moans of ecstasy were drawn from her with each deep, rhythmic stroke.

He was driving furiously when her jaw went lax. The convulsive tide of climax rocked her. A moment later Sam collapsed atop her. "God, Roxy, you're good!" he said in a gin-laden breath.

With that, he rolled off her and was asleep like an old dog in a matter of minutes.

She lay stiff and still and chewed the cud of her resentment against him. The reek of gin and cheap cologne filled the night air. At that moment she had no hope left. She wondered whatever had led her to believe the gin-sodden Sam Brady could help her. She wasted no more idle dreams on a quixotic plan of him helping her interview Villa or find Angelina Asunsolo.

Whatever she hoped to accomplish would have to be done on her own. But first, she was going to get even.

20

Late afternoon found Sam lying like a corpse facedown on the cot. He slit one eyelid, still gummed with sleep. The liquor-soaked muscles at the corners of his mouth and below his cheekbones dragged down, the force of gravity tugging them loose from his skull.

His head was a solid lump of red-hot pain. Worse, it felt as if it were nailed to the floorboards, so that any attempt at raising it caused him agony. His mouth was parched and his throat ached.

He pressed his teeth together and rolled to one elbow and reared up. "Jesus!"

His eyes could not stand the light streaming through the screen door. With a groan, he shut his sandpapery lids. Behind them floated the Junoesque Elsa Griensen de Alvarado, shouting, "Villa, Villa!" and berating the Mexicans for allowing the vile gringos to defile their city. She had hurled other insults and obscenities, but fortunately the troops of the Thirteenth had not understood.

Someone had taken a potshot, hurting no one. By that time

the strong Carranza force there at Parral caught the contagion to fire away, and Whittington was backing K and M Troops of the Thirteenth out of the pueblo. It may have looked like a retreat, but Whittington had instructions from the Old Man: "Don't get trapped into a battle with the Mexicans. It's what both Villa and Carranza—and the Kaiser—want. All for different reasons."

Sam had to hand it to Elsa. Later that night the broad had matched him gin bottle for gin bottle. If she knew anything, she certainly wasn't spilling it, although toward dawn she spilled— or poured—a bottle of some god-awful cologne over his head. Just sat there on the edge of the bar and doused him and laughed. Then she passed out, sprawled lengthwise along the bar.

He knew now what it must feel like to be sprayed by a skunk. After two days the stink of the cologne still clung to his clothes, even seeming to ooze from his pores. No wonder Roxy had been infuriated about—

Where the hell was she? He shot to his feet and felt the impact of what had to be a bag of cement that slammed against the inside of his head. "Sonafobitch!"

"Mr. Brady?"

He cracked open one lid again. The stocky form of a soldier was silhouetted on the screen. "You told me to get you when Lieutenant Patton returned. He's just driving in now."

Sam thanked the orderly and walked gingerly to the screen door. He thought he might live after all. The desert sunlight was excruciatingly bright and gave the landscape a washed-out look.

Well, well, another fine day.

He blinked several times, attempting to focus, before he finally made out Patton at the wheel of the dusty Dodge. Trailing behind were two more touring cars, loaded with the interpreter and the six privates he had taken with him.

The lieutenant had left, ostensibly on a corn-buying expedition, but the two dead Mexicans draped over the Dodge's fenders like deer attested that Patton, a crack shot, had been too busy to purchase corn.

Sam ran his fingers through his rumpled hair, trying to smooth it into place, but the caramel-colored lion's mane had never been obedient. Gritting his teeth, he stepped into the furnacelike sunlight and made his way over to the Dodge, surrounded now by curious soldiers.

Patton, sitting atop the front seat, raised a leather-gloved hand to hail him. "What do you think about what I've bagged, Sam?"

Sam rested his hands on his hips and surveyed the two dead Mexicans. One had a bullet hole between the eyes. For all Patton's brashness, the young man appeared to have a future with the Army—though a "future with the army" could mean anything or nothing, Sam thought wryly, as his own personal history testified. He looked back at Patton. "Villistas or Carranzistas?"

"Villistas. The one on the left fender is General Cardenas, the commander of Villa's bodyguard."

"Look, George, I need some help. I'm trying to locate a woman."

"Aren't we all," a freckle-faced private chipped in cheerfully.

Sam fixed the private with one of his black looks, which was especially mean that morning, and the soldier sheeped away.

Patton climbed from the car, saying, "The woman can only be that strong-willed, obstinate creature who claims she is a journalist; Miss Roxana Van Buren."

With a half sigh-half grunt, Sam shut his eyes, then opened them. "You had a run-in with her?"

"About forty miles south of here. She's gotten a guard, young Dreyfus, to finagle her a ride back to Rancho San Geronimo with Truck Company Number Seventy-three."

Sam swung around and started for the Remount Depot, where the cavalry's mounts were picketed. After riding the width and length of Chihuahua his skewbald was stove in and wasn't going to make five miles, much less fifty. He would get his gear and catch the next convoy out instead.

He halted in midstride, five yards from where he had picketed his stallion. "Jesus!" he screamed out.

His stomach roiled in response to the sight of such wanton destruction! Roxana—it could be no one else. The woman had dragged the gin bottles from each saddlebag, stripped the lead foil, and poured out the stuff! Out of reach of the horses, the empty brown bottles were neatly positioned like ten pins.

Deep parentheses formed from the corners of his flaring nostrils to his compressed mouth. He felt a cold rage that the memory of her sweet bosom did nothing to mollify. He was going to bring that woman to her senses!

Within three hours he was sitting in front of Captain Foulois, who had winged the Curtiss JN down the Rio Santa Maria valley.

His eyes protected by goggles, Sam scouted the checkered terrain, so different from that perspective. Below, too far below, the arroyos and hills were as tawny and wrinkled as an old mountain lion, and off to the right torturous railroad tracks ran through the valleys like the lifelines in the palm. Farther to the right, the Sierra Madre mountain ranges looked like minarets and pyramids.

The air currents and wind turbulence vibrated the light, open aeroplane, and in that high altitude the low-horsepower engine strained, coughed, and wheezed, and several times sputtered out, only to catch again.

It was only Sam's second flight. Unlike the first time, when he'd been dazed with exhaustion, now he was wide-eyed and alert. The sky was an incredible colorbook blue with patches of angel hair. The wind tornadoed past his ears, lifting and dropping the light machine painted with the Stars and Stripes.

First four-wheel vehicles, now aero squadrons and even submarines. Somewhat sadly, Sam Brady reckoned that the romantic era of the horse soldier would soon be drawing to a close.

He was only thirty, but he felt a millennium older. He had come to maturity in a different era. He wasn't ready for the fast-paced world of cosmopolitan people like Roxana Van Buren, damn the bluestockinged, straitlaced spinster to everlasting torment.

Like a stubborn mule, she was following the carrot that the Villa interview dangled before her. She could only think in terms of success, of becoming a full-fledged journalist for the *Post*; but not in terms of failure: death before an adobe wall, or worse, at the hands of the Yaquis. Hadn't she learned firsthand that they delighted in stripping the flesh from live victims and other fiendish acts of torture?

And what about the five thousand dollars? With the Villa interview so close at hand, she was forgetting Angelina Asunsolo and the reward! But he wasn't. Nor was he forgetting the sensitive matter of the destruction of his gin stock. By golly, he was going to find that woman if it took him the rest of the year!

He could only hope he reached her before she inveigled a ride out of Rancho San Geronimo with one of the reconnaissance troops.

He didn't.

Pershing and his limited staff had already set out southward, to establish a new advance base. When Foulois's Curtiss caught up with them at Satevo, a mule train was attempting to pull Pershing's touring car across a stream. Pershing was bivouacked in a cornfield, and the three cavalry troops had fanned out earlier in their search for Villa. Worse, Pershing had not seen Roxana. No one at the advance base had seen the woman.

How could a thousand soldiers possibly miss seeing one woman?

She could be with any one of the three flying columns, anywhere in a hundred square miles. However, sheer logic pointed to the fact that she couldn't have made it as far as the advance base without someone noticing her.

Sam cursed with feeling and eloquence, obtained a mount— a ragged buckskin—and started backtracking. Within an hour he tracked down a column of pack mules ladened with machine guns, but although all the soldiers vividly remembered Roxana Van Buren, none had seen her lately.

Half a day later he came across Truck Company Number Seventy-three, which had left that morning, returning to Colonia

Dublan—or attempting to return. A broken axle on one and a flat on another had halted the string of trucks in the red-burned hills.

With a disgusted grunt, the American captain in charge of the truck convoy pushed the dust goggles back on his campaign hat. "Sure, the woman was with us—if that was a woman underneath that bizarre getup. Hobnailed hunting boots, loose Mexican trousers held up with a rope, and an Army shirt she must have wangled from some poor S.O.B. Oh, and a pith helmet right out of an African safari."

"That's her," Sam said grimly. "Where is she?"

The captain shrugged. "Beats me. Last time I saw her was yesterday, twenty miles outside the pueblo of San Antonio. I stopped the convoy there to request permission from the commander of the Carranzista force to pass through his town. He's friendly enough to Americans. Friendly enough to talk to the woman for a few minutes."

That was just grand.

Late afternoon clouds had boiled up by the time Sam picked up her trail, and that of the Carranzista soldiers. They had moved out of San Antonio and were headed southwest. In pursuit of a force of Villistas?

Sam spent another two hours dogging their trail. In Chihuahua the sun died hard and twilight came late. He camped at a bosque of spindly manzanitas along a finger gully. For a while he lay on his back in his bedroll, watching shooting stars arc above like showers of stardust. He wasn't too worried about losing the trail. A person always found what he was looking for in the desert if he kept after it long enough and knew what to look for in what place.

When he broke camp that morning, the stars had not turned off yet. With daylight he was on the trail again. He knew how to use the faculty of vision upon the distance, knew that the ground gave great reflected glare. By holding the forearm just below the eyes, a shadow that would have been an impeding glare was slanted upward, enabling his eyes to see much farther.

The spring wind all but obliterated the tracks, but he also knew that if a stir of dust drifted steadily aside with the prevailing wind, it was caused by movement of bodies, but if it rose and vanished after a while, it was merely a desert gust of whirlwind.

The former was the case: a thin corkscrew of dust that drifted steadily in the far distance to lose itself in the lavender blue haze of the mountains. But when the bright Chihuahuan sun was high overhead, he lost the skyward trail of dust altogether.

Roxana sat comfortably in the bottom of an arroyo, a four-foot trench, making friends with the Carranzista soldiers, most of whom were without uniforms and clothed only in what rags they had been able to scrounge up. Several miles away the Villistas had fortified a large encampment about a string of crude irrigation ditches.

None of the Federal troops in the trenches seemed excited that a battle would soon take place. It was as if the soldiers were going to have a huge picnic.

On her left a Mexican officer, dressed in remnants of a Federales blue uniform, was all smiles and white teeth. "You must try the *tuna, amigo,*" he encouraged, handing her the pulpy red cactus fruit. He lifted his arm in order to bulk the muscles beneath the mustard-colored cloth, then pinched her forearm. "You American newspapermen are runts, eh?"

In her scrambled getup she had been mistaken as a scrawny male, which was fine with her. She borrowed a cigarette from the soldier on her right, a man called Fidencio, whose gentle face was hidden behind a barbarous-looking mustache. He leaned forward to view her notepad. "What is that you are writing?"

"I'm going to tell the readers that you have lent me a cigarette and that I like it."

"*Bueno!*" he laughed, slapping her on the back. "Tell them that in the last battle we had, I broke my gun while smashing the brains out of a Villista."

"I've already written that."

"*Caramba!* But you write fast. It takes me an hour to sign my own name."

She turned back to the officer. "You think Villa himself is with this bunch?"

He shrugged his massive shoulders. "*Quién sabe?* Some say he has gone farther south."

Suddenly the peaceful quiet of the evening meal was broken by the enemy's first shell, fired as a feeler to get the range of the trenches. Her stomach knotted, like an attack of stage fright. The officer's next remarks did not reassure her.

"The cannons will come nearer each time."

The prospect of a terrific cannonading didn't seem to bother him. He wiped the dust from his rifle and prepared his cartridge belts, five in all, so he could withdraw the clips more easily.

The red in the sky had turned a deep purple. Little fires gleamed brightly in the dusk. Then the Villista artillery on the right began to boom. It was difficult for her to see what she was writing, even more difficult to think that a thousand or more human beings were engaged in a death struggle, she among them.

She should have stayed with Sam, the weasel. Still, he *had* come back for her, niggled a little part of her conscience. Only because he realized he would need her when it came time to collect that five thousand from Don Asunsolo, argued the logical part of her brain.

Away to her left there was heavy rifle fire. Each shot sounded like two because it echoed against the hills. First one single report, followed by two, and then many, until it sounded like big hail, falling on a large tin roof. Would it soon be like that in her part of the trench?

No one seemed to worry. Next to her Fidencio was asleep. He lay on the sandy slope, his face covered with his big sombrero.

At that moment a young captain, not over eighteen years of age, rode up, shouting orders. He looked curiously at her and galloped away to shout the same orders farther down the line.

The first sergeant repeated them for her in his broken English. "The enemy, it is sending a column in this direction! There is a column of our own men to the rear. They'll shoot down anyone who attempts to flee if there is fighting in this trench." He smiled apologetically. "Only death is a valid excuse for failure to fight."

Fidencio, awake now, began to curse heartily, at the same time examining the rifle. A bandolier of ammunition was slung over his shoulder. The first sergeant took his position, resting his rifle on the trench bank, after placing two large rocks on either side.

"You see, I stand less chance of being hit this way," he smiled.

"Don't you ever get afraid?"

"Afraid?" he asked. He spat in the dirt contemptuously. "We Mexicans are never afraid—except maybe during our first battle. If this is your first battle, *amigo*, I understand how you feel."

Farther down the lines a fat man worked a machine gun on a tripod. He loaded a clip, and a snake of bullets dangled out of the machine gun's side.

The fighting came. Strangely enough, her fear crept away to crouch like a cat somewhere beyond. Most of the bullets went whizzing by, and few were hurt in the trenches. From her left she could hear the rat-a-tat-tat of the machine gun's black snout.

The first attack subsided. Down the line the fat man was hit in the shoulder, and the loud mutterings she heard could only be those of his profanity. In those interminable moments of waiting, she was surprised that she felt as calm as a Trappist monk.

Then once again the Mausers whistled overhead. The guns sounded nearer. Just one terrible, ominous roar. She reached for the *botija* of water, only to drop it. Fidencio retrieved it and held it for her while she drank. His hand was trembling.

Then, what had to be a thousand bullets hit the bank at once and ricocheted the dirt into the ditch. A fragment of stone hit her on the cheek. She could feel blood trickling down her face but was more preoccupied with watching Fidencio—the way his hand, still trembling, reached for his cartridges.

The enemy's cannon had been turned on their trench. Shells were exploding with hellish roars all around her, but she couldn't see them.

Then Fidencio was hit. Shot in the throat, he fell beside her. Blood gushed like red foam from the hole while he gasped. The man on the other side of Fidencio's body implored all sorts of virgins to protect him.

Overhead a shell burst to the right with an ear-shattering blast; its splinters whistled on their mission of death and maiming. The air was heavy with an indigo pall of dust. "God has gone against us!" the first sergeant cried.

Now, no one seemed calm. Everybody was yelling. Sounds of men weeping mingled with groans and cursing. Nearby, fleeing horsemen went down like dominoes under the staccato rattle of machine guns.

The first sergeant shouted hysterically that the enemy was upon them. "Run, *amigo!*"

Paralyzed, she watched as he joined the other soldiers, retreating along the trench. They trampled the fallen bodies. Another shell burst near where she sat. She was afraid to move for fear a bullet would hit her. The world seemed to be coming to an end. If she could continue her writing, it might keep her from going insane.

From nowhere a man in a canvas duster suddenly grabbed at her waist and yanked her bodily up the bank of the trench. When she beat out at him with harmless fists, he yelled at her, "That damned white helmet sticks out against the black earth like hulled cotton."

"Sam!" she shouted. She wanted to hug him, right there in the midst of all the death and destruction. Behind him she saw a Mexican infantryman, red bandana flapping about his neck as he charged with a glinting machete in his upraised hand.

"Sam, watch out!"

He spun, her forearm still in his grip. His free hand came up smoothly from beneath the duster at the same time he thumbed back the Peacemaker's hammer. Its bullet found the center of its target, and the Villista dropped almost at their feet, his machete next to his outstretched hand.

Only then did Sam release her. He grabbed at the rearing buckskin horse and jerked the bit down in its mouth. In the flash of a second he had swung his lithe body into the saddle and hauled her up behind him. The buckskin bounded forward, passing the fleeing foot soldiers. Her hands locked about Sam's muscled stomach. At any moment she expected to feel a bullet slam between her shoulder blades.

"Sam!" she cried. "My notepad! I left it back in the trench!"

"Jesus!" she heard him mutter as he spurred the horse away in a tooth-jarring gallop.

21

The black of night curtained the battle scene behind them and the interval of miles and mountains dimmed the sounds of the firing and the screaming and agony until there was just the two of them, riding the buckskin on a nocturnal trek. The only movement was the horse nodding its head in time to its gait; the only sounds, the sandy whispers from its plodding hooves, the creaking of the tack, and the low clanking from the canteen and Sam's spur chains. Occasionally when the caterwauling of a coyote joined the other sounds, a shiver would course its way up Roxana's spine.

"Where we heading, Sam?"

"South, to Durango. Villa's old stomping grounds. When he gets his hide in a tight spot, he always heads deeper up into the mountains, where he waits it out with his Yaqui friends."

His tone of voice told her clearly that he was none too pleased with her, and she knew why. The destruction of his beloved gin. "Sam."

"Huh?"

"I think we need to straighten out the terms of our partnership." Heavens, but she sounded prim. "I mean our business deal needs—"

"This ain't the time nor place to hold a profound conversation. Not with Yaquis and Villistas and Carranzistas all itching to claim our carcasses."

"All right, later. But I do have just one question."

He sighed. "What?"

"Were you with that German woman the entire two weeks you were gone?"

With the stretch of silence, she guessed he was deciding what to tell her. When he finally did speak, she knew it was the truth.

"Only the last day or so. Before that—your father had me hauled up to Washington. Wanted to talk me out of helping you."

"I should have known. He stops at nothing!"

Sam chuckled. "Neither do you."

"What happened between my father and you?"

"I convinced him that you were better off with me than running around alone in Mexico like some nitwit."

"Did . . . did you see Rowena?"

"Yes. Her husband died recently."

"Oh. I'm sorry about that."

Silence.

"Sam?"

"You said just one question, Roxy. But I'll answer the next one anyway. Whatever I felt for your sister is over."

Roxana rested her cheek against the broad back, where his curly butter-churned mane tickled her forehead. For the moment she let herself relax, leaving it all in Sam's capable hands. As the night deepened, so did the cold, so quickly that the rocks cracked, sounding frighteningly like rifle shots. A mystery of calm and vastness lay over the desert and its mountains. High above rode the ghost of a blue moon.

Suddenly another kind of ghost rustled in the salt cedar and cane break. Sam reined the buckskin up short. Roxana felt Sam's stomach muscles knot beneath her palms. Then the moonlight revealed the ghost was only a long-horned, bony steer rambling through the chaparral.

"A *corriente*," Sam said, expelling his breath in a relieved whoosh. "An unbranded cow. But it's just as well. We'll pull up for a breather."

He dismounted and drew her down beside him. He didn't release her for a moment, and, held that close to him, she felt his strong heartbeat—a beat that entered her own veins and moved into her blood. When he finally set her down, his fingertip traced the ridge where the rock kicked up by the flying shrapnel had grazed her flesh. "You've been hurt."

His touch did funny things to her. She shook her head and pulled away from his embrace.

"It's nothing."

Her rejection obviously frustrated him, because he braced his weight on one leg, hands low on his hipbones, and said, "Roxy, now's as good as time as any to tell you I didn't appreciate what you did to my stock of gin. If you'd've been a man, I'd've given you a drubbing. If you'd been a child, I'd've tanned your bottom. But you're a woman, and I don't know how the hell to handle that."

Her mouth tightened. Her teeth gritted against each other. "Well, Mr. Brady, I didn't exactly appreciate what you did earlier that night either."

His dark brows pulled down and the blue eyes zeroed in on her. That Black Look appeared again. "Don't tell me you didn't enjoy what happened, Roxy, because you and I both know different. And despite that you're a woman and all, I've always set great store by your honesty."

Under other circumstances she would have burst out into laughter at Sam's stereotyping of women. But the subject was too intimate for levity. Her chin lifted proudly. "I won't pretend otherwise. I did enjoy what happened."

He couldn't have been any more surprised by her forthright statement that she was. "I enjoyed it very much, in fact," she continued briskly. This conversation was very difficult for her, and the only way for her to approach it was logically, practically. "I'm only angry because you didn't give me the chance to refuse you. If I had been a man, I would have given *you* a drubbing."

"Well, I'll be damned."

"And the fact that we went through a farce of a marriage doesn't give you the privilege of practicing your conjugal rights on me at your whim. Come to think of it, even if we were really married, you still wouldn't enjoy that privilege except by my consent."

They were nose to nose like two prizefighters. "Well, we aren't married, so don't go getting any crazy ideas about that wedding. What happens here in Mexico doesn't necessarily make it legal in the United States."

"And don't you go giving me that Black Look of yours, Sam Brady. I think we can agree that it's best we keep our affairs strictly businesslike from here on out."

His face looked haggard and tired. "You don't know much about men and women, Roxy, if you think you can pull that off." He turned his attention to unstrapping the bedroll. The one bedroll.

"If you've got it fixed in your mind that you're going to get me in that bedroll with a repeat performance of the other night, you're very mistaken."

Bedroll in hand, he turned and eyed her wearily. "Roxy, a eunuch could do more than I could right now."

"Ohh!" She couldn't think of anything appropriate to fire back and ended by grumbling, "Oxygen is wasted on you."

They were both exhausted. Nestled against him like a spoon cupped inside another, she fell asleep immediately, her head pillowed against his arm. Her last confused thoughts were how despicable the man was and how cozy and secure she felt in his arms.

That security evaporated when the morning sun leaped blisteringly into the copper sky and she bared her eyes to see three Mexican *vaqueros* standing over her. The barrel of some obsolete musket stared down at her. "Sam!" she whispered and punched him in the ribs with her elbow. "Sam, we've got trouble."

"Shut up, Roxy." So, Sam was already awake.

The middle *vaquero* grinned, showing a row of decayed teeth beneath a big, floppy sombrero. "Ah, *Norte Americanos!*" Without taking his gaze way, he began talking rapidly to the other two vaqueros.

"What's he saying, Sam?"

"He wants to put us in some hoosegow. He's telling his compadres that our heads'll be worth a reward next time a Villista band rides through."

The memory of the news story about the Carranzista who had paraded an American soldier's head on a spike hit her square in the lungs. "Do we have to go along with his idea of jailing us?"

"You're damned rootin' tootin' we do. The alternative is even less appealing."

The vaquero broke off his discourse and prodded her in the stomach with the blunderbuss. Another vaquero searched Sam and took his pistol and knife, and confiscated her cork helmet for his own use. "*Vamos,*" he growled. "*Ahorita.*"

For the better part of an hour she and Sam were herded afoot before the three *vaqueros*, who trailed Sam's buckskin behind them. In that empty sunstruck desert, she was thankful for the hobnailed hunting boots. Without the protective helmet, her scalp was blistering where her hair was center-parted. Sam removed his Stetson and clapped it over her head. Above them, the turkey buzzards wheeled in the white-hot sky. It seemed as if a lid had been closed over the earth, shutting off the air supply. It was so thin, she wondered how she could draw another breath. But she did. Just as she kept putting one foot in front of the other, like Sam did. By the look on his face, it was as if he were out for a pleasurable stroll.

At last, irrigation ditches and a wooden windmill that whirled slowly in the searing breeze announced the presence of a pueblo. Dogs began barking at their approach. The bony curs slunk along beside her and Sam, snarling, and a woman, balancing a fat clay *jarra* atop her head, stopped to stare.

"*Norte Americanos,*" boasted the captor wearing her helmet. At that, an old man with a gunnysack of gathered firewood brush bundled on his back paused to spit at the prisoners' feet.

The scattered clumps of gray-brown, mud-baked adobes were little more than hovels, although the ever-present cantina and a small, crumbling chapel lent a little dignity to the grassless, barren pueblo.

The jail was as big or bigger than the chapel, which didn't exactly testify to the good character of the pueblo's citizenry. However, the jail's interior left a lot to be said for any comfort. It was a large one-room office furnished with a crudely made pine desk. The floor was packed earth.

The vaqueros turned them over to the jailer, a cherubic little man with a deadly .45 automatic tucked into his belt. He officiously escorted them to the rear of the room, the width of which was occupied by one cell, and unlocked the barred door. The cell was bare; without a bench or stool to sit on, nor a window for ventilation. The adobe's flimsy slatted door was the only way in or out.

After the little man settled himself behind the desk, his cowhide sandals propped on its scarred top, she turned to Sam. "What are we going to do?"

"Nothing." He slid down against one flaking mud-brick wall, long legs stretched before him, and tilted his hat down over his face. "I'm going to rest," came his muffled voice. "The first real rest I've had since I met up with you. You should do the same."

She couldn't believe it. Why hadn't she learned by now that the man was unreliable?

Incredibly, a few moments later, there came his soft snoring. A large horsefly buzzed about the cell, but Sam slept undeterred. Impossible! She allowed herself the comfort of a few choice French swear words she had learned at boarding school.

The rest of the afternoon she paced the cell while Sam slept. Fifteen steps one way, eight the other. Fifteen and eight. Eight and fifteen. The jailer, whittling away at a piece of wood, never looked up. What she wouldn't have given for a cigarette.

At last Sam stirred, nudged his Stetson up. "Should be just about sunset."

She glared at him, hands planted on her hips. "I take it that's of import. Do they hang their prisoners at sunset?"

"No, but it's the best time for us to try to escape, before a night relief comes on duty."

"Oh, and I suppose you have a key?" she continued in her caustic tone.

"Something almost as good." He bent forward and stuck a hand down inside his boot.

"A weapon!" she breathed. "I knew I could depend on you, Sam Brady!"

"Not a weapon. This." He held up a pint of gin.

She wanted to pummel the self-satisfied look off his face. "Damn you, Sam! I'm not going to sit here and drink myself into a stupor while I try to devise a way to escape. I'm going to do something. Anything!"

She looked about her wildly. Two feet of mud-brick walls on three sides, a sturdy iron grill on the fourth. She crumbled to her knees, hands over her face, and sobbed.

Sam gently touched her shoulder.

"Go away," she said, without lifting her head. She hated him for his irresponsibility, but she hated herself more for reacting to her fear in such a foolishly feminine way. And for reacting to him in such a typically feminine way. He made her weak, where she should be strong.

Sam's lips brushed her exposed nape before he plucked a hairpin from her coiled tresses. Startled, she lifted her head to see him bending the U-shaped wire into a straight line, then curving one end into a fishhook. She glanced back at the jailer. He was still whittling. His piece of wood had taken on the shape of a guitar.

"Even if you manage to pick the lock, Sam, we would never get past him."

He smiled serenely and pocketed the altered hairpin. "Hey, *hombre!*" he called out to the jailer.

The man paused in his carving and looked over his shoulder. Sam held up the pint of gin. The Mexican came to his feet and ambled over to the cell. But when he struck out his hand for the bottle, Sam held it just out of reach. The Mexican tilted his head to the side and narrowed his eyes. "*Que quiere?*"

Sam pointed to the whittled guitar the Mexican held.

His rotted teeth appeared, and the jailer quickly made the trade, the piece of carved wood for the gin, sure he had gotten the better end of the deal from the gringo. Sam settled back against the wall and, strumming on nonexistent strings, began to sing:

"*We started at the border, and we chased to Parral,*
We were after Pancho Villa and Lopez and his old pal;
Our horses were starved and dying; we lived on parched corn,
Oh, it's damned hard living in Chihuahua, where Villa was
    born."

She barely recognized the semblance of the tune to "Tipperary," but apparently the jailer didn't care. He drank and listened and hoisted his bottle each time Sam began a new song. Some of them were in Spanish, and she guessed the words must have been pretty raunchy, for the Mexican would cackle drunkenly at certain places in the songs.

"*Esta loco!*" he called out cheerily to Sam and tipped the bottle again.

Sam was playing the jailer like he did the guitar, plucking an imaginary string and leaning back and watching him. At last the jailer's head nodded, and Sam put the mock guitar aside in favor of the hooked hairpin. She held her breath as he went to work on the cell door lock. It was a simple mechanism, but it was built as solidly as the cell's bars and the bolt's latch could possibly be too heavy for the hairpin to lift. For all Sam's former insouciance, beads of sweat popped out on his forehead as time and again the hairpin hooked the latch only to slip loose.

She felt the strain he labored under. What if someone walked in at that moment? What if Villa himself walked in? These weren't exactly the conditions under which she wanted to interview him.

The lock gave, and the door creaked as Sam swung it open. She froze. He caught her by the arm and pulled her on cat's paws past the snoring jailer. Outside in the darkness, the street was deserted. A candlelight flickered in one of the *jacales* that had a window. "Now what?" she asked.

He grimaced. "You can bet the buckskin has already been sold down the road. We have to find the next available means of transportation."

That turned out to be a pair of burros chomping on tufts of fireweed that sprouted about the jail's adobe base. Dubiously, she looked at Sam, who unceremoniously hefted her over the jenny's back. Sam boarded his burro, his long legs almost touching the earth, and kneed the burro into a fast trot. Her jenny shot forward behind the lead one, and Roxana anchored her fingers in her mane to keep from being bounced off.

Into the moonlit desert they rode. Her hungry stomach rattled protestingly at the burro's jarring gait, but she was too thrilled about their Great Escape to grumble. She was alive! She laughed aloud, exultantly. "We did it, we did it, Sam!"

His deeper laughter wrapped about hers. "That we did, Roxy old girl!"

On into the night the burros plodded. Roxana's derriere was on fire and her thighs were sore again. But her high feeling of exuberance never did diminish.

At last Sam felt it was safe to stop for the night. He had chosen the back side of a mesa that afforded them protection from any sudden desert windstorm. She slid gratefully off the jenny and slumped beside him against the sloping mound of sand. Sam's eyes were already closed, his long lashes a dark curve above the high ridges of his cheekbones. A pleasurable tiredness, the kind she had never known, was settling over her, yet she wasn't really sleepy.

In the desert, nothing stirred. Nothing moved. After the heat of the day, a refreshing breeze cooled the night. Ahead lay the dark humps of the mountains. Nearer, Indian paintbrush and cactus blooms waited quietly in the moonlight. For what? It was as if the whole world was holding its breath in anticipation of something. "Sam?"

"No, Roxy."

She turned on her side to face him, her forehead wrinkling. "How can you say no, when you don't know what I'm going to say?"

"I know what you're feeling," he said, without opening his eyes. "I'm feeling it, too."

"What is it I'm feeling?" she asked, slightly short of breath, as if she had been dancing all night.

His lashes lifted, revealing those blue eyes, terribly clear in the silver moonlight, fastened on her lips. "It's the same thing soldiers feel after a battle, Roxy. It's as though some grand, delicate balance needs to be restored; that after going through the motions of destruction, a soldier is gripped by the powerful urge to perform the motions of creation." His gaze raised to hers. "Do you understand?"

Her answer was the brushing of her mouth over his. For a moment his lips were unresponsive. She wasn't unsure of herself; nor did she regret laying bare her intimate feelings. Instead, she found she rather liked taking the initiative. Sam's hands gently closed over her shoulders, drawing her against his length, and he kissed her. A tender, searching kiss . . . one that gave instead of took. Her mouth parted and his tongue ran softly over her bottom lip. Her tongue stole out to play with his.

She could feel his heart beating rapidly against her breast. So this was what made women swoon. It no longer seemed silly, that lightheaded feeling that claimed her. He drew back and his strong, callused fingers cupped her jaw. "Roxy, I don't think another man has ever kissed you."

She shook her head. "You were the first."

"Then I'm probably the first to tell you that you are an extraordinary and beautiful woman, but I want you to believe me."

Unbidden tears flooded her eyes. "Thank you, Sam. I believe you." And this time she really did believe it when a man said she was beautiful.

Almost reverently this time, he removed her clothing. The stars seemed to pause in their course across the sky while Sam made love to her. He stroked her face and throat and kissed her lips, her palms, and the insides of her arms. He made her forget everything but her need of him. Mounting him was awkward, but once her fingers guided him in, his hands reassured her love-starved body. Sitting on his hips, crouched on her heels, she arched into him, recoiled, and arched again. Her hair lashed his chest and face.

Anticipating her waning strength, he pulled out and, easing her onto her back, reentered her slowly. Their pleasure at being alive was great, their relief extravagant. So it spoke through their lovemaking, as their bodies knit in passion. His preoccupation with her at last released her into that unsustainable plateau of intense pleasure. Then he joined her, his orgasm gyrating inside her. Toward dawn, they slept, her head tucked into the hollow of his shoulder, one arm flung across the expanse of his chest, his heavily muscled thigh clamped over her leg.

With the morning sunlight, the sand and hills mutated to a brilliant rust. She lay for a moment on her back, missing the warmth of Sam's flesh against hers. Several yards away he stood naked against the sunlight, his back to her and his hands on his hips, as he boldly watered a clump of bear grass.

She laughed. With a grin he faced her, and her breath drew in at the beauty of his lean, well-sculpted body. She thought she must look a fright with her hair tumbled about her head like a loft of tossed-about hay. But the lusty look in his eyes told her otherwise.

"Hungry?" he asked, fully aware of her discomfiture.

She could play the game, too. Smiling, she met his gaze and drawled blithely, "Well, Sam, a cup of tea would be marvelous."

He chuckled and began donning his clothing. "I can remember, in Manila, how eagerly I looked forward each afternoon to a shared pot of tea."

"Well, for once I'm glad it was gin you had stashed away last night and not tea."

Her toes curled into the warm sand for balance, she stood on one foot and slid her free leg into the loose cotton trousers. Her bare breasts bobbled with her movement, reminding her that she was standing in the midst of a desert, naked, before a man who, the night before, she had loved with wild abandon. Not for the first time, she was astonished at this new side of her, this new woman.

"You know, Sam," she said, "I think I'm acquiring a taste for dangerous living."

"The dangerous living is finished, Roxy."

At his dry tone, she looked up. He was buttoning his shirt. "I intend to sell my life dearly. And after the close call we just had, I've decided five thousand isn't dear enough."

"You can't be serious?" Now her career was at stake. "Sam, you can't back out now. Hey, the team of Van Buren and Brady makes a good pair!"

It was the wrong thing to say, of course. "Pair" suggested marriage. She watched disconsolately as he mounted up on the burro and sat looking coldly down at her. "Finish dressing, Roxy. It's a long way back to Dublan."

22

Villa was at his most unheroic in the vengeance he inflicted upon a woman who had once borne him a son in the little town of Santa Rosalita. After several years had passed, he returned there, only to find that during his absence, his señora, Maria Amelia Baca de Villa, had taken a new husband with whom she was living happily.

The Centaur of the North calmly ordered his men to execute this new husband; next he coolly presided over the burning at the stake of the mother and the child. Word was passed that, as the flames engulfed the two victims, no expression crossed Villa's face; not remorse, nor pity, nor anger, or at least so the story goes.

This was the same Villa, the Wraith of the Desert, who, during his siege of Juarez in 1911, held off his final assault for several days after an American newspaperman told him the World Series was about to begin and his prospective victory would be pushed off the front pages.

"We shall hold off the attack, boys, until the Americans finish their ball games," Villa had told his staff.

This was the Dictator of Chihuahua who, at the request of the United States State Department, had given up millions of dollars in American mining and ranching companies in Mexico that he had confiscated. Of course, that was early in the revolution, before Wilson became a bed partner with Carranza.

"*Pues*," Enrique had consoled the affronted Villa, "what can you expect from two former schoolteachers?"

Throughout April and May, Villa and his handpicked Dorados laid low while the despot recuperated from his knee wound, which at one point had been threatened by gangrene. Villa and his men moved periodically from cave to cave, from pueblo to pueblo, always in a southwesterly direction toward the protective mountains of his home state of Durango. Only when they reached the wooded mountainous country of pines, junipers, cedars, and oaks would Villa feel really safe.

And Enrique. With a certain instinctual knowledge, he sensed that they were being followed. The Yaqui scouts would have detected a large body of soldiers, such as one of Pershing's cavalry troops, or even a smaller Carranzista detachment. Nevertheless, Enrique couldn't shake the ominous feeling.

Beneath the hot, humid sky Villa's soldiers slogged along the road corkscrewing over the Sierra Madre Occidental. The desert rabble from Chihuahua and Sonora were comprised of a ragtag assortment of Mexican peons, *muchachos* fourteen to sixteen, and the fierce Yaquis. The soldiers revealed all stages of picturesque raggedness; some wore overalls, others the charro jackets of peons, while one or two sported tight vaquero trousers. A few had shoes, although most of them wore only huaraches; the rest were barefooted.

Every so often, a spring would pour from the rocky slope that walled one side of the trail, and, after the officers had their turn, the other soldiers would scramble for a place in line to fill their canteens, calabash gourds, and palms with the pure, clear, cold water.

Behind the soldiers followed the *soldaderas*—and the lovely but lethal Angelina.

In the heat of summer days the flowers unfurled their buds; just so Angelina. She was a precocious bud upon a diseased stalk, straining ever toward that moment when the petals would burst savagely asunder to reveal the exotic flower of evil.

And, *Madre de Cristo*, Enrique's love and need for Angelina had fully consumed him now. He wanted her as nothing else, above all else—above even his zealous love for his country. For Mexico. Now, Mexico was for him only the grandeur of poverty, the misery of politics, and the fury of Latin passions. Yet he still clung to hope and he fought. Only in the heat of battle could he slake the passion that he refused to spend on Angelina, God help him.

Late afternoon, the last day in May, or so Enrique reckoned, Villa bivouacked his army of almost two hundred in a high canyon that would serve well as a fortress should a surprise attack be mounted. Little campfires leaped up throughout the canyon and along its meandering stream. The soldiers who weren't posted on the rocky parapets as guards settled in with their saddles for back rests and *sotol* to ease their parched throats.

The Yaqui detachment would make their own separate campfires and draw on the *marihuana* weed. Then the cruel warriors would squint across the mists of long centuries to regain the glory they had lost with the arrival of the mounted white man.

Even the Villistas had taken to smoking the weed. "La Cucaracha" was a sprightly corrido that the Villistas now sang as they went into battle. Though *cucaracha* meant "cockroach," in the sense of the song it was slang for the *marihuana* addict.

Enrique knew that Angelina was becoming dependent on the weed. He suspected that she even occasionally used the heroin, whenever a village was ransacked and the fine powder could be found. Yet her dependency seemed only to make her entire being glow with an incandescent beauty, a beauty that drew the coveted glances of all the men.

Even young Tonio she had made her adoring slave. It was an

adoration that Enrique instinctively knew as unnatural. Some last shreds of decency had prompted him to abandon the boy into the care of the good padres at the last pueblo they had taken. Then there was Molly. Despite Angelina's assertion that the Mormon girl had died in the crossfire of the Americans' attack, he was certain Angelina had played a part in Molly's death. But there was no way to prove it.

And if he could? What would he do? Destroy Angelina?

That night, like any of the other nights, Enrique could have had his choice of the camp followers. In the flickering light of the leaping flames, more than one feminine pair of dark slumberous eyes followed him, watching and waiting and hoping. Even so, he left the congestion of the throng, seeking privacy to confront the unrest that ate at his soul. In the twilight, he climbed among the strewn boulders and wandered among the deepening shadows of the spruces and firs.

Below him, he could hear discordant voices from the nearest campfire singing a corrido from the song that had become the revolutionary war anthem.

> *"La cucaracha, la cucaracha,*
> *Ya no puede caminar,*
> *Porque le falta, porque no tiene*
> *marihuana que fumar . . ."*

. . . the poor cockroach couldn't travel anymore because he had no *marihuana* to smoke.

Enrique's catlike tread surprised the Indian woman gathering firewood a dozen yards ahead. About her forehead was knotted a band of leather from which hung a burlap bag filled with kindling sticks. It was impossible to tell from her face whether she was young or old, so quickly did the mountain people age. Her dark sloe eyes took in the twin Lugers riding his hips and the sheathed knife at his waist and she turned to run.

The hunter in him urged him after her. For a few minutes

her moccasinned feet skimmed the rocks in the places his boots slid. In the dusk he caught glimpses of flesh where her long skirts hiked above her ankles when she scaled a rock. But when the path she followed opened into a small canyon, he knew he had her. His longer, heavier muscled legs would shorten the distance between them.

The Indian woman knew it, too. She whirled to face him and, squatting, began shoveling the dirt into her pudendum in frantic hope it would revolt the would-be rapist.

Enrique stopped and threw back his head and laughed. A deep laughter that was filled with the agony of the soul. *Jesus Cristo,* he wished that he did want the woman! The dirt would not have stopped him. He simply didn't want her, wanted nothing but . . .

Slowly he turned his steps back to the camp. His boots crunched long-dead pine needles and their redolence of age and decay drifted upward.

Another battle. Only then did he, and would he, find forgetfulness. Some said he fought like a demon in battle, taking risks that not even the bravest, or most foolhardy, dared to take.

Night had fallen and the woodsy, fecund smell of the Sierras was pungent in his nostrils. In the sinister slivers of moonlight that shafted between the needle branches, Angelina rose up before him. Her arms were outstretched, her palms open. With the moonlight upon her, she appeared as a figure of crucifixion. Indeed, the blinding moonlight was reflected into his eyes by the black-pearled silver crucifix shimmering between her naked breasts.

He sucked in deep drafts of breath between his parted lips and watched her walk slowly toward him. Her long raven-black hair swung wantonly about the curve of her hips. The corners of her lips curled with the mystery that was hers. Her fathomless black, sultry eyes were luminous, smoldering with the intensity of repressed passion. She stopped only inches away from him. "Enrique."

"No, I would kill you first, Angelina." The words were spoken in a raw whisper that was almost lost in the rustle of the pine branches overhead.

She made no move to touch him. "I've waited for you a long time." Her voice accompanied the eerie whistle of the wind through the pines.

Of their own accord, his hands closed about her throat. She relaxed and tilted her head farther back. There was a perfect understanding between them that he could extinguish the life from her. He would squeeze until her eyeballs popped, her face blackened. . . .

With a groan, he sank to his knees and buried his face in the fragrant thatch of curls between her widespread legs. His wide-open mouth covered over the furred lips, but his kiss was savage, brutal. Her fingers, lined up alongside his jaw, held him, urging him on. Her head lolled back. When her breath came in short gasps, she fell to her knees, whispering, "Now . . . now . . ."

Instead of taking her in the age-old position of lovemaking, he clamped one hand on her hip and forced her onto her stomach. He slammed his body atop of her and his hand guided the appendage of hard flesh into her, violating her in a way no man had ever done.

The Indian's black pupils were dilating with some faraway dream. His hand, engrained with accumulated dirt and blood and food stains, lifted another heroin-laced cigarette. He inhaled with a deep grunt. The pale-fleshed woman, whose legs were tangled with his, clawed at his hand. Her greed for more would keep him from making the mind's sweet journey.

He cuffed her, and she fell back panting. As the hallucinating substance took effect, his eyes fastened on the woman's brown nipples. He could see them with exact and detailed clarity, the small wrinkles about the edges that increased with the night's chill. Then the nipples expanded into giant mushrooms, dark and poisonous. In the dance of the firelight they contracted to small but deadly desert spiders. The woman was a *bruja*, bending over him, offering him her twin flesh-bound cups of poison for him to drink.

He was quickly bored with the vision, and his mind left the smoky campfire and its wreath of naked, sweating bodies to flit in and out through time and space. The cold, yellow moon was drawing near him, so close that its actual form could be made out, that of a grinning skull. He recoiled in horror, and the apparition shrank back into the small golden disk that moved across the waning night sky.

The Yaqui's hearing was acute. He could hear the crickets' movements through the pine needles, the worms furrowing the earth, the woman breathing at his groin. Her breath was like thunder. She wrapped three fingers and the heel of her hand about the hard ridges of veined flesh that was wet at the tip. Her palm was cold and he wanted to withdraw his body, but by no amount of effort could he move his limbs.

The drumming of another warrior's breath joined that of the woman, and with disinterest she relinquished his shaft of flesh. With a mind that was unusually clear, he watched as her mouth became a sacred vessel for the other warrior. The vessel altered form, becoming a cave, and the warrior crawled inside. Time elapsed and melded with the fire, and from the now grotesque vessel crawled the repulsive outcasts of the animal world that thrived in the desert—the snake, the vinegarroon, the tarantula, the lizard, and the gila monster.

The Yaqui watched, paralyzed with fear and with the substance's awful effects. Above him, only inches away, the blindingly brilliant moon shattered with a horrendous noise and sprayed his stomach with its searingly hot liquid.

Angelina attempted to move her left leg, but a naked body was sprawled across it. When she attempted to open her eyes, her lids were crusted shut. Through the after-haze of the heroin, her vision slowly focused. The chilly gray-pink of dawn was spreading its tentacles across the sky. Around the smoldering fire the bodies of the Yaquis were entwined. A sweaty, musky odor, sickeningly sweet, pervaded the campsite.

She could smell the same residue of odor on her own flesh. Her mouth tasted salty, fouled. Blurred scenes of the night drifted back to her: the frenzied orgy of sex, a multitude of Indians taking her one after another, sometimes more than one, making use of all of her body's orifices.

Beyond those scenes, before that revelry of drugs and copulation and drink, was one scene . . . a horrible memory that sliced clear through her like a razor-sharp machete. The degrading memory of Enrique taking her, coldly emptying his seed, and then giving her over to the Yaquis without a trace of feeling showing on that marble-hard face. That was his way of ridding himself of wanting her, but her pain was unbearable.

Enrique had taken her—and he had rejected her.

While the bodies strewn about her gradually came to life, she lay there and plotted. Plotted her revenge, plotted the destruction of her beloved.

23

The tropical rainy season arrived that morning like the onset of the Biblical flood. Sam sloshed along the overgrown trail, head down, leading the palomino. He had managed to exchange the two burros for the big stud. But not even the strong palomino could carry both Roxana and him through that quagmire, and he had been forced to dismount.

The water channeled from the dip in his Stetson's limp brim and sloshed over his back. Overhead the rain pattered loudly on the palm leaves, then slid off to soak the wild, lush vegetation beneath. So dense was the foliage that the sky, or rather the clouds, could not be seen. Here and there pencils of sunlight broke through the lush overgrowth. Once a huge dinosaur-looking iguana scampered before the palomino and Roxana had to cling tenaciously to the reins of the rearing horse.

Sam cast a backwards glance. Roxana sat perched on the stallion, her lips compressed stoically.

Of course, she wouldn't complain. Aristocrats didn't. The stiff upper lip and all that. But he was no aristocrat and he could damn well complain. He could complain that he might as well be put out to pasture like a gelded stud for all the good his body was doing him these days. Since the morning following their escape from the hoosegow, he and Roxana had treated each other with a distant cordiality.

As the day wore on and the rain tapered off, he castigated himself a hundred times for not hightailing it back to Dublan when he had told Roxana that was what he was going to do. He still wasn't sure exactly what had made him change his mind. It could have been the sight of her lovely breasts heaving with her furious breathing.

Or it might have been the sweeping shadow of one of those reconnaissance aeroplanes that had changed his mind. In that flash of a second he had realized all over again that progress was closing in on his world. And he didn't like the idea. At that point the idea of the Rio Grande rancho retreat had once more become strongly appealing.

What was equally appealing at that moment was a bottle of gin to warm his cold, bone-tired body. At thirty he was too old to be traipsing around a jungle, looking for a woman. If he found the Asunsolo woman with the Dorados, how in the name of Saint Anthony was he going to get her back?

For five thousand bucks, he'd figure out a way.

He felt real sympathy for Roxana, because the one thing that extraordinary woman wanted so badly, that interview with Villa, she wasn't going to get. At least not get and walk away alive. When he started feeling sympathy, he knew for certain his brain was pickled by the formaldehyde that was passed off as gin.

It had to be really pickled when he slipped up, at that very moment, and walked right onto a small Carranzista encampment.

The five soldiers sprang to their feet, rifles aimed at his gut. In that steamy mist they looked like ghosts. Ghosts or not, he doubted they would be friendly to *Norte Americanos*. All classes and factions of Mexicans hated the foreign exploiters. Without turning, he muttered to Roxana, "The French you said you learned in school: you'd better damn well speak only French now."

He addressed the soldier with the stripes of a captain on the sleeves of his tan Federales uniform. In his best Spanish Sam explained that he was an exporter from Chihuahua and that the train he and his French wife were on had been attacked by guerrillas.

The captain's swarthy face closed over. His eyes narrowed, looking pointedly at Sam's clothing—hardly that of a businessman; and the wife wore the khaki blouse and hobnailed boots of an American soldier and the trousers and sandals of a peon.

Sweat that had nothing to do with the humidity gushed from Sam's pores. "In the confusion of the attack we were lucky to escape in the jungle with some *peónes*, who provided us with clothing."

The captain's heavy-lidded gaze lingered dubiously on the palomino. The time for explanations was over. "*Capitan!*" Sam barked imperiously. "We are tired and hungry. Would you be so good as to direct us to the nearest settlement."

For a long moment the officer wavered, but apparently Sam's hauteur satisfied him. Unfortunately, rather than direct Sam to the nearest settlement, he and his men delivered them to the family hacienda of the General of the Federal Army of that district.

Mounted astride a fine Arab stallion, the general's aristocratic father met the captain at the arched entrance to the estate. He wore the traditional riding costume of jodhpurs and knee-length boots and he sported a magnificent Don Quixote drooping mustache beneath an imperious hooked nose. With the rest of the detachment, Sam and Roxana waited while the captain rode forward and presented himself to the old hidalgo. What if the *hacendado* didn't buy the story Sam had fed to the captain?

Sam's eye caught the hangman's noose dangling from the arched gateway of wrought iron. The soldier waiting with him noticed the direction of his gaze and volunteered the information that many a *bandido* had been hanged from it, which didn't paint a favorable picture for Sam's hopes.

The *hacendado* edged his horse forward. "*El capitan* tells me you and your wife barely escaped a Villista attack," he said sympathetically. "I am sorry I was not here to welcome you personally. I was out inspecting the rain's effect on our crop. Please, let me offer you the comfort of my humble home until you have rested."

Sam's guts eased their knotting at Don Ferdinando Gomez's generosity. Custom demanded a polite exchange of amenities—talk of the weather, a glass of home-grown wine, an inspection of the hacienda. The humble home was more like a palace with its cream-colored walls; the estate, a medieval fiefdom—the kind Villa sought to destroy. However, the hacienda of the general's family was a bastion defended by the Carranzista forces firmly entrenched in the state.

The don's ancestors had made their fortune in rice. Their wealth was evidenced by the opulence of the place. Exotic birds in brilliant hues strutted about well-manicured lawns bordered by gardens of blue hibiscus, pink oleander, and flaming vine. Marbled tiles, Moorish fountains, and arched porticos provided shade and protection against the sultry air and steaming sunlight.

At Don Ferdinando's orders, servants scurried to wait on the couple, and Sam found himself and Roxana installed in a large guest room carpeted with the traditional handwoven *jergas*. A dividing screen of carved teak separated the satin-swathed bedroom from a sunken tiled bath.

One *mozo* brought a platter of tropical fruits and a carafe of wine, then opened ancient spooled and slatted shutters to let in the sunlight. Another servant entered with a change of some kind of fancy clothing for both him and Roxana and then proceeded to draw the bath water, which was fed by a venerable Roman aqueduct system. When scented soap and towels were left on the tub's tiled rim and fresh clothing laid out, Roxana royally told them, "Merci."

He hoped that wasn't the extent of her French.

After the *sirvientos* departed, their huarache sandals slapping softly down the tiled hall, she turned to him. "Well?" Her voice was hushed. "What do we do now?"

He spun his hat toward one of the bed's four-posters and fell back onto the deep mattress. "Nothing." Locking his hands behind his head, he looked up at her. "We rest and partake of the don's hospitality. Tonight we'll be gracious guests and dance at Doña Gomez's birthday ball and learn what we can about the political atmosphere. And tomorrow we'll be on our way again."

After a moment, she nodded. "That sounds sensible enough. Let's just hope none of the other guests is fluent in French."

His eyes narrowed. "You told me you learned French."

With a husky laugh that he unwillingly found enchanting, she picked up a ripe mango from the tray of assorted fruits and moved to sit on the far end of the bed. "I learned to conjugate the verb *aimer* and a few other totally useless phrases."

Aimer: to love. He probably remembered more French from his West Point days than she did. He wondered what other French words of love would sound like on her lips. Intoxicating, coming from such a prim exterior. Fascinated, he watched her bite into the mango, licking her lips with a delicate swipe of her tongue that ignited a spark in his combustible lower part.

He stifled a groan. "Pass me a banana."

"What? No wine?" She raised a derisive brow. "Or are you missing your gin?"

He caught the banana she tossed. "I'm easing up on the booze until the Asunsolo girl is found." He felt her startled gaze but concentrated on peeling the yellow fruit.

After a long moment, she quietly replied, "I see."

He wondered if she really did see. He had been looking for something because he was smart enough to see he didn't have anything. In the last few weeks he had sobered up enough to realize that that ranch up in the Rio Grande valley was his last chance.

Unlike most females, Roxana did not prod the point when he volunteered no further insights into his personal life. Finishing the mango, she rose from the bed and slipped behind the scrolled and paneled screen. "I think I'll bathe now. Mmmm. It's the one luxury I've missed most."

He closed his lids. Not because he was tired, but because, listening to her clothing slither to the floor, his imagination was roaming in fields that would do it no good. With a grunt, he rolled over onto his stomach to deflect his throbbing erection. The heavy, lush scent of oleander lacing the window ledge acted like a narcotic to his weary body.

He awoke sometime later, when the sunlight had all but deserted the room. Roxy was seated before the dresser's mirror, wearing only a lacy white underthing and, beneath that, a corset that lifted her alabaster mounds until they looked like twin bullets. He mumbled something about taking a bath, and she called out, "When you're ready, let me shave you, Sam. I pestered Wally until he taught me how."

"I don't trust you," he said, his voice muffled by the shirt he was peeling off.

Roxana's reflection frowned petulantly from the mirror.

Just for the shock value, he thought about stripping down all the way in front of her. He also thought about bedding her. He thought about . . . hell, making love to Roxana was only intensifying an intimacy that would take some readjustment when this idiotic quest was over.

He sank to his shoulders in the warm water and reached for the scented bar of soap. It wasn't like some of the soap bars he had had to resort to, soap that would curl the hide off a rhino. When his own hide was wrinkled by the water, he eased out and dried off with the towel.

"Sam?"

"Hmmm?"

"Could you hook me up?"

He looked up. Roxy was watching him in the mirror. After a long, breathless moment, her lashes lowered, blocking his gaze into her eyes. He wrapped the towel about his waist. Some vestige of civilized behavior was necessary if he hoped to continue this relationship on a businesslike level.

She rose and crossed to him with a natural grace he doubted she was aware of. Damn't, if she wasn't a beauty.

She was wearing an ankle-length skirt with a long train and puffed sleeves in a style that had gone out five years before. The dress was too short for her tall frame, short enough to provide a peak at her well-turned ankle. The mauve-gray material, some kind of satiny stuff, had been tailored with a wasp waist, and it clung and shimmered about her lissome form. To alleviate the tightness of the tubular skirt, there was about a foot-long fancy slit up one side.

She hadn't put up her hair yet, and it clouded down about her shoulders, so that he was tempted to grab great handfuls of it and . . .

"Would you, Sam? Hook me up, please?" she repeated, turning her back to him.

He was lost. Below his stomach's inverted arrow of fur, the towel jutted tautly. With a deep breath, he fastened the hooks in her silks of London Smoke. He tried to concentrate on what his fingers were about. But her shoulders were pearly and bare and softly curved, and simply made for kissing.

Wordlessly and rapidly, he completed the task and set about shaving and dressing himself. Even as he drew on the gray striped trousers, which, amazingly, were almost long enough; even as he slid into the linen shirt and gray waistcoat; even as he fastened the links into the French cuffs, his gaze was drawn continually to Roxana, who was distractedly arranging that silky mass of chestnut hair atop her head. Jesus, how did newlywed husbands last until the end of the evenings?

Resolutely, he went in search of a fresh stock for his collar, which was a shade too tight.

"Sam?"

He looked up from pulling on the hand-cobbled boots that had been set out. Fortunately, they fit. Roxana was in the act of drawing on long white gloves. "What?" He didn't mean to sound so harsh.

"Did a woman ever tell you that when you shave and clean up your're extremely good-looking?"

"They've told me a lot of things, Roxy, but I can't recall in the heat of those moments just what they were."

She smiled, and dimples formed below her cheekbones. "I believe you're a rogue, Sam Brady. Shall we join the other guests?"

Whatever disruption the revolution might be causing on Mexican lives and the rest of the countryside, it certainly did not seem to be affecting the tobacco and rice planters of Sinaloa and Durango. Spanish gentlemen and their grand ladies had turned out in all their finery, most of which was newly ordered from the Paris and London fashion houses. The women were lavishly clothed in gowns of soft soie-de-chine and shimmering watered silk. The gentlemen wore elegant evening dress coats, vicuna dinner jackets with silk facings, and even the traditional embroidered hidalgo's costume.

The French doors were thrown open and soft fragrant mountain breezes cooled the crowded ballroom. Don Ferdinando introduced Sam and Roxana to the other guests first and then to his olive-skinned wife, Doña Ysabella, who had bovine eyes and was plump from too many siestas. To Sam's relief, Roxana managed to rattle off impressive bits and phrases of French that no one questioned.

The guests were all sympathetic for his and Roxana's plight, and he felt not a small amount of admiration as he listened to Roxana embellish in badly accented French on his original tale of the guerrilla attack.

"*Mon Dieu*," she breathed, "the man held a—how do you say it?—a knife, right here at my throat. And, ohh, the horror of the killings—*non, non*, I do not wish to talk about it. It is too, too terrible!"

Of course, as was the nature of the human race, the guests vicariously enjoyed speculating on such a catastrophe and added their own tales, which interested him more. But none of the incidents was recent and no one reported actually having seen

Villa, though all had been sure the guerrilla attacks over the past few years had been Villa-inspired.

The guests talked more of the old days—of Diaz and his government, how it had been highly respected in Wall Street, London, Paris, and Berlin. Railroads, mines, smelters, and cattle ranches had all prospered, producing a golden stream of profits. Mexican bonds, once worthless, had become gilt-edged investments under Diaz's wise and beneficent dictatorship.

Sam wondered that the guests did not see that they were gauging progress in terms of dividends and profits; that their profits had been enormous because of the cheapness and docility of Mexian labor; that the poverty-stricken peasants still lived in virtual servitude, in near chattel slavery. Their aristocratic obtuseness to the realities of the situation soon bored him.

Musicians imported from Mexico City were stationed behind the concealment of colorful, palm-planted *macetas*. They played the waltzes of Johann Strauss, and Sam escaped the dreary conversation by asking Roxana to dance.

With her left hand she picked up her dress's train to keep from stepping on it. "Why, Sam, I didn't know you could waltz," she teased, her head tilted back, her brown eyes glowing.

He wanted to pull her close, to feel her lovely body next to his. "I learned at the West Point hops."

"Your face closes over when you talk of the past."

"The past is better where it is: in the past." He whirled her rapidly to the crescendoing tempo of the waltz.

"But Sam." Her voice was so soft it was difficult to hear above the romantic strains of the violins. "The past is what makes you . . . you; what makes you special."

He looked down at her face. Beneath the shimmering prisms of crystalized candlelight her face was tanned and radiant with health. An amazing woman. She hadn't broken under the strain and stress of battle conditions; she had never complained or grumbled. A determined, spirited woman. A beautiful woman. He was surprised that he had never really noticed that loveliness years before. Perhaps it just took age to bring out the real beauty in a woman.

He realized he was staring, that her lips were parted, as if she were waiting for something to happen. He ceased the rapid spinning about the room and, standing there with her still held firmly in his arm, with the other guests whirling about them, he said, "It sounds as though you might find me likable, Roxana Van Buren."

She caught up the ivory fan attached by a thin silver cord to her wrist and, fanning herself, stepped away from his embrace. "You might say that, Sam Brady."

So, Roxana Van Buren was learning the art of flirtation and coquetry!

Entranced, he followed her to the banquet table, where a few other guests had already assembled. Whatever he had on his mind to say was promptly forgotten at the sight of the mounds of succulent foods being set about by discreetly hovering servants. It was well past midnight and he could have eaten a side of beef. After months of skimpy rations of stale hardtack, rancid bacon, and coffee, his mouth involuntarily watered.

Centered on the table, a three-foot-high cake was slathered thickly with creamy icing and topped by birthday candles. Surrounding the cake were other delicacies along with steaming *guajolote asado*—baked turkey encircled by red chiles, the pungent *lechoncillo*—suckling pig stuffed with apples, onions, and cornmeal, and what had to be easily a hundred other delectable treats.

However, he never got the opportunity to sample any of it, because suddenly a blood-curdling scream burst from the open French doors a few feet away. All heads swiveled to behold Doña Ysabella, locked before a near-naked Yaqui warrior. Beneath her doubled chins the Yaqui pressed a machete. Tears of fright welled over her lids and furrowed her ample cheeks with a black trail of kohl.

Sam's gaze was fastened not on the hostage woman but on the

thin, young woman who stood a few paces to her left, close to the intruder. Between them was another Yaqui warrior. She was but a specter of the lovely young girl Roxana had described, yet he was certain the two were the same. Angelina Asunsolo. The black-pearled crucifix that lay on the dirty peasant blouse confirmed it.

Her long, dark hair was tangled and matted with filth. The pupils of her eyes were tiny pinpricks, the irises a washed-out dusty black. The whites looked like smashed milk glass with red ink funneled into the cracks. She stepped away from the Yaqui, and the smell of sour stale sweat emanated from her.

"If you want your wife, Don Ferdinando, if you want Villa, your soldiers will find them both in the old mining town. In the small canyon southeast of here." Her voice was thick, slow. "But if your soldiers seek to follow us there, my Yaqui will kill your wife on the trail and deliver her heart up to you."

The stunned silence of the ballroom was interrupted by smothered gasps of shock. Don Ferdinando, ashen, cried, "Wait! If it's a ransom you want, I can offer—"

But the night intruders were gone, vanishing like apparitions, taking with them the *hacendado's* wife.

Roxana clutched Sam's sleeve. "That was Angelina, I'm certain! What did she say?"

"That we'd find Villa holed up in some mining town." He spun around and ran for the bedroom and his revolver. The guests were speaking frantically, groping for their partners, and moving aimlessly like cattle ready to stampede.

In the corridor that led to his bedroom, Roxana caught up with him. "Sam, wait! I'm going with you."

He shook off her hand at his arm. "No, you'll only slow me down." The soldiers already had a head start. Most likely they would spook off Villa.

"Sam, it could be a trap. Why would Angelina give away Villa's hiding place?"

He whipped off the dinner coat and buckled on the holster,

not bothering to knot the rawhide about his thigh. "I don't know, but I'm bringing her back. And Villa. You can get the interview then."

"No! I'm part of this team, remember? Van Buren and Brady?"

He crooked a grin at her. "Brady and Van Buren. Be back soon, Roxy."

She followed him down the hall, beseeching him. "Sam Brady, you listen to me. I'm going, and you can't stop me!"

He halted and turned on her. The woman was a curse. An albatross about his neck. The worst part of it was that he was growing accustomed to it. To like it, even.

"Roxy, it's too damned dangerous for you to go. And I *will* stop you. If I have to, I'll throw a punch that'll deck you. Do you understand me?"

Without waiting for her reply, he swung around to leave. But as he loped down the hall, he heard her yell, "I'll get even for this, you—you weasel—you four-flusher—you, you—ohhh!"

24

Enrique rolled away from one of the sleeping women and lay on his back, listening. Outside the fractured bank walls a wild burro clip-clopped down the silent, deserted street. Through the gaping holes in the roof the stars twinkled serenely, as though the Villistas' acts of death and destruction and war did not take place within light-years of their life span.

Dawn was not far away and with it would come the raucous cry of the forest birds, the yellow-eyed juncos and parrots and dusky-capped flycatchers. Only within the past hour or so, the Dorados and their *soldaderas* one by one had fallen asleep, aided by the maguey's potent *pulque*. Most of the Dorados slept in the open in Los Alamos's Plaza de Armas. Enrique and Villa and Ramon Cordoba had taken possession of the few buildings left standing in the ghost town.

Once a brawling mining camp, Los Alamos was only a gentle whisper of the past. It was a storehouse of legends concerning lost mines, buried treasures, and fabulous extravaganzas. Perched halfway up a mountainside, it clung tenaciously even when the

rainy season descended and plowed the earth with sluicing fresh-
ets. Eventually, a hurricane would no doubt sweep through the
canyon and level the remaining stucco buildings.

The plodding of the burro faded off. Enrique rose naked from
the bedroll and, stepping over the other sleeping woman, picked
his way through a rubble of adobe bricks and wooden debris. A
broken roof tile crunched beneath his bare feet, but his two female
companions never stirred. He had ridden the sisters hard and,
later, indifferently, morbidly, watched them amuse themselves
with each other.

The bank's door and windows, like the other buildings, had
been carried away over the years by vandals. The crumbling
wall he leaned against smelled strongly of urine. His penis,
crusted white in places from the night's activity, was stiff with
his need to piss. He took his own turn splashing against the
wall.

Off to his left, horses were hobbled in the weeds in front of
the weather-ravaged post office, where Villa and Ramon were
quartered. Incongruously, parked next to the cropping horses was
an Indian Scout motorcycle, Villa's newest toy. First the private
railroad car, then the Pierce Arrow touring car, and now the
motorcycle.

Enrique shrugged, his gaze moving farther up the moon-sil-
vered street to what had once been one of the many cantinas in
Los Alamos. All that was left was one time-scarred wall with a
scrap of a shutter that swung slowly, crazily, in the pre-dawn
breeze. The Yaquis were camped in there—and so was Angelina.
He had thought that by taking her as he had, by giving her to
the Yaquis, he would have debased her to the point that he no
longer wanted her. He had told himself that at last he would be
content; maybe even slightly amused to observe her disintegra-
tion.

But he found, to his anger, that he was disintegrating along
with her—more slowly perhaps without the heroin to speed the
degeneration process, but nevertheless he was falling apart inside.

His knuckles raked down the peeling stucco wall. "Damn her!" he muttered softly. "Damn her to everlasting hell!"

The nocturnal scent of the warm earth and scorched grass drifted over Angelina. A few feet away, crouched in the weeds that encroached on the ghost town, the two Yaquis stripped the body of Doña Ysabella Gomez of its valuables: her rings, her pearl necklace, her sapphire bracelet. One Yaqui rose from the weeds to prance about like a child, preening with the *hacendada's* tall tortoiseshell comb anchored in his greasy locks.

Angelina's attention wandered back to the sleeping ghost town. Soon. Soon her vengeance would be accomplished. She estimated that she had had twenty, maybe thirty minutes on the Carranzista soldiers. Time was so difficult to judge anymore. It was warped for her, unless it was the dream-drifting time of the delicate powder.

She wanted the heroin now; her very bones were splintering from the need of it after more than twenty-four hours without. Purposely, painfully, she had abstained until she had implemented her revenge. Acrid sweat leaked from her pores; her hands shook—or at least one hand shook; the other seemed atrophied and lay lifelessly on her thigh.

The pre-dawn stillness was interrupted by the ghostly whistle of the light breeze moving through the rubble. No, wait, it was the soldiers she heard! Straining her eyes, she could just barely make out the drab olive of the Rural Federales uniforms slipping in and out of the trees and slithering through the grass. Just then came the first crackle of gunfire. Then the charge.

She sprang to her feet, tottering as her vision spun. Then, steadier, she began to walk hurriedly in a broken gait toward the embattled town. She would not miss that precious moment of Enrique's death.

In the semi-darkness, spurts of rifle fire flared among the crumbling ruins of Los Alamos. Flashes and flickers and sparks in the darkness. But they were deadly. In the Plaza de Armas, sleep-groggy Dorados staggered to their feet, groping for weapons. The *soldaderas* among them reached for their own weapons, for some merely knives. Within the plaza's bandstand a Villista machine gun opened gunfire on the attackers. The flaming sheet of its chatter lit the gray dawn, and its staccato ripping reverberated from the town's shattered walls.

Clumsily, Angelina picked her way among fallen adobe bricks toward the tumbledown portion of the bank. She had to be there for that final moment. She wanted him to see, to know that it was she who had betrayed not only him but his hope for the Cause.

With the first burst of dawn's bloody-pink light, she saw him silhouetted momentarily against the blackness of the bank's doorway, slapping a clip into his Luger. His warrior's sun-browned body was naked; primitively beautiful, hard and masculine.

At that instant she realized the life would soon be extinguished from it. And with the snuffing of his life, her own would hold no meaning. What had she done?

She shot up from where she crouched, but he was already springing across the street and loping in a zigzag line toward the post office, bent on protecting Villa. Looped about one muscled-striated shoulder was slung a *bandolero*, and in one arm he cradled a lever-action rifle, besides the Luger in his hand.

Behind him, three soldiers dashed out into the street, rifles raised.

"Enrique!" she cried, but the shouting and gunfire drowned out her warning.

The Carranzistas' bullets geysered dirt about his bare feet. He bellied down behind a rain barrel. Just beyond she saw Villa and Ramon and two or three other officers make a dash from the post office for their picketed mounts. The Federales' shots puckered the ground, harmlessly short of the Lion of the North. Even with all the noise of the battle, the shouting of the combatants, and the zinging of bullets, she could hear Villa's wild laughter as he scrambled onto the motorcycle. A lucky shot sent his big hat spinning off.

Then Villa blurred from her vision as she turned her gaze back to Enrique. He slipped a cartridge into the rifle's breech and snapped up the lever. When a shot sent a stream of water gushing from the bullet hole in the rain barrel, he heaved up and streaked for the one remaining horse. From behind her, rifle fire ripped the air. Enrique spun. To her befuddled mind, the scene transcended time. His hands released the rifle and Luger, and the weapons appeared to float end over end through the air.

For an eternal moment his glittering eyes held hers; in their pale brown depths first questioning, then disbelief, and, lastly, great pain succeeded one another rapidly. Then he crumpled to the dust with glacial slowness.

Tears stinging her eyes, she half ran, half stumbled toward him. His lids were partially open. Blood seeped from between his lips. She gathered him to her, cradling his head against her breast. His chest was sticky with the blood that drained from the bullet-blackened wounds.

"Angelina." His lips barely moved.

"Enrique!" she choked. "Please, tell me you love me!" Her fingers dug into his flesh. "*Dios mio*, tell me!"

His eyes rolled back and his body went limp. She was left alone, totally alone, in her mad world.

"Nooooo!" It was a piercing animal wail, a shrill keening that made the Federales who gathered around her shudder.

In the blinding sunlight the features of a face coalesced above her. She closed her eyes, tilted her head back against the sun-heated, pockmarked wall and took a deep drag of the cigarette. The *marihuana* wasn't as soothing as the heroin, but it did help to obliviate that body lying just a few feet away in the dusty street.

Around her she could hear fragmented sentences exchanged between the Federales as they moved about the buildings. She was dimly aware that they were turning over the bodies of the dead and wounded, making identification, rounding up the Dorados who had not escaped into the brush, and searching through the ramshackle adobes for Villa.

"Angelina? Angelina Asunsolo?"

She opened her eyes wide. Overhead the carrion birds swooped and circled, waiting with their eternal patience. Directly before her a man seemed to waver in and out of her blurred vision. Illogically, he was wearing dinner trousers and ruffled linen shirt.

He took the cigarette from between her lips and held it out of her grasp. "Are you Angelina Asunsolo?"

A hand—her hand, though it didn't seem a part of her—reached out to take back the cigarette, but misjudged the distance. "Yes. Give me the *marihuana*."

The hand flicked the cigarette out of sight and she made her fingers arc to claw at the man's flesh. In reality her hands produced only palsied tremors.

"Your father is looking for you."

"Tell him you found me."

"He wants you to come home."

The fingers of her hand fumbled at the necklace about her throat. With monumental effort she managed to remove it. She shoved the crucifix in the direction of the man's hand. "Tell him you found me . . . tell him I am home . . . tell him to go to hell . . . and . . . give me back the *marihuana*."

25

Roxana sawed on the reins, certain she heard the low rumble of an engine off to her left in the hills above her. She had to strain to hear over the horse's heaving. The bay, made for light carriage work, was already blowing puffs of foam. It was winded from the wild ride from Don Ferdinando's hacienda. The guest who owned the bay would be surprised to find his carriage shafts empty.

Yes, there it was, again. But the drone of the engine was diminishing, moving away from the direction in which she was riding with the tail end of the Federales, toward Los Alamos.

She hesitated, wavering between logic and instinct. One of the straggling Carranzista soldiers turned in his saddle to motion her to catch up. Instead of joining the soldiers, she swerved the mount from the road and took the path that struggled through the undergrowth and zigzagged upwards. A quarter of an hour later she intersected with the main road, leading up and out of Los Alamos. Far below her she could make out through the lacework of branches the movements of the Federales. From that height they looked like wind-up miniature toy soldiers.

She kneed the horse forward. The lather from the bay's steaming flanks soaked her bare thighs. She realized she looked like an Amazon, with the gown's tight, tubular skirt hiked about her hips and her hair streaming in all directions. But that was only a passing acknowledgment. For all she cared, she could look like Medusa, if only she could get that interview with Villa.

The few people she had talked with who had seen Villa said he sometimes traveled in a luxurious Pierce Arrow touring car. A hunch told her the automobile she was pursuing belonged to Villa.

If she was wrong, if he had not escaped the town, then she would find him below, either dead or alive. Whichever, she'd have her story.

At times she believed she had lost the automobile altogether. Then she would catch the sound again, but always farther away than before. She knew that her horse could not continue its pace before she rode it into the ground. In her urgency, she had been foolish. She slowed the bay to a walk, as Sam had taught her. Villa would be forced to match his touring car's speed to the horses of his Dorados. Eventually she would catch up.

At one point, possibly half an hour later, the road passed across a shallow riverbed. For but a moment she paused, letting the bay drink only the smallest amount of water. As she did, she noticed in the damp earth fresh hoofprints—and a tire track. A single track! She was chasing not an automobile, but a motorcycle.

Through the gap in the thick, leafy canopy overhead she could judge the progress of the sun and she knew that it had to be nearing midmorning. She had gone more than thirty-six hours without sleep. Her stomach was growling and her temples were throbbing.

Her head had begun to nod when the screech of a parrot jerked her upright. She shook it to clear the cobwebs and forced herself to pay attention to the road. What if, at some point, Villa and his Dorados left the road and she missed their turnoff? Worse, she was bothered that she could no longer hear the engine's drone.

Still, she pressed on. She thought about Sam. By now the Federales would have captured the village; by now he must have found Angelina. He would get his five thousand dollars and his dream, his rancho. And she . . . ? She plodded the bay forward. The months of following Villa were drawing to a close. Once she had the interview, she could return to civilization.

A reporter's desk job in Washington, D.C., was going to seem pretty tame, especially after everything she and Sam had been through together. Incarceration and wild Indians. Blizzards and bordellos. Even a shotgun wedding. She mustn't forget that. As if she ever could. The recollection of Sam's suffering face, the expression that announced clearly he had resigned himself to a fate worse than death as he took his part in the wedding ceremony, caused a small chuckle to escape her parched lips. No, that she wouldn't forget, not if she lived to be a very old woman.

By the slant of the sun shafts through the trees, it had to be getting close to noon. When she rounded a jutting clump of pines at the crest of the road, she was busy cursing herself for traipsing off on a wild goose chase. Then, below her, she saw a scattering of *jacales*. Rustic-looking with their adobe walls and thatched roofs, they were centered about a crude sawmill.

Quickly she reined the bay back into the concealment of the trees. She counted maybe a dozen ragtag Dorados in the small lumber camp. They sat or sprawled on the ground, lazing or eating. Next to the mill's steps a motorcycle was perched on its rear stand. So, it *had* been a motorcycle and not an automobile she had been chasing.

She had seen Villa's picture on the wanted posters at Columbus, but from that distance she was unsure which of the Dorados below was he. To get closer she had to desert the road and pick a path down through the trees, circumventing the lumber camp.

Below the lumber camp was a creek that both paralleled and, at times, crossed the road. Back of the camp, the stream was wider and deeper. And at that point she encountered a bather, who stood submerged just past the hips. He was humming to himself as he lathered soap first into one armpit, then the other. That cockroach song. She left the bay and crept down through the underbrush to get a closer look.

Villa! There was no doubt about it. The handlebar mustache, the pugnacious chin, the slightly protruding teeth. Surprisingly, his body was not as corpulent as his rounded face led one to suspect. It had been honed by the years of living off the land, of staying just a step ahead of death.

Her gaze was diverted by a glint of metal reflecting in the sunlight. Mounded on the bank were his clothing and boots. But it was the shiny bullets in the *bandoleros* that had drawn her attention. She knew then what she would do.

Keeping carefully within the perimeter of the undergrowth, she circled around until she was behind Villa. His clothing and gunbelt were mere yards away. She wondered how many people had tried to corner Villa and had failed. What made her think she could succeed?

Well, it was now or never. An opportunity as perfect as this would likely not present itself again.

On hands and knees she crept toward the mound of clothing. Villa stopped humming and she froze. But he had only ducked his head beneath the water. He came up, sputtering, and began to lather his hair. He was singing, now. Something about a woman named Adelita.

Her hand closed on the pistol's grip. She eased it from the holster and cocked the hammer. She rose to her feet. Steadily, as she had been taught, she leveled it at the area between Villa's shoulder blades. "Turn around." Her voice sounded like a croak.

His singing stopped. Slowly he turned. A stare of incredulity widened his eyes. "You call out," she warned in English, "and I pull this trigger."

His eyes locked on the length of leg, exposed where the gown's slit had ripped all the way up her thigh. A wide grin of uneven, yellowed teeth split his swarthy face. "*Ejoli!*" he breathed. "A woman! A most beautiful woman." He cocked his head. "Who are you?"

She never took her eyes off his face. "I'm a newspaperman for the *The Washington Post.*"

"You are no newspaperman, I think. A newspaper woman, no?" He laughed at his joke. She didn't. Sobering, he put his fist on his hips. "You come after me for the reward, eh?"

She was thinking hard. She had never planned further than getting the interview. Like a fool, she had merely assumed the interview would come with Villa's capture. But now, with the situation the way it was, she might just be able to carry off the capture of Pancho Villa herself!

That one pause was her undoing. Swift as lightning, Villa moved. He flung the soap bar at her. She ducked, but in that time he scrambled up the bank and caught the pistol's barrel just as she brought it up again. She tried to wrestle the revolver back, but he cuffed her across the jaw with the gun.

She staggered to her knees. Above the ringing in her ears she could hear him shouting commands. His hand entangled in her hair, he jerked her to her feet. He saw her stare briefly at the limp column of flesh and its wrinkled bag dangling from his crotch, and laughter erupted from his barrel chest. "We have a little sport, eh. I give you an interview, but in return you give me and my Dorados a little *panoche*, eh?" he asked with a grisly attempt at humor.

Her mouth parched dry as tinder. Suddenly all the horror stories about Villa came back vividly. Villainous Villa. His murderous rages. His cruelty. He had had his own butcher shop once in Chihuahua City. He would know how to separate a body's limbs efficiently with a machete . . . while the victim still lived. She searched somewhere deep inside her for strength, for the courage to face what was to come.

Behind her, she could hear the men he had summoned hustling down the slope with shouts of "*Que pasa?*" and other Spanish phrases she couldn't follow. But when he turned her to face them, she understood their leers quite well. He flung out another command that elicited a snickering response from the soldiers. She was grabbed by several pair of hands and dragged up the embankment.

She tried to jerk away, but the soldiers, one at either side of her and another behind, shoving at her back, hauled her along. She lost one slipper; the other was already grass-stained. The guard posted before the sawmill rattled out a question and there was laughter from the gold-toothed soldier on her right. The soldier behind her ran his hand beneath the skirt's split and groped for her buttocks. She twisted and kicked out at him. With a chortle, he shifted aside. But at least he withdrew his hand.

A sickening knotting in the pit of her stomach told her this was only the beginning. She would endure tortures as exquisite as Villa had devised for his other captives. Perhaps he would have new ones just for her.

A ragged Dorado prodded her up the sawmill steps. She stumbled and floundered to her hands and knees in the sawdust where the half dozen or so male prisoners sat huddled. The shed was redolent with the pine shavings, but the fresh scent could not overpower the odor of fear that clung to the passive group of men.

At the sight of her, various expressions showed in their faces. Surprise. Apathy. Pity. The last was the worse. Her courage collapsed. She covered her face with her palms, and wept. Silently. Deep, gulping breaths that seemed to last for hours.

Beneath the tin corrugated roof the tropical heat was unbearable, and her tears coalesced with the perspiration that streamed down her face, soaked her underarms, and collected in the valley between her breasts. This was indeed the *tierra caliente*, the hot land.

The straw hat of the peón next to her was full of fleas, and she tried to defend herself against the invading creatures. Momentarily, the activity took her mind off the fate that awaited her. After a while she gave up and subsided into a morose state, uncaring of the fleas or the heat.

A sandal-shod old Indian, who had only stubs of teeth left, touched her shoulder and mumbled something about the Virgin Mary. She raised tear-glazed eyes to find him crossing himself. Perhaps he had meant to console her, but she began to tremble uncontrollably. Forgotten phrases came to her from the Protestant creed she had learned by rote as a child. She repeated them in her mind and in the repetition found a sort of comfort; at least a deliverance from the horror of her imagination.

A younger Mexican, with the muscled arms of a lumberjack, locked his hands about his doubled knees and murmured, "*Que sera, sera.*"

That phrase she understood. She wanted to deny its veracity. People did have choices in their lives. But the sight of Villa at the foot of the stairs sealed the words in her throat before they ever took form. As he slowly mounted the stairs, he tucked his shirttail into his trousers. He wore a sort of charro costume with a black bandana beneath his belligerent chin. His dark kinky hair was plastered to his forehead. His too-long arms hung low, and his short legs were slightly bowed. Behind him were two Dorados with multi-caliber rifles braced in the crooks of their arms.

A dozen feet away from her Villa stopped and sat down, legs crossed at the ankles. His face wore a look she could only define as anticipation of amusement, the kind the hunter must wear as he gradually brings his quarry to bay. The old cat-playing-with-the-mouse pleasure.

"So, you are a newspaperman? I give you an interview, okay? I tell you about the great *El Centauro del Norte*, Pancho the Puma." He stretched out his hands, palms up. "What do you want to know?"

He was trifling with her. She forced herself to hold his smiling gaze. He admired bravery, if she remembered one of the tales rightly. Still, she could actually taste fear on her tongue. An acrid, metallic taste. Strange, that fear should have a taste.

"Where is your paper? Your paper for notes?"

"I left my notepad and pencil behind in my haste to catch up with you."

He canted his head and narrowed his curly-lashed eyes, as though considering the truth of her statement. "All right. I tell you about me. I tell you that, like you, I can write my name. Doroteo Arango. That's my name. I learned to write in the sand. After much, much practice.

"I tell you that I do not drink or smoke. Coffee—bahh! I like tea. Did you know that I had tea once with your General Pershing? And now he hunts me like I am a criminal." His fist smacked his chest. His big brown eyes looked soulful. "Me! The Liberator of my people. What business is it of your United States, this revolution I lead?"

Why, the cockiness of the bandit was extraordinary! And yet, appealing. That he possessed a charisma was undeniable. "You attacked an American town, killed American people. You became our business."

His heavy brows lifted in an expression of surprise; genuine or not, she wasn't certain. "Not me. Another guerrilla band, maybe?"

She did not press. "Maybe."

"I tell you I like women. I have five, maybe six wives. Bahh, I don't remember the count. I like you." He clapped his hands like a Chinese warlord. "The interview, it is finished. Now it is your turn to amuse me."

His congeniality had sidetracked her. So did his unexpected shift of subject to focus on her. No wonder they compared his military genius with Napoleon and Alexander and Stonewall Jackson. She forced the breath back into her solar plexus, although it felt as if it had been slammed by a giant fist, then she said, "If you kill me, how can I carry your story back to the American people? How can I tell them about the great general you are?"

With an outburst of laughter, he slapped his knee. "You American women, you are too smart for your own good. You appeal to the man's mind, eh? And not to his cock."

At the confused look in her eyes, he said, "Ahh, I see you still don't understand what I am saying. Come. Come along, now."

She should have known. At his command, the two soldiers

behind him gripped her arms and propelled her down the steps after him and out into the open area before the sawmill. The intense sunlight at first blinded her, and she put both hands up to shield her eyes.

"I will ride you, American lady, like I ride my motorcycle there, okay?"

She swayed—from lack of sleep, food, or stark fear, she didn't know. Maybe all. But her knees were unable to hold her. She sank to the ground, only to be pushed onto her back by one of the Dorados. She could smell the garlic on his breath. The other—he was pinning her arms above her head. A shoulder seam tore. One breast was bared to the mob's greedy eyes.

Outrage replaced her fear. They had no right to look at her. Much less to touch her. But what were abstractions like rights or decency or respect in a primitive land like Mexico?

She tried to lash out with her feet, but her skirt only rode higher on her limbs. Her remaining slipper went sailing through the air to land somewhere beyond her vision. She could hear Villa's grisly laughter.

"That woman is mine."

Villa's laughter ceased. His head snapped around. She lifted her own head, her eyes following the direction of Villa's. "Sam!" she breathed.

He looked like hell. His fine linen shirt was bloodstained, his face gritty, his hair curling wildly, his eyes dark and tired. The .45 he trained on Villa was steady, but a muscle flickered in his jaw, and she could see he was trying to control the fury that raged inside him.

"Damn't, Roxy, I'm tired of chasing after you. Now get up and move around behind me."

Despite the way he snapped at her, she recognized with something of a thrill that his rage was directed at Villa for daring to touch her. The Dorado squatting behind her released her wrists, and she struggled to a sitting position. "How did you know where to find me?"

Sam's mouth flattened. "Not too many women go tearing through the mountains at dawn wearing nothing but a ballgown. You were on the tongue tip of every Federal soldier who rode with you. When you didn't show up at the ghost town, I reckoned you were hot on another trail. I swear Roxy, your hare-brained—"

"Hey, *amigo*," Villa said, spreading his hands amiably, "we can share the woman, eh?"

The outrageous offer was enough to divert Sam's chagrin from her to Villa. "The woman is my wife, and I don't share her," he said with a lethal calm. But she could almost hear the flames crackling inside his head.

Unfortunately, his anger, which he had never let get the best of him, made him careless this once. "Sam, look behind you!"

Too late, she called his attention to the Dorado who had circled the sawmill and crept up from Sam's rear. Sam spun and fired the gun. The lunging Dorado fell at Sam's feet, his body flapping like a headless bird. But in that instant the other Villistas closed in on Sam. In the scuffling that ensued, Sam swung a mighty punch and leveled one. A beefy Dorado hurled himself at Sam. Sam's leg shot out and up in a way she had never seen done, and the Dorado went somersaulting across the ground.

Sam's pistol was knocked from his grasp, and she scrambled for it in the sawdust. But Villa was quicker. His boot crunched her hand. Needles of pain shot through her arm and the breath whooshed out of her lungs. He collected the pistol and aimed it at Sam. "That's enough, *amigo*," he said with a genial, toothy smile.

Sam straightened from his crouch. With the back of his arm he wearily wiped the dirt and streaks of blood from his face, never once taking his gaze from the cyclops eye of the revolver.

"Now," Villa said, "we are going to have a first-rate execution. 'Dobe-wall style. You—you, *amigo*—go first. Then your beautiful wife."

He barked an order in Spanish, and Sam was shoved toward

the nearest *jacal* and backed against its peeling adobe-bricked wall. "We will do this the civilized way, eh?"

As Villa went from Dorado to Dorado, emptying the chambers of their rifles, Sam simply stared coldly at him, saying nothing. Villa looked up at Sam and smiled. "Now, in only one rifle have I left the bullet which shall kill you, okay?"

"Just grand," Sam said.

The six Dorados fell into a line maybe thirty paces away. Villa retrieved some charcoal from a dead campfire, walked over to Sam, and drew a black circle on his linen shirt over Sam's heart. "So the one with the bullet will not miss, *amigo*."

Still Villa was not satisfied. He ordered his soldiers to take three paces forward, then three more. Roxana stood beside the sawmill steps, paralyzed in her living nightmare. Twilight was nearing, that time when animal vitality is at its lowest ebb, when the sick often died, when the healthy prepared to sleep; the hour when all nature seemed to stand poised for a moment.

At last Villa appeared pleased with the arrangement of the firing squad. From somewhere he had produced a kumquat, and he complacently nibbled away at it as he ambled out of the line of fire. "Do you have any last words, my friend?" he asked.

Sam grinned broadly at him and said, "My fine *Generalissimo*, you are a royal asshole."

Villa's eyes widened, but the Dorados, who spoke no English, did not understand the insult. Villa threw back his head and laughed. "I like you. Too bad we have to shoot you, eh?"

Swallowing another bite of the kumquat, he ordered his men to take aim. His swarthy face glowed with a benevolent sadness. Their rifles came up.

Roxana had no idea what she was doing. Her limbs simply moved of their own volition to some deep-seated, primordial command. She flung herself onto the seat of the motorcycle parked next to the steps and rocked it off its stand. She knew nothing about hand brakes or clutches or throttles or gear shifts. What she did know was that Sam was about to die.

Villa, the Dorados, Sam, the captives beneath the shed—all heads yanked with surprise in her direction. Frantically her hands worked at the handlebars. She stood up, thrust her bare foot against the kick starter, and the Indian Scout motorcycle roared to life. Her wild hand movements somehow gnashed it into gear and it bucked and shot forward. Her thighs hugged the tank. Dorados dove away from the path of the wildly careening machine.

She was headed straight for the adobe *jacal!* "Saaammm!" she screamed. Eyes closed, she waited for the inevitable impact.

Then, impossibly, Sam had swung on behind her. He wrenched the handlebars about in a sharply angled turn that fanned dirt and sawdust everywhere. One outstretched foot dragging against the ground, he gunned the engine, and the bike leaped onto its back wheel, the front pawing the air like a rearing stallion.

Suddenly, at that instant, the day finally ended, as if in a great hurry, as if it had been waiting for that business of the execution to be concluded. The armed Dorado's single bullet pinged the air, completely missing the cyclists. Wind roared past Roxana's ears. In the darkness Sam's arms were braced about her own, his hands lapping over hers on the handlebar grips. Her tangled, streaming hair lashed about his face. But his exultant laughter mingled with hers.

"You did it, Roxy, old girl! You did it!"

26

The tension of May and June, which had brought the United States and Mexico to the brink of warfare, caused Pershing to draw his forces into a fairly restricted area in the vicinity of Casa Grandes and Colonia Dublan. At General Funston's order, Pershing concentrated his force in order to be ready to resist any attacks.

It was late, actually near dawn, but a light still burned in the general's tent. He withdrew one of his cigars from their wooden box and leaned back in his canvas chair. "Catching Villa would satisfy the nation's honor, Sam, but we've done what we were ordered to do: smash the major guerrilla bands. And the expedition's trained a hard-core cadre of experienced soldiers who will be available for our war against the Kaiser, which I'm certain will come."

Sam rose from his camp chair. "Who can say what the outcome would have been, Jack, had we not entered Mexico."

At Sam's side, Roxana put out her hand. "Thank you, General, for allowing me to participate in what has been the adventure of my life."

A rare smile creased the usually stern face. "You've added immeasurable adventure to ours, I can assure you, Miss Van Buren."

Outside, the desert night air was cool. The flower-print house frock Roxana wore was too light for the hour and she shivered slightly as she walked with Sam toward the truck park. Sally Henson had contributed the dress earlier that day, when Roxana and Sam had cycled into camp.

Their precipitous arrival on Villa's motorcycle, with Roxana almost naked in her tattered ballgown, and their hair-raising escapade with Villa himself, had been the talk of the entire base camp. They were celebrities. The Signal Corps had already wired El Paso, and radiograms were going out across the nation about her and Sam's encounter with the Lion of the North and his Dorados.

A stringer for UP wanted to do a story on their adventures. Charley Rooney sulked. And Private Dreyfus shyly asked her to pose for a snapshot with him. Her one major regret was that the Army had impounded the motorcycle. She also missed her cork helmet and would liked to have taken it with her as a souvenir.

Sam draped his arm about her shoulder. "Cold?"

She nodded, relishing the snuggling warmth of his larger body blocking out the chilly breeze. She just liked his body. Period.

The truck convoy was ready to depart, its headlights spotlighting clumps of maguey, feathery palo verde trees, and stalky ocotillo. In order to avoid the heat of the day, which the soldiers claimed could fry a tortilla on a truck dashboard, the convoy was leaving early for Columbus, before dawn.

Roxana was scrunched between Sam and the lead driver, a hired El Paso civilian. That early in the morning no one talked. But there was so much she wanted to say.

Do you remember trying to teach me to shoot, Sam? Well, I knew all the time how to; Wally taught me, but I liked having your arms around me. . . . I wish I could have told Hell Yet-Suey and Sergeant Chicken good-bye. And gotten to see old Ah Moy one more time. . . .

What do you think'll happen to Villa? You know, one couldn't help but like the irascible scoundrel. Do you remember, Sam, that night at the Caballo Blanco, the first time you held me? Or that time in the outhouse, when you first kissed me? Or the night, our "wedding" night, when you placed a paper cigar band on my finger? I'll never forget those times, even if I live to be a ripe old maid a hundred years old. Hunh! An old maid who rides a motorcycle. I think I shall be quite eccentric.

Despite the truck's jouncing, at last she fell into the sleep of exhaustion, her head cradled in the hollow between Sam's bicep and his chest. Early evening brought into view on the horizon the multicolored, plastered buildings of Juarez and, beyond that, Mount Franklin, with the lights of El Paso wrapped about its slopes like iridescent pearls.

The driver dropped his two passengers on the El Paso side of the International Bridge. Suddenly, Roxana realized there was no time left to talk. She had a train to catch for New York. And a brilliant future waiting for her at *The Washington Post*.

She couldn't bring herself to look at Sam when she said goodbye. Instead she looked down at the Rio Grande, lapping gently at the sandy banks. The river was much prettier by twilight. Beyond the soft light of the gas street lamp, fireflies lit the summer night. To the people crossing the International Bridge, she and Sam might have looked like lovers, out for an evening stroll.

Her fingers curled about the rusted railing. "I guess you'll be on your way to see Don Asunsolo?" Oh my, how inadequate, when there were so many more important things that could be said.

Sam removed Angelina's crucifix from his shirt pocket. In the light of the lamp, the crucifix's black pearl gleamed hypnotically.

"I don't think so."

Startled, she stared at his rugged profile.

"But Sam, you can still collect the five thousand. You found Angelina Asunsolo. The necklace proves it."

Sam juggled the necklace in one hand, as if reckoning its

weight, then tossed it over the railing into the sluggish river, as he had tossed his father's Medal of Honor into the Sulu Sea years before. "Tell Don Asunsolo his daughter is dead, Roxy. That would be much kinder to the old man than the truth."

From across the bridge she could hear the trolley approaching that would take her to the depot. Oh, so little time! "Sam, we made a good team, didn't we? Van Buren and Brady."

He grinned down at her. "Brady and Van Buren. That we damn well did, sweetheart."

The trolley squealed to a halt beside them.

She had gone through hell to prove herself as a professional journalist, to obtain a prestigious job on *The Washington Post*. She stepped onto the trolley's first step and looked down at Sam. "Well, good-bye, Sam."

Sam took her hand. "Good-bye, Roxy."

The conductor clanged his bell impatiently.

Gently, sadly, she tugged her hand from his clasp. To settle for anything less, to settle for a man without any prospects was sheer foolishness.

One of the passengers coughed discreetly, and toward the back of the trolley a tot began singing a lilting nursery rhyme.

Well, she supposed she had always been somewhat foolish. But the more she thought about it . . . anything less than Sam she didn't want. He gave her complete fulfillment, where everything else was partial.

"Sam, old man, do you think we could earn enough running our own news press to buy that cattle ranch in the upper valley?"

She was afraid he wasn't going to answer her question. After all, he had never told her he loved her, that he wanted her to stay with him. But then, neither had she told him. And the word *marriage* was anathema to him.

His two big hands reached up and encircled her waist and swung her off the trolley to press her body against his. Her toes dangled above the pavement. "Roxy, like I said, Brady and Brady make a great team."

She was startled to see the suspicious glistening in his eyes. Then, before the conductor and all the trolley passengers, he kissed her. A greedy, passion-hungry, elated kiss that left her lungs breathless, her head spinning, and her legs rubbery.

In those fairy tales that begin "Once upon a time . . ." they always promise that at the kiss of True Love or of Prince Charming or for that matter of a troll, if the recipient happens to be a female troll . . . anyway, at that Kiss, one supposedly hears cymbals clashing, violins playing, and bells ringing.

Roxana Van Buren heard the trolley bell and the cheers of its passengers—and that was quite enough for her.

Sam and Roxana didn't exactly live happily ever after. But they came as close to it as any two earthbound people can. Sam gave up his gin, shaved close every morning, and was forced to shoulder the responsibilities that came with being the wealthy proprietor of a modest cattle ranch forested with oil derricks. Civilization caught up with him after all. But he had Roxana to ease the pains of the inevitable encroachment of progress.

And Roxana? Well, she shocked the Southwest establishment by successfully producing an influential newspaper with a good circulation, by successfully producing seven children along the way, and by riding a motorcycle about the town like a circus daredevil.

Truly, of such events are fairy tales created.

AUTHOR'S NOTE

The Punitive Expedition was recalled from Mexico in February 1917, after a year of chasing Villa. The experience in motor transportation gained by the American troops south of the border served them well later that year when the United States entered the Great World War.

Pancho Villa never was captured. In 1923 he was murdered by his former followers in Hidalgo del Parral, south of Chihuahua City. Villa's last words were, "Don't let it end like this. Tell them I said something."

Interestingly, two of the aristocratic Spanish-Mexican refugees from Villa's rampage went on to become film stars: Gilbert Roland from Chihuahua and Dolores Del Rio from Durango. Miss Del Rio's family name, Lopez Negrete, was the same as that of the Durango *hacendados* whose son Villa claimed had raped his sister. Coincidence?

Tom Mix, one of Villa's lieutenants at the First Battle of Juarez in 1911, rode off on his horse, Tony, to become one of the heroes of the early Hollywood westerns.

Finally, the troops of the Punitive Expedition had the lowest rate of syphilis among American soldiers, due to Pershing's insistence on the use of prophylactics. Pershing, in recognition of his service with the AEF, received the highest rank ever awarded an American officer by Congress, General of the Armies of the United States.

Parris Afton Bonds
New Mexico, 1984